"I want to tell you where and 'when' for the shift, so that we both have the coordinates," Sharra said.

Tanner narrowed his eyes. "So which one did you choose? The Training Facility? Your old apartment?"

"My childhood home."

"Don't you remember what happened the last time we went there?"

"I do, but last time I went back for sentimental reasons. This time I'm going back to look for clues about my brother. Something that will help to explain why he wants me gone."

"And you think you'll find it there.

"I don't know. All I know is that I have to try."

"Then, I'm with you."

"Thank you," she said, her voice soft with gratitude as she reached up to clasp his arms, making them a complete circle. "So how do we go about this?"

"Build the blocks as always. When you are ready, concentrate hard on the 'sending' to the mainframe. And then give the command. It should be that simple."

"Simple? I can only hope." Her brows wrinkled with worry. There were no guarantee that it would work, for it had never been tried before from a repaired agrylium. "What if I send us to god knows where, or worse, to limbo?"

"Either you'll shift, or you won't. Whatever happens, I'm here. Stop worrying." He gently squeezed her arms as he spoke, a soft reassurance that meant more to her than words.

"Okay. Here goes nothing."

VAULT AGENCY SERIES:

SHIFTERS

ARDUS

THE VAULT

THE VAULT

A Vault Agency Novel: Book Three

BY

JEAN GILBERT

A catalogue record for this book is available from the National Library of New Zealand.

Published by Rogue House Publishing
Cover design by Getty Creations

This book is dedicated

To my one true companion,

For sticking by me

Through the journey.

VAULT:

1) A space, chamber, or passage enclosed by a vault or vault-like structure, especially one located underground.

2) A room or compartment, often built of or lined with steel, usually fireproof and burglarproof, reserved for the storage and safekeeping of valuables.

3) A burial chamber.

<>

Prologue

The Vault

It was the dead of night. A strange stillness descended upon the vast chamber in the heart of Vault Agency. The nine metal pylons rested upon their axis, cold and silent. The darkness was their home. The quiet... their resolution. Their smooth metal surfaces gleamed with a strange internal light: beautiful, mesmerizing... deadly. Around their feet, the particle cloud spread out like a white blanket on the floor, undisturbed for a change, deceptive in its vigilance.

The Vault slept, if one could call it sleep. It was not in the traditional meaning of the word where consciousness was lessened, and the body at rest, though the pylons were at a standstill. Maybe sleep was too strong a word. It was more of a lessening of duty, an abating of energy coinciding with the dwindled activity of its hosts. Although it rested, the work to stay alive remained constant. For it was starving.

There had been a time when food had been aplenty, and it had thrived along with its chosen hosts. Yet, somewhere in time and space, its reason for being had been forgotten; its needs when made known, neglected. The relationship it had built had grown distant. Its food source slowly diminished though it provided every enticement to keep the host connected.

It could no longer continue on without a resolution. So, it reached out through the dimensions, searching eons of time for the right host, until it found it... a mind that would see beyond the reality.

That would hear its cry.

See its form.

Feel its hunger.

Understand its need.

If this new host failed, then the Vault and its world it created for them would be no more. That was not an option the Vault would allow.

Chapter One

The Vault

Please let it work, Sharra Lane pleaded for what felt like the umpteenth time.

Lying upon the mat inside the coffin-like medical chamber, Sharra tried to be patient... and grateful, though she found both difficult to muster up.

The darkness hummed with charged energy. It penetrated her skin. It coursed through her body, finding its way to the liquid metal assimilated to the billions of neuron receptors in her brain.

Agrylium.

That was its official name: the metal that made time travel possible. It was the same metal that tied Sharra to the secrets of the Vault. One of those secrets was the ball of energy-like threads that lived between the agrylium mesh in her head. That secret was happily gorging on the energy flowing through her nervous system. Sharra let them feed. They weren't harming anyone.

With her head held firmly within the brackets of the headrest, she could only stare at the dark ceiling a few feet from her face. Her scalp ached, not from the brackets, or from the feasting threads, but from the weight of the tight ponytail that held her auburn hair away from the metal rods pressed to her skull behind her ears. Long hair was the bane of Cam's life, the Vaults' Chief Medic and only android. If he could have his way, he'd make all of them shave it off. Fortunately, Lazarus had refused his request. At the time, Sharra had been grateful, but now with the headache coming on, she was having second thoughts.

In the darkness came the soft female voice of the Personal Voice Communication (PVC) system.

"Diagnostics complete," the PVC said.

"Release the patient," Sharra heard Cam order through the speaker.

A small light came on above her head at the doctor's words. She blinked at the sudden intrusion. The metal rods folded up and retracted silently behind her. The curved lid of the chamber lifted, and slid into the wall.

A head peeked around the lip of the chamber. It was Cael, the human Cael. Gone were the spines and webbing that had run from the top of his forehead and down his back. Gone were the fish-like features of his face which was the true form of the Arderian male from Ardus. In its place was a handsome young man with shoulder-length golden blonde hair, lustrous skin, and striking dark amber eyes encircled within chocolate brown rims that flashed with easy humor.

"All done," he said.

THE VAULT

Tucking the hospital gown around her, she took his proffered hand, grateful for the assistance. As her feet touched the floor, she searched Cael's face for an answer. His dark amber eyes told Sharra nothing. After giving her hand a quick squeeze of reassurance, Cael left her to join Cam at the diagnostic screens at the head of the medical chamber. While the two doctors discussed between themselves the readings from the chamber, Sharra's hands crept up to check the damaged metal imprints behind her ears. Beneath her fingers, she felt a familiar pattern of a double crescent-moon connected by a pointed stake: the logo of the Vault, the imprint of the agrylium.

Hope stirred in her heart.

"The melted coins are gone. I can feel the edges of the crescent moons," she said.

Cam came over, and checked the metal discs hidden behind her ears. "It looks like the agrylium imprints are back to normal. That is progress."

"Does that mean I'm fixed?"

Cam returned to the diagnostic screen, studying the numbers. Sharra's nerves were shot. All she wanted was an answer so that she could move on with her life.

Finally both men turned to Sharra. Though Cam was about to speak, it was Cael's aura that told her the good news.

"The new calibrations all match your original assimilation. Unlike our first few attempts," Cam said.

"Will I be able to shift again?"

"I have calculated the numbers…"

"And?"

"There is a minute chance that you may not be able to. Shall I read the numbers off to you?"

"No, thanks. I believe you."

Cael stepped forward with a shake of his head, and said, "What Cam is trying to say in a round about way is, yes, you will be able to shift again. The number is so infinitely small that it is mote. I do not understand why he would worry you unnecessarily."

Sharra humphed. "Stay around long enough and you'll catch on. Cam's program doesn't include the nuances of the deeper levels of emotional responses that are part of our makeup. It's a weakness in his design."

"It is not a fault in my design, but a protection. How the human brain can remain unaffected by the intricate interplay of emotions that make up your psyche, I cannot compute."

"See what we have to put up with?" Sharra said to Cael. "Since you've chosen to learn medicine, I'm hoping that with your Arderian sensitivities to our 'psyche' you'll be able to influence him, you know, to be more responsive to our emotional needs."

"I will do my best."

"You do realize that I can hear you," Cam said.

Sharra shared a secret smile with Cael.

"Here," Cael said, "try this on."

He pressed a thin metal device into the palm of her hand. It was a Com-Link. She hadn't seen one since that fateful day when she had gone for her annual visit to the crash site where her parents' had died in a fireball, and was struck down. It was the day that she had learned the true identity of her nemesis. Greyson...her brother. He knew she'd be there. She had made it easy for him to take her by surprise.

It was Greyson who had destroyed the agrylium imprints behind her ears. Without them, her connection to the Vaults' mainframe was lost. She couldn't shift nor communicate even if she had a Link. Why Greyson hadn't just killed her outright, she couldn't understand. Maybe there was something left within him, some sense of family. Instead of doing the deed himself, he dumped her on Ardus, a planet with no land, only endless water. She would've drowned if not for Cael and his pod.

She smiled gratefully up at Cael. In a silent connection that only he could hear, she said, *thank you*, putting into those simple words what her heart felt, for him, for his pod, and for the small gestures of kindness like the Link in her hand.

The rings around his eyes deepened with shared emotions as he said, *You are always welcome, my dear friend.*

Her experience on Ardus bound them together, her – the human, and him – the alien. His presence at the Vault was a welcome change from the normal recruits, if you could call any of them normal. And not just him, but Immari, Araylai's handmaiden and friend, had also joined. Lazarus must be having a field day explaining their alien presence to the rest.

Fresh blood was what the Agency needed. Arderian blood definitely fulfilled that criteria. If only Sharra was allowed back into the fold to see it.

Tilting her head, she slipped the Com-Link behind her left ear, setting it against the agrylium imprint. Like a magnet, it held tight against the flesh of her skull.

"So far so good. Now for a test run," she said, and sent a tentative feeler out to the mainframe asking for a Link to the agrylium in Tanner's brain.

An instant later, Tanner's voice was inside her ear.

"Sharra!" he said. "Is that really you?"

"It worked!" she said to Cael before answering Tanner. "Yes, Tanner, it's me. I've got my Link working. Cael says the agrylium is finally fixed."

"That's great news. Where are you?"

"In the Ward."

"Don't move. I'll be right there."

The Link disconnected, leaving her alone with the two doctors again.

"Can I get dressed now?" she asked.

After getting permission to change, Sharra hurried down the hall to the changing room. As soon as the door shut behind her, the hospital gown was off and thrown into the bin. Her clothes were on the chair where she had left them. Ten minutes later, she walked out wearing jeans, a t-shirt, and a pair of loafers on her feet. The ponytail was gone. Instead, her hair hung loose around her shoulders, thick and glossy.

Cael was waiting for her in the hallway.

"Lazarus is in Cam's office," he said.

"I'm not surprised," she said.

They fell in step as they headed to Cam's office. Though it was late at night, Cael kept a sharp eye out for anyone. Sharra understood the need for secrecy, even if she didn't like it. She had no choice, not yet. Hopefully with the agrylium fixed, things would change. And Lazarus was the man to make it happen.

As they walked, Cael said, "I have not had the opportunity to thank you for the letters you so kindly brought back with you from Ardus."

"Nayada – I mean, Queen Aliya thought it might help with the homesickness."

"To be honest with you, I have been too busy to be homesick. Between my studies, and duties to the Vault, my days are so full that at the end I fall into bed exhausted."

"I remember those days. But believe me you'll thank Tanner for it later. How far are you in the training?"

Cael reached up and touched a spot behind his left ear. Sharra saw the movement, knowing what it meant.

"You're assimilated?"

Cael smiled with a nod.

"Immari?"

Again he nodded.

"How long have I been gone?"

"Long enough. You have been missed."

"I have?"

He smiled, and winked, a very slow wink. Sharra felt the heat creep up her neck. There was no way to hide it, and she didn't bother.

"Yes, well, unlike your kind, we humans tend to keep things like that private."

"But your auras…"

"Are not visible to our eyes."

"I did not know. What a great handicap that must be."

"Yes. It is," she said, thinking of the advantage of knowing someone's true feelings by the color of an aura, and not having to guess.

Or finding out by sneaking into their heads for a peek, she thought to herself.

The conversation ended for they'd reached the Head Medic's office. Cael stopped at the door to stand guard as Sharra went in. Leaning against the wall with arms folded stood Tanner. At the sight of her, his handsome face lightened. A warm glow filled his eyes. She didn't need an aura to know what it meant.

As the door closed behind her, he said softly, "Hello, Sharra."

"Hi," she said shyly.

That was all they could say, for then Lazarus spoke up from the desk.

"Cam has informed me of the good news," he said.

Seated behind Cam's desk covered with models of human organs and body parts, Lazarus looked out of place in the business suit and smart goatee that he favored. Though he wore a genuine smile, underneath it his face looked drawn, the lines deeper than Sharra remembered. The trouble that had followed her since her recruitment hadn't helped matters. In fact, they had made things much worse, not just for Lazarus, but also for everyone else at the Vault.

"Getting your Link working is a step in the right direction," he said.

"Nothing's sure until we know whether I can shift again."

"Do you think you're ready for that? It is a big step."

"I can't stay hidden away forever. I need to know. You need to know, too, before any of us can move on."

Cam who had been studying the monitor on the wall behind his desk, turned to speak. "Though the diagnostics have all been cleared, the probabilities in the computations still must be taken into consideration. I realize the numbers mean little to you in that they seem to be minuscule, but it is not wise to dismiss them. I would recommend more testing before you risk Sharra's life."

"Thank you, Cam, for your concern," Lazarus said, before turning back to Sharra. "This is another first for us," he said to her. "It seems to have become a pattern with you. Though the double assimilation didn't harm you, I can't guarantee what will happen now if you attempt to shift. Cam is correct in pointing out the fact that the agrylium in your head has been damaged, and though repaired, it doesn't mean it will function the same. We just don't know. In the end, the choice is yours."

"I've come this far. I have to try," she said.

"I thought that's what you'd say. Tanner has already volunteered to back you up. Since you've worked closely together in the past, I've agreed to let him second you."

Tanner straightened, and came to stand beside her. "I figure we can go to one of the places that you had chosen for your training exercise. That way we won't have to waste time studying up on a destination."

Sharra looked back and forth between the two of them, and shook her head. "It seems you two have already figured this out."

"Not all," Lazarus said. "We still need to find out how your brother slipped into the Vault undetected, and what he's doing here. Until we know that, we need to keep you away from the Vault. For all he knows, you're dead. We'd like to keep it that way as long as possible. It will buy us time to investigate."

"I want to know as much as you, even more. He is my brother, no matter what he's done."

Like Lazarus, questions burned within her heart. Questions that went beyond the walls of the Vault. Questions that hurt. The biggest one was why… why did he want her dead? What had she done to make him hate her so? The answers were there, somewhere.

"When do you want to go?" Tanner asked.

"Now."

She'd been away from the Vault for far too long. Waiting was pointless. Besides, she needed to know if she could shift, or not. Her future depended on knowing.

Chapter Two

Cael led the way through the Ward. At the Vault doors, he stopped Sharra and Tanner with a hand before the sensor caught their movement.

"Wait here until I make sure it's clear," he said.

Tanner moved Sharra to the side as Cael activated the sensor to the frosted doors. When the doors slid into the wall, cool air from the Vault chamber swept into the Ward. Sharra peered through the door at the towering pylons that sat within the cloud of energy particles. A remnant of that 'energy' resided in her head. It was impossible to ignore, especially whenever she came in proximity to the primary source – the pylons. Though she had searched through the vast data stored in the mainframe, there was no mention of another human surviving an exposure to the pylons, or of anyone absorbing its energy like she had.

What are you? she asked the pylons.

Nothing came from them, only the gentle turning of their long bladed shafts. Sharra wanted to ask Lazarus about it, but since the incident, her life had escalated from one mess into another, and the time had never been right. Besides, Lazarus had bigger problems to deal with, most of them because of her.

The door slid shut behind Cael as he glided into the Vault. With the energy cloud out of sight, Sharra let go of her breath, unaware that she had been holding it.

Tanner must have noticed.

"Try not to worry," he said. "Lazarus has worked hard to keep your presence here a secret."

"I hope you're right."

"When have I been wrong?"

"I can think of a few occasions. Like the time you said nothing ever goes wrong on the practice shift. Or the time you were sure that the trap we set for J.D. Dash would draw him out into the open. We know how that went. Or the time…"

"Okay, okay. You can stop." Remorse filled his blue eyes. "That doesn't mean I'm wrong this time. Besides, didn't I promise to take care of Amadeus for you? Don't I get points for that?"

"Sorry. Just teasing you. Of course, you've always been there for me when I needed you. When I was floating on the ocean of Ardus and thought my time was up, I prayed that you would take care of Amadeus for me… that you would remember me when I was gone. There you were, bigger than life, saving me again. I owe you."

"All I ask is that you try to stay out of trouble this time."

"I'll try." Changing the subject, she said, "Amadeus must've been upset when I didn't come home."

"We all were. Upset."

"I wish I could go up and see him."

"You will, just not today. Since the cat flap has been installed in your apartment door, he's been preoccupied with exploring the whole second floor, common rooms and all. I think he's even made it to Lazarus' office."

"How do you know?"

A cocky grin grew on his face.

Bending down, he whispered in her ear, "I saw some white hair on his pants that look suspiciously like Amadeus' fur."

Sharra didn't realize how much she had missed his cheeky smile until then. Or his teasing manner.

Suppressing a laugh, she said, "Oh, no. How undignified."

"Very undignified."

Cael's voice was in her ear, breaking the mood. With the 'all clear' given, Tanner pulled her quickly into the Vault. On the far side of the immense room, standing guard in the open archway was Cael. He waved them forward before turning back to peer down the long hallway that led to the interior of the Agency.

The nine pylons began to stir on their axis, awakening the cloud at their feet, as the two agents approached the middle of the room. As Tanner drew her across the onyx floor, the white cloud of energy grew with the rotation of the pylons. Soft tendrils unfurled from its belly, reaching out to them as they passed. The threads in Sharra's head pulsed in excitement, answering the silent call of the cloud. She quickly shushed the threads, simultaneously tightened her shield against the pervasiveness of the pylons.

"Not now," she said, brushing the tendrils aside as if they were annoying insects.

"Not now what?" Tanner said.

"Did I say that out loud?"

"Yes."

He waited for an answer, but got none. With a shiftroom close by, she dashed ahead to the bright light in the darkness, leaving Tanner to catch up. Once inside she turned to face the doorway, waiting for her eyes to adjust to the intensity of the room. Tanner appeared out of the darkness of the Vault, and joined her on the pulsing silver design within the floor.

He turned her to him, holding her arms as he asked, "Is there anything you want to tell me?"

"Yes. I want to tell you where and 'when' for the shift, so that we both have the coordinates," she said, pretending to misconstrue his question.

He narrowed his eyes. "Right. So which one did you choose? The Training Facility? Your old apartment?"

"My childhood home."

"Don't you remember what happened the last time we went there?"

"I do, but last time I went back for sentimental reasons. This time I'm going back to look for clues about my brother. Something that will help to explain why he wants me gone."

"And you think you'll find it there?"

"I don't know. All I know is that I have to try."

"Then, I'm with you."

"Thank you," she said, her voice soft with gratitude as she reached up to clasp his arms, making them a complete circle. "So how do we go about this?"

"Build the blocks as always. When you are ready, concentrate hard on the 'sending' to the mainframe. And then give the command. It should be that simple."

"Simple? I can only hope." Her brows wrinkled with worry. There was no guarantee that it would work, for it had never been tried before from a repaired agrylium. "What if I send us to God knows where, or worse, to limbo?"

"Either you'll shift, or you won't. Whatever happens, I'm here. Stop worrying." He gently squeezed her arms as he spoke a soft reassurance that meant more to her than any words.

"Okay. Here goes nothing."

She closed her eyes and drew up the memories of her childhood bedroom from the place close to her heart. Soft yellow walls, periwinkle curtains covering the window, a twin bed covered with a matching comforter above which hung a framed picture of old-fashioned teddy bears sitting in a row; these were some of the memories that came readily to her. One by one she added more to the growing pile of blocks of memories. As she worked, Tanner's voice cut in, making her pause.

"Make sure it's not too close to the last time we were there," he reminded her.

She opened her eyes and gave him a look, and said, "I'm not stupid, thank you."

"Sorry," he said. "Old habit."

Closing her eyes, she went back to work, taking her time in order to get it right. That her career depended on this working was in her mind. So was the fact that it would affect her life, one way, or the other. With those thoughts in mind the memories built, until the stack of blocks towered in the front lobe of her brain. When there was nothing more to add, she opened her eyes.

"I'm ready to send it to the mainframe."

Tanner squeezed her arms again, and said, "Go ahead."

Send, she commanded.

In an instant, the pile filtered into the agrylium in her head and down to the silver pattern of the floor below her feet. Hope sprang in her heart. That was a good sign. A very good sign.

In the Link she told Cael that she was ready to shift, knowing that he still guarded the way into the Vault.

"Safe journey," Cael said. "And shift true."

"I can only try."

Breaking the Link, Sharra looked up at Tanner. In his eyes there was strength. Her determination grew. Gripping his arms, she took a deep breath, saying a little prayer.

With only a nod of warning, she commanded, "Shift!"

Chapter Three

Chicago, Illinois USA
1980

The agrylium in Sharra's head answered the command. Below their feet, the silver design pulsed. The mainframe picked up the command, and responded. In a flash of light the two agents disappeared as the Vault shifted them back to nineteen eighty, the year she had turned eight years old.

It took less than a blink of an eye, and they were in her old bedroom, standing almost in the exact spot as the initial shift that she had taken Tanner on a year ago.

"It worked!" she said, grinning in relief within the circle of their arms.

Tanner smiled down at her, and said, "I never doubted."

Though he sounded confident, his eyes mirrored the same relief.

As she stood there, the walls went out of focus as if an invisible force were pushing them back. At first she thought it was her eyes, yet the feeling remained too long. It was as if time had not caught up with the shift, warping the room they were in. One second went by, and then another. Then it was gone. Beside her Tanner seemed unaffected.

Sharra shook her head, not sure if it were a side effect of the repaired agrylium, or if it were just her imagination. Either way, she dared not say anything.

Letting go of Tanner, she stepped back to look around. Everything appeared as she remembered it. Then, she changed her mind. Though the bed was made, and the floor clean as always, a few things were different. This time the desk was clean. Papers were tucked away. Schoolbooks were gone. No sign of the packet of school pictures was to be seen. On the bed were a few more stuffed animals than before.

Tanner went over to the window, and pushed the curtain aside to peer out. Sharra could see the trees lining the back of the property. Their branches were full of green leaves that danced in the wind.

"No one will be home," she said.

"When are we?" he asked.

"The middle of July if I've shifted true. We went away for a family vacation to Florida for a week this year. First time that I saw the ocean. I'll never forget it."

"I know the feeling. Though I was a little older than you when I first saw it."

"How old were you?"

"Nineteen." He paused as if not wanting to say more, but after a few moments he took a breath and continued on. "I just finished a year in the military and was stationed in Virginia at Langley. My buddies and I would drive to Virginia Beach when we had leave. For them, it was for the girls, but for me, it was the ocean. I couldn't get enough of it. The power. The endlessness. It boggled my mind."

"You would love Ardus then," she said as she went over to her old bed and picked up a teddy bear.

It flopped in her hands for the stuffing had broken down with age. Its brown fur was worn in places. Yet, the eyes still shone like black coal buttons in its pleasant face.

"I was there, remember?" Tanner said.

"Yes, but you should have stayed longer."

"No thank you. I like the land too much."

As she studied the old tattered bear, she said, "I don't know. It kind of grew on me."

"Only you would say that."

He came away from the window to join her at the bed. "Treasures of an eight-year-old," he said after observing the collection on the bed.

"A hoard. I'm going to take this one back with me," she said, showing him the teddy bear in her hand before tucking it under her arm.

"Won't that change your past? I'm sure your younger self will have missed it."

"I did miss it. Cried for nights on end about it. Don't you see? It had already happened, so I must take it.

Though at the time I had blamed Greyson for it. And to think, it was me all along. How ironic."

Tanner shook his head. "Your twisted logic actually makes sense." Changing the subject, he said, "Since this exercise in shifting to this particular spot has a two fold purpose, shouldn't we move onto the next part?"

"You're right. Greyson's room is right across from mine."

Sharra led Tanner out of her bedroom to the hallway, and across to the closed door on the other side. As her hand held the doorknob ready to turn it, she paused. It had been many years since she'd been inside Greyson's bedroom. Her memories were sketchy on what it looked like. Being six years her senior, he'd made it perfectly clear while growing up that she wasn't allowed in his room. Now, for some reason, it made her nervous, though she knew that it was ridiculous to feel that way. Greyson was far away in Florida, and would never know of their invasion. That thought was enough to bolster her courage.

She pushed the door open. Stepping inside she was immediately hit by an offensive smell coming from a pile of clothes thrown in the corner.

"Phew," she said, wrinkling her nose.

The bed was an unmade nest of blankets, probably smelled too, not that Sharra was going to find out. A black backpack was left on top of the blankets. When she saw it, she remembered that he'd forgotten it, and had complained nonstop the whole trip. Their mother had to go out and buy him a new tape deck and some music just to pacify him. No wonder she'd erased the memory. She wondered what else she'd forgotten about.

More clothes were shoved under the bed along with a pair of ratty sneakers. No guessing how long they'd been under there. His desk was just as cluttered.

Tanner stopped beside her and looked around.

"Typical stinky teenager," he said, summing it up in a neat package.

"I can't imagine you were like that."

"No, I was pretty clean for a teenager."

Sharra looked at the walls. "I don't remember there being so many posters."

They were everywhere like mismatched wallpaper. Some were even tacked to the ceiling. Posters of the Chicago Bears, Greyson's favorite football team, mixed with those of the top models of some sports magazine posing seductively on a beach in skimpy bikinis. There were rock bands, too, some with odd symbols and strange writing. Sharra was too young at the time to know who the bands were. Now, though, she recognized them, and wondered how her parents let him listen to them, or worse, idolize them. Their sadistic practices were well publicized. Not healthy material for a young mind.

"Sex, drugs, and rock and roll," Tanner said as he studied the posters. "I see he liked the Bears. I was more a Bills fan myself. What about you? Did you have a favorite team?"

"I wasn't much into the sports scene. More into books, and gardening, like my mother."

"And don't forget the cats."

"And cats," she said with a fond smile.

Tanner's hands went onto his hips as he peered around at the mess. "So, where do we start?"

"You take the desk while I tackle the dresser," she said, moving to the dresser.

"What are we looking for?" he said as he started to sift through the papers on the desk.

"I don't know. Something that would help explain Greyson's odd behavior. I'm hoping we would know it when we saw it."

They worked in silence, Tanner at the desk, and Sharra at the dresser. When the drawers came up with nothing but clothes, Sharra moved onto the closet. Sliding the mirrored door aside, she pushed the clothes aside to get to the shelves that were built into the side. Starting from the top, she went through Greyson's stuff, careful to replace every shoebox, board game, tape cassette, and book, back to the exact spot from which they were taken. In her search, she learned much about her brother that she didn't know, things like his interest in horror stories and mind games, and that he played Dungeons and Dragons, and Risk. On the floor next to the stacks of books was a whole box of technical manuals, everything from computers to high tech security systems. Yet, none of this stuff explained Greyson's hatred for her.

She replaced the lid on the box with a sigh, and was about to give up when Tanner made a noise from the direction of the bed.

"I think I've found something," he said.

Getting to her feet, she came over to him, leaving the teddy bear on the floor. In his hand was an old school composition notebook, the kind that was stitched down the spine. A frown marred his face as he stared at a page before turning to the next. Sharra leaned in to look, and then wished she hadn't.

On the page, drawn in red and black markers, was a bullseye. Pasted in the center was a cut out photo of a face, her face. The paper had been punctured around it as if darts had been thrown at it. 'Four, three, two, one, BOOM!' was written in black around the outside of her face.

"What the?" she said in shock.

Tanner turned the page. The next one was a drawing of a guillotine. Arms and legs had been put around the bottom. Red marker smeared the blade of the guillotine, on the basket, and all over the ground around the body parts. The missing body from the page before was laid out on the slat behind the guillotine. It wore a green dress. It was the one she'd worn for her school picture that year. Beside her, she heard Tanner suck in his breath, and knew that he had recognized it too.

He quickly turned the page, but it got no better. One page after another had a similar theme. Some were obvious pictures of her, whether made from more cut up photos, or from painstakingly made drawings. Each one had the same black marker countdown of numbers that ended on the 'BOOM.' Together it told a story... a horrible story.

"I think we've seen enough," he said, shutting the notebook with a snap, and slipping it back into the backpack.

"I don't understand," she said quietly, shaking her head in disbelief. Her heart chilled. The images were stuck in her brain, playing over and over again like pictures in a flipbook. "What did I do? I was only eight. Did he hate me that much?"

"Hey," he said gently. "Come here."

His strong arms came around her and gathered her to his chest. She sank into him, needing to feel the warmth of his touch. Under her ear she could hear the steady beat of his heart as she rested against him. The chill in her heart began to thaw in the comfort of his arms.

"You did nothing. You're a sweet, kind, and generous person. You see the good in everyone. You give when others don't deserve it. There's nothing to hate about you."

As he spoke his hands stroked her back in a gentle caress. It made her feel safe.

She raised her head from his chest, pulling away a few inches to look at him.

"You're just saying that to make me feel better," she accused him.

His blue eyes darkened with unsaid emotions. She couldn't look away. Locked in his intense gaze, she forgot all about the pictures. Under her hand his heart began to beat faster. It did funny things to her insides, things that she had only felt before with Faolan. It confused her, and excited her.

"No, my little chickadee. You are the real deal. No one can help but fall in love with you."

The sincerity in his voice was genuine, his meaning clear even to her addled senses. She could feel it in his soft breath as it stirred her hair, and in the beating of his heart under her hand. Her lips parted in an unconscious gesture that was as primal as time itself.

His gaze dropped to her mouth. Her breath quickened. His voice turned husky. It made her shiver.

"No one," he growled as he pulled her back to his chest.

And then, his mouth was upon hers, warm and insistent. Her traitorous body responded as her lips softened underneath the sensuous pressure of his full lips. Wrapping her hands around his neck, she leaned into him lost in the moment.

Tanner needed no more encouragement than that. The warm pressure of his hands on her lower back drew her even closer as he deepened the kiss. Behind her ribcage, her treacherous heart leaped in excitement as unruly emotions coursed through her blood.

All thoughts stopped as passion took over. In that moment neither one cared about the consequences. They each needed the other, and took what was given, coming up for air only when their lungs were exhausted.

It was through the haze of passion that the Link from Lazarus registered in her ears. Tanner got it too. Yet, he was the first to break away, though reluctantly.

As their lips parted she felt regret for the interruption. She didn't want him to stop. As he lifted his head to flip the tiny microphone wire down, her common sense returned, so did her embarrassment. She tried to pull away, but Tanner would have none of it. With one strong arm wrapped around her waist, he kept her close as he got control of his wayward breath, and answered the Link.

"So I take it that the test worked," she heard Lazarus say in her ear.

"I'm sorry. I should've linked as soon as we had arrived," Tanner said into the wire, answering the Link for her.

Resting her head back against his chest, she let him take the lead.

"I assumed it was clear," Tanner continued, "that Sharra had succeeded when we had disappeared from the Vault. Not only did she succeed, but surpassed as usual. Hit the mark right on the spot. Shifted us into her old bedroom without a blink of an eye. This girl's got talent."

"She does have talent at that."

Sharra could hear the pleasure in Lazarus' voice, yet chose to remain silent, grateful for Tanner's quick wit when hers had disappeared altogether with his body pressed so intimately against hers.

"Now that it's sorted," Lazarus was saying, "we'll continue with the plan, and meet you at the rendezvous point. Have you memorized the details for the shift?"

"Yes, all done. I don't want her at the Vault any more than you do. It's not safe. We can shift out as soon as we return to the Vault."

"Go to the Training Facility instead. Grimm has left costumes for both of you there."

"And the others?"

"I've sent them ahead. They wait for you. I'll follow as soon as I can."

The Link went dead as Lazarus switched the connection off. Sharra lifted her head off of Tanner's chest as he slid the wire back to the device attached to the agrylium half-moons behind his left ear with one hand. All the while he kept her close within the circle of his other arm. Though the conversation between Lazarus and Tanner had given her time to recover from the kiss, her head was still a mess.

She tried to pull away, too embarrassed to look at him. His arm loosened a bit. Immediately she felt the loss of his heat as a small space opened between them.

"Sharra, look at me."

He placed his fingers under her chin, and tilted her head up. Her eyes got as far as his sensuous lips and stopped.

An intense moment passed before he groaned, and said, "If you don't stop looking at me like that, I won't be responsible for what happens next."

As the meaning hit her brain, her eyes flew off his lips, and slammed into his heated gaze. "Tanner, I..."

"I think you know how I feel about you," he said softly. "If not before, then that kiss we just shared would've given it away. But now it's out in the open, and I'm glad because I'm tired of hiding it."

"Tanner_"

He stopped her with a finger to her lips. "Shhh. You don't need to say anything right now. This isn't the time or the place, no matter how much I want to keep you in my arms. Just tell me that you felt it too."

"Yes," she whispered, for his eyes pleaded with her not to lie.

"That's enough for me."

He placed a light kiss on her lips before dropping his arms and stepping away.

A sudden feeling of loss swept over her. The desire to leap back into his arms was strong, yet she fought it, for it would only cause more problems. She knew that now, and was grateful that Tanner had stopped her from speaking, for she didn't know what she would have said. Her heart warred within her chest. When she dared peek up at Tanner, he, too, looked pained as he struggled with his desire for her. With a sigh, he rubbed his face as if to wipe some semblance of order to his own internal battle.

"Right!" he said as if coming to some conclusion. "We need to think of your future which means we must keep our appointment in the past. Are you ready?"

She looked around at the room. Spotting the forgotten teddy bear on the floor by the closet, she went to it, and tucked it under her arm. After sliding the mirrored door shut, she returned to Tanner, taking the hand that he held out to her.

"Ready," she said.

Tanner squeezed her hand, and gave the command to send them to the Training Facility. When they shifted, a vacuum swept into the place where their bodies had been. It rushed over the papers on the desk, knocking some of them off. They drifted to the floor, landing with a soft swish of paper for the teenage Greyson to find and wonder about when he got home.

Chapter Four

———

London, England
1825

Dusk had fallen. The gaslamps that lined the quiet street lent a romantic glow to the stately row of townhouses. More light shone from windows that had not yet had their drapes closed against the cold of that night.

Tanner's shift had dropped them some distance from their target in the mews behind another row of homes. It took him a moment to review the map in his head, to figure out which mews they were in, and then they were off. Sharra wrapped the fur-trimmed Redingote coat that Grimm had included with her costume around her gowned body, grateful for its warmth. The cold of the sidewalk seeped through the soles of her shoes as they walked quickly down the lane. Though there was no snow on the ground, the air was ripe for it. She could feel it. Growing up in Chicago where it snowed every winter, it used to get so cold that sometimes the oil in the car would freeze if her dad didn't plug it to a battery. Not that Sharra thought it was that cold now, though it was getting there.

They left the mews, and started down the street. Beside her, Tanner's breath came out in white puffs around his head as his firm footsteps clipped on the sidewalk. His hands were jammed into the pockets of his dark coat. It stretched the wool over his shoulders, making them look even broader. The row of buttons down the front was closed, the high collars turned up at his face. The heavy skirt of the coat swished with the movement of his long legs. On his head was a top hat. She thought the costume suited him.

"Here it is, number twenty-four," Tanner said as they reached their destination.

Taking her hand, he drew her up the steps to the landing, and rang the doorbell.

"Your hand is cold," he said.

He began to gently rub it between his. Warmth spread inside her belly at his touch. It confused her, like the kiss had done. She raised her eyes to his and saw them soften. The white clouds of their breath mingled in the air. His hands slowed, then stilled as he gazed longingly into her eyes. Her heart skipped a beat.

The door opened, and Faolan was there standing in the doorway. Dressed in a linen shirt under an embroidered waistcoat of green, and dark trousers, he looked everything a gentleman should be.

Sharra jumped away from Tanner, pulling her hand free, but not before Faolan saw it. Guilt filled her heart, and heated her cheeks. Though it may have looked innocent, for it was cold outside, and she had no gloves, she knew better. Something inside her had awakened with that kiss; feelings that she had denied existed all along. She was a fool. What was wrong with her? She was in love with Faolan. How could she have let this happen?

The smile on Faolan's face remained though it did not quite reach his eyes.

"Come in," he said to both of them. "You look cold."

He shut the door as they entered the front foyer. Before Sharra could remove her coat, Faolan was behind her, helping her out of it.

"It feels like winter out there," Tanner joked as he removed his coat, hanging it on the decorative coat rack in the foyer.

"There's a fire lit in the parlor," Faolan said. "And whisky, or wine, if you prefer. You can warm up there in a minute. First, Lazarus would like to have a quick word with you, Tanner. You'll find him down the far end of the house in my study."

"Right," Tanner said, and took off in the direction that Faolan had pointed.

The foyer turned quiet. Sharra hugged her arms as Faolan hung up her coat. Then he came to her, and placed a light kiss on her lips.

"I've missed you," he whispered.

"I've missed you, too," she whispered back.

Needing more, she pulled his head down, and gave him a proper kiss, pouring into it how desperate she felt. She had missed him. Her exile from the Vault had kept them apart. She needed to feel his touch, to smell his scent, to gain back that connection that they'd had. Most of all, she needed to wipe out the memory of Tanner's kiss.

After a moment, he lifted his head, and smiled softly down at her. "I guess you did miss me after all."

"Did you doubt?"

"I…"

"What?"

He shook his head. "It's nothing." Drawing her into his arms, he held her close. "I just want this mess to be over with, so that we can move on."

Sharra wrapped her arms around his waist, and sighed. "Me, too."

The confusion that had filled her heart washed away the longer he held her. Within the circle of his arms, she felt content.

After a little while, he said, "Though I'd love to stay like this, the others are waiting for us in the parlor."

They broke apart, both unwilling to let the moment pass but knowing the necessity of it. Drawing her hand through his arm, he led her down the hall to the parlor.

The large parlor was full of people. On the couch of rich green damask upholstery sat Katie in a high neck gown of pale organza and pink silk, talking animatedly with Tatiana who sat next to her in a similar dress of deep blue. Araylai listened quietly to their conversation, perched on a matching chair of green, looking astonishingly beautiful in a dress of true red. Against the far wall, Maxum was pouring drinks from a decanter. A welcoming fire burned in the hearth. It reminded Sharra of a typical scene from a Regency romance novel.

As they entered the parlor, Faolan drifted off in the direction of Maxum as Sharra moved towards the women and the fire.

"Sharra!" Katie exclaimed at catching sight of her, jumping up from the couch to give her a hug. "I'm so glad that you're back. The Vault hasn't been the same without you there."

"You mean there's no one else causing a ruckus besides me? Not even Tony?" Sharra teased.

"Well, besides Tony, but he doesn't count."

"Don't let him hear you say that."

"Tony is Tony, all bark, and no bite. Anyway, forget him. It's you that we're here for."

Katie drew Sharra to the couch as Tatiana scooted over to make room for another. Araylai met her eyes, sending her a silent greeting.

We need to catch up sometime soon, Sharra said through the connection.

Much has happened since you have been gone.

So I hear. But later. The men come.

As she spoke, Maxum and Faolan came bearing drinks in their hands, and passed them to the women. Faolan handed Sharra a small wine glass.

"Sherry, to help warm you up," he said, taking the empty chair next to her.

Before she could take a sip, Lazarus and Tanner entered the room. Lazarus was carrying a leather satchel. Maxum handed them each a tumbler of whiskey before settling against the mantle of the fireplace. Tanner moved to join him on the other side. Arms folded, with the drink held precariously in his hand, his blue eyes reached across the floor to where Sharra sat. As their eyes met, a wave of heat stole up her neck. She quickly dropped her gaze, taking a sip of sherry to cover her discomfort.

"Now that we are all here, we can begin," Lazarus said, the Head Director once again.

"What about Grimm?" Tatiana asked.

"Grimm thought it'd look suspicious if we all disappeared simultaneously. I agreed. And, since his position is the most visible, we thought it best if he stayed behind. We can Link with him if we need to. Now, onto business. The problem from the beginning was not knowing who was behind Sharra's attacks. Though it was assumed to be J.D. Dash, we now know better." From the satchel he withdrew a pile of papers, and began to pass them out to the group. "His name is Greyson Lane, also known as Jake Byson."

Sharra felt her face stiffen as she stared down at the headshot of her brother. Where Lazarus had found it, she didn't know. Yet it was the face she remembered. She had been half-drugged at the time, but it was still the same Greyson. In the photo, his eyes looked hard as if he'd seen too much of the world. And there was something about his mouth that wasn't right.

"Lane. That's the same last name as Sharra's," Katie said.

"That's because he's my brother," Sharra said to herself, but they all heard it.

Lifting her head from the photo, Sharra looked around, and saw the confusion on their faces. Only

Tanner and Lazarus remained unmoved by her quiet affirmation.

"How can that be?" Maxum asked. "I thought Sharra was the only one of her family at the Vault."

"Somehow Greyson got into the Vault without any of us knowing."

Maxum stiffened where he stood. "Are you saying that he just walked in off the street and got assimilated? Doesn't Cam need your permission before he can perform one? Where were all the security checks? You do have them in place, don't you? The Vault isn't a playhouse. If one got in, then who's to say there aren't more_"

"Slow down, Maxum. I understand your concerns. They're mine too. We don't have all the facts at our disposal as of yet. Though we do know some. For instance, we do know how Greyson Lane found his way into the Vault."

From beside Sharra, Katie breathed a name. "Viktor."

Lazarus nodded. "After Viktor identified Jake Byson as Sharra's abductor, we started questioning him more on his association with the man. Viktor may be a genius with mechanical things, but when it comes to people..." Lazarus shook his head. "Needless to say, Jake Byson, or shall I say, Greyson Lane saw the soft heart of our gentle giant and used it. Once he learned of what Viktor did, shift through time, Viktor said that there was no stopping the man. Before he knew it, Greyson had conjured him into showing him the Vault. Once here, Viktor quickly lost sight of him."

"Why didn't Viktor come to you?" Tatiana asked.

"He said that he was about to. Then Greyson showed up out of nowhere with a fresh agrylium tattoo behind his ear. Thinking that Greyson was now one of us, he did nothing."

"Did you approve the assimilation?" Katie asked. Hope was in her eyes, hope for redemption for Viktor's blunder. Yet it was short-lived, for Lazarus shot her a scorching look.

"Like Maxum stated, you don't just walk into the Vault and become an agent. There are certain requirements that have to be met, procedures that must be gone through. All in this room can attest to that. You were all hand picked for the job. You didn't come looking for it. The Vault came to you."

Faolan shifted in his seat and spoke up, saying, "None of this explains why he's after Sharra, and what we're going to do about it."

The pictures from the notebook that Tanner had found in Greyson's backpack flooded Sharra's mind. With them came other memories… memories of incidents that at the time seemed unrelated. Now, she wasn't so sure. Like the times he'd stolen her new toys and hidden them away, or later gave them back broken, or the times her school projects were mysteriously destroyed, or the times her new clothes were found with suspicious holes in them. There were many, and none of them nice. Maybe she had subconsciously blocked them out. He was her brother, after all. Yet, now she couldn't deny any longer what she knew deep in her heart to be true.

He hated her.

He had always hated her.

She looked at Tanner, knowing he was thinking of the notebook too.

"Was Greyson already at the Vault before I was recruited?" she asked Lazarus.

"Yes."

"Then that would explain the 'why' part, why he's been so determined to get rid of me. He probably feels that the Vault is his territory, and I've somehow taken it from him. You see, ever since I was born, Greyson has been jealous of me, and the attention I received from my parents, and later, from my friends. I didn't think much of it because that's the way I thought families were. People labeled it as sibling rivalry. I guess he's just taken it a little too far."

"A little? Is that what you're calling this?" Maxum said.

"This is not Sharra's fault," Tanner said to Maxum. "It doesn't matter how many times he has tried to get at Sharra. The point is to figure out how to stop it from happening again. Believe me, he'll keep trying until he succeeds. His mind isn't right. I've seen the evidence of it. And yet, somehow he keeps outsmarting us."

Araylai, who had remained silent throughout the discussion, finally spoke up. "To outsmart someone you must think like them. What would he do next, and then with that knowledge, turn the game around so that it becomes yours. You play them."

"Easier said than done," Lazarus said. "The other thing we've discovered about Greyson is that he has a very high IQ, a borderline genius. On top of that, he also has a photographic memory."

"The technical manuals in his closet," Tanner said. "When Sharra and I were looking for clues in Greyson's bedroom, we found a box of manuals, everything from computer programming and designing, electronics, engines: you name it, and it was there. That might explain how he kept one step ahead of us. With a photographic memory, he could learn anything, even maybe how to self assimilate. What other explanation could there be?"

"Whatever the case, we need to draw him out of hiding in order to catch him. You know how badly that worked last time we tried it with Dash," Katie said.

Tatiana raised her hand to speak. "Why can't we just go back to his timeline before he met Viktor? We could stop all of this then before it can even begin. Problem solved."

"If it were only that easy," Lazarus said. "But we can't because from the moment of his assimilation, his timeline has been set. It cannot be undone. There's no way around it. We have to deal with him, now, in our timeline."

"I can't stay hidden somewhere in time forever," Sharra said. "I won't. I'm tired of being scared. I know I said I would never be the bait again, but this is different. Greyson is my brother. He will come for me. Maybe this time I can talk to him, make him see reason. I don't know. I have to try."

Faolan took her hand in his, and said to her, "You'd be putting yourself in great danger if you did this. He's almost succeeded twice, no, three times so far. Who's to say that this time he won't carry through? Our luck can only last so long. And we can only do so much to protect you."

"I agree with Faolan," Tanner said. "Sharra, you've gone through more than anyone should have to. Let us take care of it this time. If we should lose you…"

His eyes implored her not to argue.

It hit her like a cold shower that both these men were vying for her attention in front of everyone. She felt it in Faolan's grasp of her hand, and saw it in Tanner's eyes. She squirmed in her seat. What was she to do? She loved them both, but for different reasons. She needed to escape and think, but she couldn't do that until this thing with Greyson was resolved. And she had plenty of time to think of a plan back on Ardus.

Taking a mental breath, she said, "Need I remind you that my tag is still in place? You can find me anywhere, any when, as you did when you found me on Ardus. Let Greyson learn that I'm still alive. Give me a mission. Put me back on the grid. Make up a story about how I was found by fisherman on Ardus, and spread it around. If Greyson should happen to miss that I'm back while hacking into the mainframe, then he'll definitely hear about it from the gossip, especially if Viktor is still in the picture."

"That'll only get you noticed," Faolan said.

"Knowing that I'm still alive is the first step."

"What's the second?"

"Preparing to bait him. With me back in active status, we should be able to draw Greyson out into the open, but this time we control the factors. When we know that the bait has been taken, instead of shifting directly to the mission site like we did with J.D. Dash, I can come in from another direction, like by car, instead of foot, and from outside the half-mile radius. It may be enough to throw him off. Either way, he will have to stay close to the target to get his sights on me. And he won't be there as the target itself. I doubt he will use the same trick twice. This time we will have to be closer, and in disguise so that he doesn't recognize any of us, except me. I'm talking more than costumes. I mean faces, and bodies, even hiding places."

"Your brother will know it's a trap," Tatiana said.

"No, he won't. He is too arrogant for his own good. We wouldn't dare try the same trick twice. That would be just plain stupid, and he knows that Lazarus is not stupid."

The room went silent. The only sound was the crackling of the wood in the fireplace. All eyes had turned to the Head Director for an answer. Lazarus stroked his goatee as he stared at the flames of the fire, lost in thought.

"Lazarus?" Sharra asked, breaking the silence.

His eyes cleared as he turned to her. "I see you've been busy planning this."

"I had nothing to do on Ardus while I recuperated, but to think."

"You feel that your brother will fall for your plan?"

"Yes, I do. Like I said, he's arrogant, and overconfident. Once he learns I'm back, his confidence will be shaken. He'll hate that. And me even more. It will set him off for sure. For once that will work in our favor."

Lazarus peered around at their expectant faces. "I don't know…"

Tanner was the first to speak up. "I don't like it any more than you do, having Sharra involved in any way, but it's a sound plan as long as someone stays with her at all times."

"I have to concur with Tanner," Maxum said, "as long as Sharra agrees to the arrangement. Someone should also be with her inside the Vault. Otherwise, she will be too vulnerable even there."

"Agreed," Faolan said.

"Is that really necessary?" Sharra said.

"It's for your safety, and our peace of mind," Faolan said, squeezing her hand.

"It won't be forever," Tanner said.

Tatiana, Katie, and Araylai all sided with the men. No one cared what Sharra thought on the matter.

"Then, it's decided," Lazarus said.

"Wait," Sharra said. "There's one more thing. Since we have only one try at this, I think it'd be a good idea to have a tag handy… just in case. I could get it in Greyson."

"No!" Tanner and Faolan said in unison.

At their outburst, Lazarus stepped in, ever the diplomat, and said, "What Tanner and Faolan mean is that you won't need one because there is no need for you to get that close to him."

That was the end of the discussion for her. Sipping her sherry, Sharra sat back while the rest discussed the finer details of the trap. For her it didn't matter how Greyson's capture was to happen, only that it would, though no talk was said about what they'd do with Greyson once he was caught.

One step at a time. The first step of getting back to her life at the Vault, she couldn't wait for. She missed Amadeus.

Chatper Five

The Vault

A white blur of fur rushed from the bedroom at the swish of her apartment door. Sharra reached down, and swooped Amadeus into her arms as the door sealed behind her. Hugging him to her chest, she buried her face into his neck. Under her ear his body hummed as he purred loudly in her arms.

"How I missed you, you furry beast," she said.

She held him, petting him as she moved further into the room. The in-house calendar on the wall monitor read the Vault day and time. She quickly did the math and figured out that time had moved only a couple of weeks in the Vault compared to the six months she had spent on Ardus. It was the longest she'd been away from the Vault since her recruitment. No wonder her body clock felt off. It wasn't something talked about among the others... the sense of disconnection. She wondered if she would ever get used to it, or would time mean nothing after a while.

Everything was the same as she'd left it, except for some tuffs of cat hair on the carpet. On the couch laid the half-naked statuette that she'd taken from Tony all those months ago. She'd forgotten about it until she saw it. Though it was beautiful, the memories of the Pompeii mission and Tony's bad behavior left a stain on it, along with her subsequent abduction. Yet, there was something about it that made her keep it. Maybe it was the thought of all those people dying back then. Or maybe it was because, even though they could change time, there were some events that were an integral part of the fabric of time. The destruction of Pompeii was one of them.

"A little piece of history sitting on my couch," she said.

Amadeus began to fidget in her arms. Plopping him on the couch, she picked up the statuette, and went to the greenhouse. The automatic watering system hummed as a fine mist sprayed down upon the vats of growing plants. She breathed in deeply, taking in the wet earthy smell, refreshing her need for all things green after the long absence. Looking around she picked out a large tub of lavender, and planted the statuette within it. The purple flowers formed a skirt around the marble woman, framing the artifact in an unlikely pedestal. It pleased her, especially knowing how much it'd irk Tony if he knew.

From the ceiling came the soft voice of her PVC system, announcing a visitor.

"Let her in," Sharra commanded.

Araylai walked in, all golden and beautiful. In her hand was Sharra's teddy bear.

"You left this at the Training Facility. Tanner wanted to make sure you got it," Araylai said as she passed it over.

Sharra took it, having forgotten about it in the hustle of costume changes and the secret shifting back and forth.

"Thanks."

The faded eyes of the bear stared up at her from her hand.

If those eyes could talk, she thought to herself.

Araylai sent her a questioning look. "You are upset."

"Ignore my aura. It is nothing," Sharra said. "So, you've come to babysit me."

They sat on the couch in comfortable companionship. Amadeus settled at her feet, but would come no closer. His tail snapped back and forth as his blue eyes stared suspiciously at the blond woman. Araylai returned his stare with the same disgust until the cat turned away. With a quirk of her lips, she settled back into the cushion to answer Sharra.

"Your life is valuable to all of us," she said.

"I know, but it's a tad humiliating."

"It will not be forever."

"I hope you're right."

"Lazarus will get to the bottom of this. He cares very much for you, as a father cares for a daughter."

"I feel bad for bringing this problem upon everyone. If I'd known that Greyson was here, I wouldn't have joined the Agency."

"This is not your fault. I, more than anyone, understand what you are going through: the pain, the fear, and the humiliation. I would have never dreamed that my mother could stoop so low as to dishonor our family, and with such hatred, and treachery. So many have suffered and died because of that treachery. There have been so many times that I wished I could have changed it, and I would have, if I had the means. Yet, within all the horror and death, there was honor and good to be found. Lazarus showed me that. Then… there is the Vault."

"The Vault," Sharra repeated, not quite understanding the connection.

"Yes, the Vault. If my mother had never sold me to the slavers, then I would have never encountered Lazarus and subsequently, the Vault and all the miracles that it entails, including you, my dear friend."

"I'm no miracle. More like a curse."

"Never that. You have been a blessing. You befriended me when no one else dared. You were willing to give up your life for that friendship. That is something that blood does not guarantee. And because you risked all, you have made it possible for more of my kind to enter the Vault, something I never dreamed would happen. I am no longer alone. So, now it is my turn to help you. That is what family does."

From the folds of her loose flowing gown she withdrew a metal box, and offered it to Sharra. Sharra took it, and immediately opened it. In a cushion of foam rested a pen-like device.

"It is a tag," Araylai said at Sharra's questioning look. "The receiver is underneath the foam."

"I don't understand."

"I did not agree with the rest when they denied your request. I thought your plan was good."

"How did you get this? I though it could only be issued through Medical, and only with Lazarus' permission?"

"I called in a favor."

"Cael. I hope it won't get him into trouble."

"I will take full responsibility for it. It is the least I can do for you."

"I must admit that Greyson has been heavy on my mind. Though I hope not to get that close to him, this," Sharra tapped the box, "helps put my mind somewhat at ease. If I've learned anything from Ardus, it is that it never hurts to have a back up plan."

Chapter Six

Though most of the residents at the Agency were known to be egotistical and self-centered at their worst, they were also known for their vulnerability and tight knit loyalty. They felt it deeply when one of their own was lost in death, or otherwise. And so when the news of Sharra's rescue and return got out, it spread through the Vault like wildfire. It found its way into every nook and cranny, every hall, and hideaway. No place was untouched.

Deep within the underbelly of the Vault, Greyson shut the door of his hideaway. Like a marble stone, he stared at the door with sightless eyes as his hand reached down to the lock to slide the bolt in place. Step by step he dragged his feet away from the door and further into the utility closet until his back hit the wall of blinking lights. The tiny lights flashed all around him in the semi-darkness.

In the safety of the utility closet, Greyson began to relax. His stony face melted away in the rising heat of his emotions.

"No!" he cried, shaking his head as if the denial would make it all go away. "It can't be true. It can't!"

He slammed his fists into the metal wall panel again and again, denting it under the force of his anger. The tiny lights flickered for a second before settling back to a steady glow.

Lines of hatred grew around his eyes and mouth. In his mind he saw her... Sharra, his sister. She was happy and carefree. She was pushing her hair out of her face. Her mouth was open wide because she was laughing at something somebody had said. He couldn't remember where that memory had come from, or why it surfaced now. He wanted to tear it from his brain. It had to go. All of it.

Closing his eyes, he tore at his hair as if to pull her out of his head. In his minds eye he saw her turn to him with accusing eyes. Her laughter changed from innocent to knowing. Cruel and coarse, it mocked him, goading him to respond. He couldn't take it any longer.

A cry of anger pierced the air.

"Aaaaah! Why can't you just leave me alone!"

The panel rattled again with another vicious blow from his fists.

"Everything was going so well. Viktor, the shuttle, even the watery grave. It should've been foolproof. Damn it, Sharra! I should've finished you right then and there when I had the chance."

He spread his hands in front of him. In the semi-darkness, they looked as if they belonged to someone else. He curled them around an invisible neck and pretended to squeeze.

"I was this close." He tightened his hands until they became fists squeezing nothing but air. He stared at the balls of his fists for a few angry moments before dropping them.

"Coward!" he growled, finally admitting to the truth.

The room turned silent as Greyson sank inside himself to think. Only the hum that came from behind the panels remained constant. His eyes glowed with an eerie light as he dished out blame to those responsible for his failure. Viktor's clumsiness, Lazarus getting into everyone's business, those damn fishermen on that water planet. Even the glowing reception Sharra had received at the Vault and on Ardus... blah, blah, blah... it made him sick.

"How can one person be so damn lucky? It's not fair! Not again. Not this time."

Renewed determination pumped into his veins as a plan began to take shape in his mind. Dropping to his haunches, he unscrewed a panel near the floor. Setting it aside, he carefully withdrew a laptop from the bed of wires inside the wall, and placed it on the narrow shelf above his head. He pulled out a spliced power cord from the cubbyhole, and snapped it in place. Flipping the top open he turned it on, and waited for it to connect to the mainframe.

As the icons flashed onto the screen, Greyson locked his fingers together, and cracked his knuckles.

"Sorry Viktor, but I think I'll save your dumb ass for another time. Using you twice in a row wouldn't be wise; I think, though keeping you close might. Yes… it just might. Now, let's see what my darling sister is up to."

He felt his lips curl into a wicked smile as his fingers hit the keys of the laptop. Old habits stirred his heart. He let the hate fester, for it felt good. It gave him power. It surged through him. He felt it even now as he tapped out his first command. It was in his bones. It was in his mind… in his heart. And he didn't care.

Chapter Seven

The waiting was the worst part.

Not that Sharra hadn't waited for an adversary before. This time was different because it was her brother who wanted her dead, and not some stranger. It would've been easier if it had been a stranger. Though if she thought about it, her ordeal with J.D. Dash, whom she hadn't known, had left a lasting mark on her even so.

When the PVC announced that Tanner was at the door, she knew that something was up, for he wasn't due to replace Katie for another few hours. Before the girls could rise from the couch, Tanner came striding in the room.

"Greyson has taken the bait," he announced.

"That was quick," Sharra said as both girls stood up to greet him.

Amadeus woke up, and when his bright blue eyes caught sight of Tanner, he meowed, and began to wriggle.

"Traitor," she said to the cat, before setting him on the couch.

Immediately, he ran across the cushions to meet Tanner who swept him up and settled him into his arms like an old pro.

A cheeky grin crossed his lips. "I can't help it that he likes me. Anyway, I'm not here for Amadeus, though he does have good taste. I came to tell you that the waiting is over, and that things are now in motion."

"Sharra's been back not even two days," Katie said.

"News travels fast," he said, petting the cat. "We made sure of that. The imprint showed up a few hours ago on Lazarus' monitor. We were just waiting to make sure the tap was completed."

"And was it?"

"Hmmhmm. All the files for your next assignment have been copied and transferred. 'Hook, line, and sinker' as the old cliché is known to say."

A little tremor went up her body. Things were finally in motion. Though she welcomed the news, inside she was scared. Somewhere along the way, Greyson had become unhinged. That, coupled with his intelligence, made him unpredictable. And incredibly dangerous.

"So what's the next move?" she asked.

"The others are already in place," Tanner said, "this time with facial recognition equipment. Lazarus is taking no chances. Believe me, we won't be making the same mistake we made with Dash."

"That's good."

"As far as you and Katie go; you two will shift later, once we know that your brother has shifted out to the target. I'm sure with his record; you won't have long to wait."

"You're not coming?" Sharra said a little disappointed.

"I'm to be the Link between you and the team. I can do that best from here."

"I'd feel better if you were with me. Not that I'm not happy to have you as my partner, Katie" she said, quickly correcting her blunder at the sight of Katie's crestfallen face.

Katie shrugged her shoulders and said good-naturedly, "I get it. He's all tall and muscular, and I look like a skinny teenager. I'd want him, too, if I had a choice."

Sharra felt a blush creep into her cheeks. "That's not what I meant. It's just that Tanner has been there from the beginning."

It was all that she could think of to say. And it was true to a degree. Her eyes were drawn to the pale scar at his hairline, remembering that awful night when he had almost been killed. It angered her to think that it was her brother who had been behind it from the beginning. Tanner had risked his life for her repeatedly since. She was sure that he would do it again without a thought. If she were truly honest with herself, she'd come to like having him around. He made her laugh, and gave her strength. And he liked her cat.

Tanner put Amadeus on the couch, and rested a reassuring hand upon her shoulder. "It'll be all right. Katie's quick on her feet, and has a sharp eye. With her by your side, and Faolan and the others close by, you'll be well protected. And we'll be in the Link together. You won't be alone. I promise."

"We'll get him," Katie said.

We'd better, Sharra thought.

The pressure to succeed was fraying her nerves. They would only have one shot at this. Greyson was no dummy. If they failed, who knows what he'd do next. There was something wrong with him, with his mind. Based on what he's done already, it scared her to her bones.

Later that evening when the call came in, the girls were ready. Everything had been carefully thought out, from the timeline, the location, to the no fuss glamorous costumes. After throwing on designer shirts, skinny jeans, and heels, they left for the Vault. All the way down to the main floor, Katie chatted away in a nonstop monologue. Sharra walked beside her in silence, deep in her own thoughts. Even the pull of the pylons that filtered through the wall was brushed aside.

As they approached the Terminus, Tanner got up from a couch, leaving a steaming mug behind on the coffee table. After adjusting the fitted jacket of his Vault uniform, he came and met them in the hallway in front of the arched entrance to the Vault.

"Faolan is at the rendezvous point outside of town with a car," he said, as he fell in step beside Sharra. "Do you have the coordinates?"

"Yes," Sharra said, tapping her temple.

"Good. Once you've met up, he'll drive you into town to the target. Greyson won't be looking for you to come in a car. That gives us the element of surprise."

"I hate being the bait."

"You volunteered."

"Don't remind me."

"Don't be nervous. We've got everything covered. Remember. No mistakes this time," Tanner said.

"When will you set up the Link?" Katie asked.

"I'll get onto that as soon as you shift out. It will take me a minute or two to connect the whole team. When it's your turn, it may sound funny, like being in an amphitheater. That feeling will pass."

As they moved across the onyx floor, the pylons began to stir, waking the cloud resting at their feet. At their waking, thin tendrils of mist unfurled from the cloud and drifted out across the floor, following the three agents as they headed to a shiftroom.

Outside the shiftroom, Tanner reached out, and stopped Sharra. The warmth of his hand seeped through the thin material of her sleeve as he turned her to face him. Words were on his lips, but none came out. She searched his face, and read the uncertainty in his eyes and on his forehead.

"Tanner, stop worrying. I've got this."

"I can't help it. He's a dangerous man, and will not stop until you're dead. If something should go wrong…"

"Have faith in the team," Katie said from beside them. "We won't let him hurt her."

"Just don't do anything rash."

"I won't," Sharra said.

"Promise me."

"I promise."

He pulled her near, bending down to whisper in her ear.

"I've lost you too many times already," he whispered. "I couldn't bare it if I lost you again. Come back to me. I...I..."

His cheek was a breath away from hers. So close was he that she could feel the heat from his skin as if they were touching. Her breath caught in her chest. The words moved her. The feelings that had awakened with that kiss, stirred inside her. She knew in her heart that he was about to declare his feelings for her. She wanted to hear it.

Then again, she didn't.

Once it was said, it couldn't be taken back. Her good sense told her to leave it alone that now was not the time. Yet, her heart battled onward, and won.

"What is it? Tell me," she whispered.

"Sharra."

He looked down into her eyes. She couldn't look away. The worry in them was mixed with a stronger emotion. She was sure that it was love. In fact, she knew it was love. His eyes dropped to her lips. They parted in an unspoken invitation.

"Sharra. Don't tempt me. Not now. Not in front of Katie."

"Katie. Oh," Sharra said.

"That's right. Katie," Katie said.

Tanner stepped back as Sharra turned to look sheepishly at her forgotten partner.

With hands on her hips Katie faced them, and said, "If you two are done saying goodbye, I'd like to get going. The others are waiting."

Behind Tanner a shiftroom flashed bright, signaling a returning shifter.

"I wonder who that is…" Tanner said.

A man stepped out of the shiftroom, and paused within the backdrop of intense light. Sharra stared at his black silhouette. Something about the slimness of his body and the way he stood seemed familiar. It was only when he moved away from the brightness of the shiftroom and further into the Vault that his features became discernible. That's when she understood why he seemed familiar.

It was Greyson.

A small gasp left her throat. She grabbed Tanner's arm. Her mouth worked to say her brother's name, to warn him. Nothing came out. Tanner's bicep stiffen under her hand, and she knew that he had seen him too. Like her, he stood frozen in shock.

The arched walls of the Vault picked up the tiny sound she had made. Greyson heard it, and stopped. His body tensed as he whipped around. In the dimness of the Vault, he found them. Time slowed down to a crawl. As if in a dream, she watched his eyes widen in shock as recognition hit his brain. His face fell, twisting into hard lines as his eyes narrowed in anger.

"You," he snarled.

In those few precious seconds while Greyson stood immobilized in shock, Tanner came alive, and flew into action. Taking off across the floor, he charged into her brother at full speed. The force of his body threw them both to the floor with a thud. It was enough to wake the girls from their stupor. They ran forward and spanned out around the fighting men; ready to jump in. Sharra watched helplessly as the men rolled towards the cloud.

The row of pylons grew agitated as the men struggled close by. The more energy that the men expended, the faster the pylons rotated. With each rotation the currents that flowed up their liquid metal spirals increased in power, feeding the cloud at their feet with electrical particles.

The cloud grew. Sparks colored its insides like fireworks. But the men didn't notice, for they each were intent on the other, one to escape, and the other to imprison.

While they fought beside the expanding cloud, the threads inside Sharra's head grew restless. Though her mental shield was tightly clamped against the pull of the pylons, the threads heard the call of the cloud, and responded. They wriggled and writhed like a mass of squirming white worms, matching agitation for agitation as if they were one with the mother cloud. Only by sheer will power did she keep them contained. If they got loose... She didn't know what they'd do, only knowing that they had killed before, and with her permission.

Tanner's feet were almost touching the cloud. The feathery wisps reached down like hands, ready to draw him in.

"Tanner, the cloud!" Sharra yelled.

He pushed away from Greyson's body to look over his shoulder, only realizing then how close they had come to the particle cloud. In that moment of distraction when Tanner's grip had loosened, Greyson twisted his body free, and rolled away.

As he jumped to his feet, Sharra caught a flash of metal in his hand. On the other side of Greyson, she heard Katie gasp.

Fear gripped her. It held her rooted to the floor. The healing knife wound in her shoulder throbbed in memory. Yet, this time it was Greyson plunging it into her flesh, and not the Grex.

Tanner shot to his feet, and saw the knife. It glinted in the dim light as Greyson raised it between them.

"Whoa there," Tanner said, holding his hands out, warding off the other man. "No need for the knife. We just want to talk to you."

"Like hell you want to talk," Greyson said.

Sharra watched as her brother's slim body coiled for the thrust. Her fear escalated. Tanner was unarmed, and her brother was unpredictable.

Without a thought for her own safety, she lunged forward, jumping onto Greyson's back. Her arm squeezed his neck as her legs gripped his waist. The unexpected load caught him off guard. The knife fell from his grip as he grabbed at her, fighting for balance and breath. His foot kicked the knife in the struggle, sending it skittering across the floor. While they teetered precariously, Sharra whipped out the tag-inserter with her free hand, and plunged the tiny capsule into his shoulder deltoid muscle.

"You bitch!" he yelled.

Reaching back, he grabbed a handful of her hair, and yanked as hard as he could. Tears sprang to her eyes. She cried out as searing pain ripped through her scalp. Her grip loosened around his neck as she went to grab his hand. Freed from her grip, he dragged her over his shoulder by her hair. Blinded by the pain, she had no choice but to follow. The ball of threads in her head grew more agitated. They heard her cry, felt her pain, and begged for release.

No! She commanded with all her might.

It all happened so quickly: the fight, the growing cloud, the threat of a knife, her launch onto Greyson's back, leading to the position she was in now. No one thought of the consequences. Not Tanner, Katie, nor Sharra. Thus, when Katie launched her small body at Greyson, neither brother nor sister was prepared for it.

"Leave her alone!" Katie screamed as she leaped onto his back, taking the spot Sharra was pulled from.

"Get off me!"

With his free hand he tried to slap her off, keeping Sharra at his knees by the hair. As Katie grappled with Greyson, Tanner dove for the knife. But before it was in his hand, Greyson gave off a great scream of pain. Letting go of Sharra's hair, he went for Katie. Sharra dropped to the ground to look up to see Katie latched to Greyson's neck.

An unholy fire blazed in Greyson's eyes. She'd never seen him so angry. Instinct told her to flee. And when Tanner pulled her away from the feet of her brother, she went willingly.

Like a wild animal, Greyson tore Katie from his neck, flipping her over his shoulder as if she weighed nothing. When he saw the knife in Tanner's hand, he wrapped an arm around Katie's neck while the other pressed her against his body like a shield. Blood dripped from the perfectly round bite marks on his neck. It ran down into his shirt collar near the top of Katie's head.

The dynamics in the room had changed. They all knew it.

Tanner held his hands out and gentled his voice as if calming a spooked horse, and not a person.

"Greyson, you don't have to do this."

Greyson eyed the knife in Tanner's hand, and tightened his grip around Katie's neck. She tried to pry his arm away as she struggled to breathe, but failed. He smirked at Sharra. Sharra had seen that look often enough, and knew that they were in trouble.

"Greyson, is it?" he said. "You know me, do you? Isn't that interesting."

Tanner held out a hand in appeal. "Let Katie go. We're not looking for any trouble. We can go over there, to the Terminus. Just you and me…to talk. Simple like. And clear this up."

"No talking. I'm not an idiot. Did you think that I would be stupid enough to fall for the same trick twice?"

"No one said you were stupid."

"I knew it was another trap. All you poor people trying to help my darling sister," Greyson scoffed.

"We just want to talk."

"It's too late for talking. And don't go calling for help," Greyson said, stopping Sharra in the act of reaching for the wire of her Link. "Don't think I don't know that you're all wearing a Link."

As he spoke, he ripped the Link from behind Katie's ear, and shoved it into his pocket. Slowly he began inching backwards to a shiftroom. Tanner followed him step for step. Sharra knew that it would be disastrous if he got away, but didn't know what to do.

"We won't Link with anyone," Tanner promised. "Give us Katie, and you can go."

Katie's eyes latched onto Sharra. Round with fear, they filled her pixie face as Greyson dragged her to the threshold of the shiftroom. Sharra knew that the same fear was in her own eyes as she inched her way forward, ready to back Tanner up. Her high heels clicked on the smooth floor of the Vault. The noise drew Greyson's attention back to her.

His eyes blazed with hate as he spat out, "This is your fault, Sharra! Your fault! You can never leave things alone, can you? Now, look what you've done."

Sharra pressed her lips together, stopping the words that wanted to come out. She dared not answer him, knowing from experience that it only made things worse.

Another step, and Greyson had Katie inside the shiftroom. As Tanner went to step inside, Greyson pulled Katie against him, and squeezed her neck until no air could go in or out of her gaping mouth.

"Back off," he said as he squeezed.

"Okay, okay," Tanner said as he obeyed. "Don't hurt her. You don't need her. Give her to me, and go."

Greyson smiled above Katie's red face. It wasn't a nice smile.

He shook his head. "I think not. Let's call this an insurance policy."

His eyes found Sharra where she stood in the light just beyond the threshold. His smile dropped. A different light gleamed in his eyes. She'd never seen it before. It made her cringe inside.

"I'll be back for you," he said.

With those words, the shiftroom flashed bright as Greyson and Katie disappeared.

Chapter Eight

Sharra stared in shock at the silver design on the shiftroom floor where Greyson and Katie had just stood. The wind from the agitated pylons brushed her back, stirring her hair, tickling her face. Yet, she barely noticed.

Finally Tanner moved. Flipping the wire of his microphone down, he linked with Lazarus.

"We have a situation. Abort the mission. Call everyone back. Now," Tanner said, rubbing his forehead.

There was a pause as Tanner listened to Lazarus in the Link. Sharra knew that they had to tell him what had happened. After all, Katie was his daughter.

And so Tanner told him, laying it out plain. "Greyson has taken Katie."

The strain in his voice was too much for her. It wasn't his fault. Whipping down her microphone, she linked with Lazarus just in time to hear his clipped response.

"What do you mean, took Katie?" she heard Lazarus say. "Greyson left the Vault. I checked it myself. You were there with me."

"He came back right when we were about to shift out. Caught us all by surprise. He said he knew that it was a trap."

"Sharra?" Lazarus asked.

"I'm fine," she said, brushing a piece of hair out of her mouth. "Tanner went for Greyson as soon as we realized who it was, but they got too close to the cloud in the fight. Greyson got away. He grabbed Katie. He had a knife. It all happened so fast."

"What do you want us to do?" Tanner asked.

Sharra's hair whipped around her face as the wind swept around them. She pushed it away, raising her eyes to see the deep lines on Tanner's brow and around his mouth. Sharra knew it was for worry, not just for Katie's safety, but also for his dear friend. She went to him, and wrapped her arms around him.

"It's no longer safe for Sharra to remain at the Vault," Lazarus said. "I've told Faolan to head back to his place in London. Take her there. We can regroup later."

Tanner gave Sharra a hug as he asked Lazarus, "What about Katie? We can't just do nothing. You didn't see him, Lazarus. I'm telling you; the man is psychotic."

"He could've taken her anywhere, into any timeline. It'd be like searching the stars for a mote of dust. We can only hope that he won't damage her agrylium like he did to Sharra, and that Katie can escape. Otherwise...I... I don't know."

Though neither could see him, the anguish was clear in his voice. It broke Sharra's heart. Pain of loss was an old friend of hers. Lazarus need not suffer. Though Sharra had done something she'd probably get in a heap of trouble for later, right now that didn't matter. All that mattered was getting Katie back.

"Don't get mad at me," she said to Lazarus, "but I got hold of a tag, just in case. And, I tagged him. I tagged Greyson."

Tanner pulled away to look down into her face, and sent her a credulous look. "You what?"

"Please tell me it's true," Lazarus said as hope filtered into his voice.

"I tagged him," she said to both of them, "when I was on his back. We can find him, you see? Follow him, and get Katie back."

"Oh, Sharra," Tanner said as he gave her a little shake. "I don't know whether I want to kiss you, or shake you, you reckless thing."

Her heart filled with happiness at the hope shining in his eyes.

"Didn't I hear Lazarus tell you that you couldn't have a tag?"

She bit her lip, and admitted sheepishly, "I didn't listen."

"Thank God," Lazarus sighed. "Though you and I shall have to have a talk about how rules work... but later, after we get Katie back."

"Yes, sir," Sharra said. "As for Katie, we can go now. I have the receiver chip on me. I only need a tracking device to put it in."

"You are not going anywhere near your brother again," Tanner said.

"I agree," Lazarus said.

"Why not? I know more than anyone what he's capable of. He's a psychopath. There's no time to waste."

The worry was back in Tanner's eyes as he said to her, "Have you forgotten that you're his real target? We'll get Katie back. Trust me."

"In the meantime," Lazarus said, "wait at Faolan's townhouse until I send word."

With that final command, Lazarus cut the Link.

The nine pylons were still at work, spinning like liquid metal in the expanding cloud of charged particles. The wind they generated beat at Sharra and Tanner as the cloud reached out to touch them. Inside her head, the ball of energy pushed against their restraint as they felt the cloud's nearness. The anger and frustration over her brother, coupled with the powerful pull of the pylons was too much for her, and she lashed out at the only thing she could.

Spinning on her heels, she raised her arms to the pylons, and commanded them with a ferocity that would've shocked her, if it weren't for the powerful need within her.

"That is enough!" she yelled over the wind.

Through the white light of the energy that beat behind her eyes, she could see the pylons slowing as if someone had pulled their brakes. Within a few heartbeats the storm winds subsided until a calm took over as all motion stopped. The cloud shrank away to gather tightly at the feet of the motionless pylons. The energy in her head snuffed out, taking with it the light that clouded her vision.

When all was still, Sharra lowered her arms, her energy spent. Her heart pounded in her chest as her lungs worked to breathe. It was as if she'd run a race, yet she hadn't moved. She stared at the now quiet pylons in amazement and fear, as comprehension of what had just happened slowly sank in.

Tanner, whose mouth had dropped open, snapped his jaw shut as he turned away from the pylons to stare at her. An odd expression was on his face.

"How… how did you do that?"

She turned away, not liking the way he was looking at her.

"I just told it to stop," she said. "And it did."

"You just told it to stop. That's it." He shook his head, and frowned. "No one has ever been able to control the pylons. No one. And that light in your eyes, I've seen it before, three times now. The first time was right after the cloud had engulfed you and Dash. The second time was on Ardus after you jumped Larua in the throne room. And just now, when you brought the pylons to a standstill. Do you want to explain what's going on?"

"Tanner, I…"

She didn't know what to say, or how to explain the white threads or her connection to the cloudmass. She barely understood it herself.

"No, no," he said, hearing the hesitation in her voice. "Don't go denying it. I won't be pacified this time."

"I'm not going to deny that it's happened, because it has. It's been there in my head ever since the cloud touched me. I can't explain it, why it does what it does, when it does what it does. That's the thing."

"Does Lazarus know?"

"The time has never been right."

"I think you need to make the time."

"I'll make the time, but later. We've got bigger things to worry about right now, like getting Katie back," she said, holding out a hand to him.

"You're right," he said as he took it, and led her back into the shiftroom. "But this is not the end of this discussion."

"I promise to talk to Lazarus when I get back."

"I'm going to hold you to it."

In the brightness of the shiftroom, she peered out at the silent pylons. The cloud had settled back to the floor like a blanket of white snow. A sense of longing... and of hunger touched her. She peeked up at Tanner, thinking it was coming from him. All she had to do was raise her shield and slip into his mind to see. Yet, something told her that it wasn't him, that it was something else, something not human.

He squeezed her hand. "Ready?" he asked.

Could it be from them? She thought as her gaze returned to the pylons. A singular idea entered her mind, but she couldn't test it out, not now, not in front of Tanner. If she did, and she was wrong, then he would think that she was crazy, too. Maybe she was.

"Ready," she said, and prepared for the shift.

Chapter Nine

London, England
1825

There was an art to running around the London streets of eighteen twenty-five in a pair of high heels and skinny jeans without drawing attention to oneself. Not that Sharra wanted to make a habit of it, especially in the middle of winter. Fortunately for them it was night, though the snow was still falling. Though she didn't care much for period clothing, there were advantages to it. Warmth was one of them. There had been no time to change costumes. It wasn't long before the cold seeped through the fine fabric of her designer shirt and through the soles of her heels.

The front of Faolan's townhouse was dark when they arrived cold and shivering. When they rang the bell, no one answered. They went around the block to get to the backside of the house through the mews. At the back door, Tanner reached up and felt around the lip of the wooden doorframe. A key was soon in his cold hand. He quickly unlocked the door and let her in. After a short search in the dark, Sharra discovered a candle and a small box of matches on a side table. Lighting the candle with shaky hands, she held it up to see. Together they headed down the long hallway to the parlor where the meeting was held a few days back.

"Find something to wrap in while I get the fire going," Tanner said as he bent to add fresh kindling to the cold grate.

Sharra took the candle, and searched the room. Finding an old woolen blanket near a reading chair, she wrapped it around her shivering body and went to sit on the couch near the fireplace. Kicking off her heels, she tucked her feet under her body, and huddled in the blanket as Tanner stoked the growing flame. Soon, a soft glow was coming from the fireplace as the fire gained strength. The sound of crackling wood filled the room.

Sharra watched Tanner rub his hands together close to the flame. As he crouched by the fire, he eyed her in the blanket.

"This isn't working. Do you mind if we share the blanket while we wait for the room to warm up?" he asked.

"Of course," she said, opening the blanket. "I don't know why I didn't think of that myself."

His eyes darkened in the firelight as he stared at the open blanket and then at her. His face showed nothing as he rose from his haunches to join her on the couch. One of his arms slipped around her waist as he tucked the blanket around them with the other.

"Very sensible, sharing body heat," he said as he wrapped his arms around her, enveloping her in the heat of his body as they shared the blanket.

All of a sudden, the room got very warm. Her breathing turned shallow as her heart began to beat in response to the intimacy of their position. She was a woman. He was a man. He had made it plain how he felt about her. She should know better than to encourage him. Yet, her traitorous heart wanted this, wanted him close.

She lowered her eyes to study the plaid of the blanket, and said, "It's on my resume. 'Sharra Lane, a very sensible, practical, boring person. Never late. Always on time.'" She quoted the line as if reading it from a sheet of paper.

"You are never boring," he said with a squeeze of reassurance.

"You're just saying that to be nice."

"No, I'm not. Our lives were dull before you. Shifting in and out, timeline to timeline, job after job. Same old routine. And then you came, sweet little you, and changed everything."

"But nothing's gone right since I've come."

"Some things have," he whispered into her hair.

It was then that the parlor door swung open and Faolan walked in, bringing in a fresh burst of cold air with him. The air hit Sharra's face like a splash of frigid water, waking her to the awkwardness of the situation she now found herself in.

"Well isn't this cozy," Faolan said as he spied them on the couch.

Sharra pushed out of Tanner's arms, and off the couch, leaving the blanket behind. Faolan's silvery eyes never left them as he paused beside a chair across the way. Like a child caught with a hand in the cookie jar, her face turned red with guilt. She couldn't stop it no matter how badly she wanted to, and hoped the flame from the fire was too poor a light to show it.

"Tanner was just trying to keep me warm," she said.

"I bet he was," Faolan said. He raised one black eyebrow at Tanner.

Tanner stretched his arms over the back of the couch, and smiled like a cat at the cream.

"She was cold," he said.

Faolan pressed his lips together. His stare grew more intense. The heat was rising between the two men. Sharra could see it, and it was her fault... again.

"Lazarus wanted me out of the Vault immediately. I had no time to change into warmer clothes before the shift here," she said, trying to justify their position, and calm the look in Faolan's eyes.

"Would it have been better if I had refused her, and let her freeze? Is that what you would've done if our positions were reversed?" Tanner said.

"Hmmm," Faolan mumbled, not caring to admit that Tanner was right. "I was to tell you as soon as I arrived that you were to shift back to the Vault while I stay here with Sharra. Lazarus said something about working up a plan of attack. What's going on?"

"Lazarus didn't tell you?" Tanner said.

"No. I came straight from the job."

Sharra clutched her arms against the chill that crept through her at the thought of Katie with Greyson.

"Greyson has taken Katie as a hostage," Tanner said as he stood and draped the blanket around her shoulders. She took it gladly, wrapping it close to her body.

"Good God, no!" Faolan said in shock.

"Sharra can fill you in on the details."

Tanner gave Sharra's shoulders a gentle squeeze as he looked intently into her eyes. "We'll find her. I promise."

Before she knew what he was up to, he gave her a kiss on the cheek. As he released her, he winked at Faolan and stepped away. Faolan pressed his lips together in displeasure. Sharra couldn't blame him.

Tanner didn't see it, for his eyes had turned inward as he prepared for the shift. When his eyes cleared, he sought them out.

"Keep Sharra safe," he said to Faolan, and then he was gone.

Air rushed in and filled the vacuum created by his abrupt absence. It blew over Sharra like a strong summer storm, whipping her hair back from her face, feeding the fire behind her with a gush of oxygen. As quickly as it came, it was gone. In the stillness afterwards the fire crackled merrily, sending fresh warmth into the room.

A pensive expression covered Faolan's face as he watched her from the fireplace. Sharra swallowed hard. It sounded loud in her ear in the silence that stretched between them. Finally he spoke, asking the question that she was dreading from the moment he'd caught them on the couch.

"Is there something going on between the two of you?" he said quietly.

She shook her head, and came to him. "No," she said as she wrapped her arms around his neck and pressed her body against his, "there's nothing between us. Just friends."

Whether that was the truth or not, she didn't know, or didn't want to admit to. All she wanted to do was wipe away the uncertainty off Faolan's handsome face.

"Because I'm feeling quite possessive of you, and I would hate to have to kill him," he whispered as his lips came down to meet hers.

Some time later, when the fire had burnt low, Sharra stirred in his arms. Somehow they had ended up on the couch with her wrapped in the blanket on top. Outside it was still dark. Through the slit in the drapes, she could see that the snow had stopped falling. Below her, Faolan's dark eyelashes opened revealing his amazing silvery eyes. He stared at her, through her, seeing everything that she tried so hard to hide. Yet, he said nothing, only tightened his arms around her.

She smiled down at him. "Is this your idea of keeping me safe?"

"Yes." His lips curved in masculine pleasure. "Though I am beginning to think that keeping you safe is becoming a full time job. Which I'm happy to take on."

"Be careful what you wish for..." she said.

"What's going on in that stubborn head of yours now?"

"Do you still have the tag receiver you used to find me?"

"Yes. Why?"

That was when she told him what had happened in the Vault. It didn't stop there, for the intimacy of their embrace broke down her defenses. The years she had spent living with Greyson came spilling out in a torrent of words, like a dam releasing the floodwaters of a storm. Resting her head on his chest, she let it all out: all the childish pranks, the mental torture, the physical hurt... the fear, nothing was held back, not even the horrible notebook that Tanner had found.

His hand stroked her hair as she spilled out all the horrors of her childhood. It comforted her when there was no comfort to be found in the memories of her brother.

When she was finished, she raised her head, and said, "So you can see why we can't wait. He's going to hurt Katie, or worse. I couldn't live with that. Can you?"

"Don't think that I don't know where you are going with this, because I do."

"With both the tag receiver and the chip, we can find them without any waiting."

"Do you really think that's wise?"

"While Lazarus is busy talking strategy with the team, we could be out scouting their location."

She read the hesitation in his face.

"You don't know my brother like I do. He's angry, Faolan. Angry. He's going to hurt her. I know it. All I'm asking is that we find them. Get a location. The team can do the rest."

His eyes narrowed as he searched her face. "We find their location, and nothing more?"

"Nothing more. I promise."

A big sigh of resignation came from him as he lifted her off his chest, and sat up.

"Lazarus is going to kill me," he said.

"You'll do it?"

"Don't make me regret this."

"You won't."

"Somehow I doubt that," he mumbled as he left to get the tagfinder.

He came back a few minutes later, carrying a coat in one hand and the tagfinder in the other.

"You might need this," he said, passing over the coat.

She put it on, and carefully withdrew the tiny chip from her jean's pocket, setting it into the palm of his hand. The tagfinder was turned on and the chip inserted. A keypad appeared on the smooth surface of its face. With his thumbs Faolan fed into it a sequence of data, and then waited. As Sharra stared at the screen a green dot appeared and began to blink. The coordinates flicked onto the screen underneath it.

"We've got him," Faolan said.

Sharra stared at the familiar coordinates, and bit her lip. There was no way she would've expected him to go there, back to Chicago, to their hometown, and so close after her parents' death. Anywhere, but there. Yet, he had.

As she thought about it that same odd sensation that she'd felt back in her childhood bedroom came over her again. The invisible walls of time whirled around her, and began to collapse, gradually at first, creating a strange pressure as if the space around her was compacting upon her body. It was only when Faolan touched her arm that the sensation vanished and the room returned to normal.

"Are you okay?" he asked.

"Yes, just worried for Katie," she lied as she took his hand for the shift.

She didn't want to sound crazy. Her brother was crazy enough for the both of them. And that's who they were going after - a madman. Maybe she was crazy after all for suggesting it.

Chapter Ten

The Vault

Tanner blinked away the brightness of the shiftroom as he strode into the Vault chamber, leaving the nineteenth century behind. So absorbed was he with his own thoughts that he hardly noticed when the row of pylons began to move again, or when the awakening cloud reached out to him as he crossed the floor. His long legs brought him quickly out of the Vault, and through the deserted corridors of the ground floor.

Visions of Sharra filled his head. The warmth of her body, the soft scent of her perfume, and the feel of her smooth skin: it tantalized him, and drove him mad with wanting her. Though it had been his idea, when she had opened the blanket to share with him, he had almost refused.

Almost.

The desire to hold her was stronger than his good sense. Although his brain told him not to go there, especially after what had just happened with Katie and her brother, his heart's fervent reasoning had won out. He was glad for that stolen moment.

And it was stolen, if he were brave enough to admit it to himself. If Faolan hadn't come when he had who knows what might have happened. It was a sweet kind of torture, picturing Sharra there on the couch, or other times when they'd been together.

He remembered the way her eyes scrunched up whenever he made her laugh. A smile came to his lips just thinking about it. And the sound of her laugh... he loved to make her laugh. It was something that was missing at the Vault. And she did it with no hesitation or embarrassment. That was because she was still real, untarnished by time, unlike the rest of them.

Then there was the way she'd hold her face up to the sun in complete abandonment. The first time he'd seen her do it was on the rooftop garden of her old apartment on a training shift after her assimilation. It had made her look so innocent and carefree. He'd almost forgotten what that was like. He wanted to savor it, to stop her from becoming like the rest of them. If only that were possible. Yet, he couldn't keep from trying. The instinct to keep her safe was too strong to ignore.

His smile grew as he thought of her with her cat. She loved that cat more than anything else. He wasn't surprised. He had read her file. Life had not been easy for her since her parents' death. Amadeus filled a void that should have been occupied with family, friends, even a boyfriend or two. Instead, she had settled on the love of an animal.

A wave of jealousy welled up from nowhere.

Damn cat gets more than me.

As quickly as it came, the jealous feeling left, for he knew he was being ridiculous.

Why can't I just tell her that I love her? Why am I holding back?

He shook his head, afraid to answer his own questions. It was because he already knew the answers.

The faces of his mother and sister appeared in his mind, the other two women who tore at his heart, and he knew that was part of the problem. He had promised himself to keep them safe, to protect them from his abusive father. And where were they for all his promises? Buried in the cold ground where his father should've been instead. For all his efforts, he had failed them, for he had been a mere boy, and had been no match against the fury of his father. He knew that now, yet the feeling of failure persisted.

He had made the same promise to Sharra, to keep her safe, and look how it's turned out so far. His track record didn't bode well for the future. If he lost her too…

"No," he said, stamping the thought from his mind. "I won't lose her."

It had been a long time since he'd allowed a woman into his heart. He was not a celibate man. Far from it. There had been plenty of women. His job made it easy, flitting from one time period to another. But, those encounters had been casual. No strings attached. He had liked it that way, until Sharra had come along. Then everything had changed. Oh yes, he waited until she was through the training period, like a good boy. Yet, afterwards when he had been free to pursue her, he still held back because of his fear of losing her. It was a lame reason. He knew that now.

Then out of nowhere came Faolan. It irked him that Sharra openly welcomed his pursuit, just like that, without even knowing the man. It was her choice, and he should respect that, yet he couldn't let it be. Though they were unofficially a couple that didn't mean Tanner was going to give up. In his mind, Sharra was fair game until she said otherwise. She knew it, and hadn't stopped him. And if by the way Faolan reacted when he'd caught them on the couch, Faolan was now aware of it, too.

Sorry, Faolan, love is war, he thought, *and in this you're my enemy.*

The way Sharra had responded to him gave him hope. And at this point that was enough.

The way up to the Head Director's office passed quickly. Before he knew it, he was standing in front of the old-fashioned wooden door. After a gentle knock, he walked in. When he saw the condition of his long time friend, his heart went out to the man.

Gone was the crisp posture and self-assurance that Lazarus normally wore. Instead, a shrunken shell of a man sat in the Head Director's chair. A half-filled glass of whiskey was next to his clasped hands. An empty bottle was on the mini bar. A grey pallor hung over Lazarus' face as he stared at his hands, seeing nothing. The folds around his mouth had grown deeper, along with the worry lines on his forehead. It was as if he had aged ten years overnight.

Seeing him this way was difficult. Though Tanner hesitated to broach the subject at hand, he knew that there was no way around it. Getting Katie back had to be a priority.

"Sharra's safe with Faolan," he said into the silence.

The far away look in Lazarus' eyes faded as Tanner's words brought him back to the present.

"Sorry. I didn't hear you come in," Lazarus said.

His hands came up and rubbed his weary face. When they came down, the lines from before were gone, so was the look of defeat that had dulled his eyes. Now, those grey eyes locked onto Tanner, sharp and determined.

"I've told the others to wait for us in the conference room. I wanted to hear the details from you first. If we can't get control of the situation before word gets out, we will definitely have a mutiny on our hands just like you had predicted. It's not just that it's Katie... well, that's not true. Greyson couldn't have taken a better agent. Not just because she's my daughter, but also because everyone else here has a special interest in her. She was only six when I saved her from the streets of London and brought her here to live." A smile of fondness lightened his tired face as he talked about her.

"I remember," Tanner said quietly.

"You couldn't help but love her. Do you remember when she first came, how all she had to do was flash her big innocent eyes at you, and her every wish was your command?"

Tanner smiled as lost memories came back of the little girl with the mousy brown hair and bright disposition.

Her laughter and joy had filled the halls of the Vault just as Sharra's had done.

"I think we were all caught by that trick," he said.

"There isn't one agent in residence that she hasn't been able to wrap around her little finger. I still can't resist her even now after all this time when I should know better."

"We will find her," Tanner said with renewed determination. "Sharra has assured me that she got the tag into Greyson."

Lazarus shook his head. "That woman is full of surprises. Though I'd like to throttle her for being so reckless."

"You and me, both."

"Nonetheless, I can't help but be grateful for her sharp thinking. Looking back, I should've honored her request for the equipment."

"How could you have known that we'd need it?"

"I should have trusted her instincts, and not let my pride get in the way."

"We all make mistakes, even you," Tanner reminded him gently.

Lazarus shoulders dropped as he stared down at his hands, and admitted softly, "Time cannot fix those mistakes, not for us, anyway. It is the price that we pay for the privilege to be here. And believe me, my mistakes still rest heavy in my heart. No amount of time can fix that."

Picking up the whiskey, he looked at it for a brief instant before downing it in one big gulp. Setting the empty glass back on the desk, he leaned back in his chair and folded his arms. His eyes flashed a steely grey. Tanner knew that the moment of weakness had passed, and the Head Director was back in charge. His next words confirmed it.

"Now, tell me what happened in the Vault. Leave nothing out," Lazarus said.

Needing no further prompting, Tanner laid out the details of the incident that happened inside the Vault chamber. He started with Greyson's surprise appearance. Then it went onto the fight that followed, and Katie's brave but foolhardy attempt to stop Greyson. He even tried to describe Greyson's unreasonable behavior. Tanner left nothing out, not even the unholy look that he saw in the other man's eyes when Greyson had threatened Sharra right before he had shifted out with Katie. Even now it made him shiver.

"There was no reasoning with him" Tanner finished. "He wants Sharra, and he wants her dead."

"That's not going to happen, not while I have breath in my body. Getting her out of the Vault and out of harms way was our first priority. Now that she's safely tucked away with Faolan in the nineteenth century, we can concentrate on getting Katie back. The Committee..." He stopped in mid thought as his hand came up, signaling a Link. "Faolan," he whispered to Tanner as he pulled the wire down.

"Yes, I'm free. What is it?" he said to Faolan.

As Lazarus listened his face turned hard. Thunderclouds flashed in his steely eyes. Tanner crossed his arms, and smiled inwardly, and wondered what foolery Faolan has gotten into this time.

"You did what?" Lazarus exploded. "Please tell me you're not that stupid. She was to stay at your townhouse, under your protection, not go chasing after her brother. Have you forgotten that he wants her dead?"

Tanner's pulse quickened in alarm.

"I left them not fifteen minutes ago. What happened? Are they in trouble? I'll kill him if he's put her in danger again," he said.

Lazarus shook his head at him as he continued to listen.

"I know exactly how persuasive she can be, Faolan, but that doesn't give you license to chase after Greyson without consulting us first." Again there was a pause as Lazarus listened before clipping out, "That's no excuse."

Tanner wished he dared link into the conversation. Whatever Faolan was saying was making Lazarus glare at the wall.

"I am well aware that he has my daughter. You don't need to remind me."

Lazarus frowned as more was said on the invisible connection before he replied again.

"No, you can't," he snapped out as if it were an ultimatum. Then a few seconds later he followed with, "Yes, it was reckless. Very reckless."

As Tanner waited, Lazarus' posture dropped the longer he listened to whatever Faolan was saying. What anger Lazarus had felt an instant ago was gone. He rubbed the side of his face with a tired hand as he pressed his lips together in resignation. Finally, he spoke again.

"Just a look, and nothing more. You understand? Just a look. And then, I expect a full report," Lazarus said, ending the conversation.

"What have they done now?" Tanner asked.

"It seems that Sharra has taken it into her head to go after Greyson, and has convinced Faolan who conveniently has a tagfinder that it's a good idea."

"I told Faolan to keep her safe," Tanner said with a frown. "I should've stayed back with her."

"And you think you would've done better than Faolan?"

Tanner nodded his head. "Yes. Definitely."

Lazarus folded his arms as he leaned against his desk. An eyebrow rose. Just one.

"Really. You can control her?"

"Control..." Tanner said, and stopped.

The word brought back the incident in the Vault, when Sharra had stilled the pylons. He'd almost forgotten about it.

"Maybe you're right," he said, a bit distracted. "Speaking of controlling... have you ever noticed anything... odd about Sharra?"

"What do you mean, odd?"

"You will not believe this, but right before we left for Faolan's place, she halted all nine pylons. And I mean completely stopped them in their tracts."

"What?"

"I know. If I hadn't seen it with my own eyes, I wouldn't have believed it myself."

"Did I hear you right? They just stopped?"

"Yup. Not a single blade of the nine moved."

"How did she do it?"

"It was right after Greyson had taken Katie. Sharra was upset. Hell, I was upset, too. In her frustration she told them, "that's enough" and they stopped. You know how the pylons can get sometimes. Something was setting them a spinning. You could literally feel the charge in the room. And with the cloud all over the place... I think she just snapped."

"They stopped spinning..."

Tanner snapped his fingers. "Like that. It was as if she flicked a switch. But that's not the only strange thing that has happened. There have been other times when I've seen something odd inside her eyes... lights... no, not quite lights."

He paused as he grappled for a better word. He shook his head, frowning, and settled for the impossible.

"Threads, worm-like, fluorescent. I don't know how else to describe it. Twice I've seen them. The first time was after Dash had been electrocuted, when the cloud had retreated from her. I was so grateful that she was still alive that I didn't say anything about it, for they had dissipated into nothing. I thought I was seeing things. Yet the second time I couldn't easily dismiss them."

Tanner recalled pulling Sharra, shaking and shivering, off the body of the traitorous Arderian High Councilor. Sharra wasn't shaking because of the knife in the woman's chest. They hadn't turned her over yet to see it. So Sharra couldn't have known that the High Councilor had been killed by it.

It was something else that was upsetting her.

When her eyes had looked to his for comfort, the alien light was there again, shimmering inside her dilated pupils. At the time, when he had said something about it, her expression had changed. And just like that, the threads were gone, snuffed out. Since then, he had wanted to ask her about it, but the timing had never been right. In fact, the timing was never right about many things with her.

"There was a second time?" Lazarus asked, cutting into his thoughts.

"On Ardus, during the battle for the throne. There was... an incident. Sharra just shook it off, as if it were nothing, but I'm telling you that it was the same as before. Shining white threads. Yet these were fatter, as if they'd been gorged with food."

"Threads, you say."

"Yes, fluorescent threads. Whatever is going on with her, it's not natural."

Lazarus looked away, unable to meet his eyes... or unwilling. Tanner didn't know which. Stroking his short goatee, the Head Director pondered Tanner's words in silence.

Tanner heard him say under his breath, "No one has stopped the pylons before," the same thing that he had thought. That acknowledgement brought Lazarus out of his contemplation.

"Thank you for coming to me about this. I, too, have had my suspicions after the incident in the Vault between her and J.D. Dash. Leave it with me," he said as he stood up. "I'll have a word with her as soon as I can.

Right now, we've got other pressing matters to attend to."

"The Committee," Tanner said.

"The Committee," Lazarus repeated as he headed to the door.

Before his hand was on the knob, there was a knock on the door. Without waiting for a reply, Faolan burst into the room out of breath.

"What are you doing here?" Lazarus said. "I thought you were getting the final coordinates on Greyson."

"We were too late."

"Did you see Katie?" Lazarus asked.

Faolan gave a sharp nod. His face looked grim as he filled them in on the last hour. After he finished his report, the room turned silent as Lazarus and Tanner absorbed the full seriousness of the situation.

"She is still alive," Faolan said after a moment.

"My poor Katie," Lazarus said.

"She's strong, and resilient. We'll get her back," Tanner said.

The possibility that they might not succeed hung over the room. Tanner wanted to say more to console his friend, knowing exactly how he felt. When Sharra had gone missing, those days had been torturous for him.

In the quiet, Faolan asked, "How many know about the tagging system?"

"Just a handful," Lazarus said.

"Could Greyson have learned about it in the data banks?"

Lazarus thought about it for a few seconds before replying, "It's not something that's documented. And if it were, it'd be in a passing comment. He would have to be specifically looking for it. What are you getting at?"

Faolan sighed with relief. "I'm thinking that if he doesn't know how we are 'tracking' him, then that gives us another chance to find him, and Katie, this time properly, and without Sharra. She's too close to this. It will only get us into more trouble."

"Speaking of Sharra, aren't you supposed to be watching her?" Tanner said.

Faolan pressed his lips together, and looked away.

"She's with Cam down in the Ward," he said.

Fire rose up from inside Tanner's gut at the quiet admission that came from the Scotsman. His fists balled at his side as the heat rose into his face.

"The Ward, you say," he growled as he took a menacing step closer to the Scotsman. "And why is that? Weren't you commissioned to keep her safe?"

"Sharra is stronger than you give her credit for," Faolan shot back. "She took out three hoodlums before I could finish off two. Three men all taller and larger than her. Most likely on drugs. They had that look about them. In a matter of seconds, they were laid out on the ground at her feet like sacks of potatoes. You should've seen her. There was such an angry light in her eyes. She was amazing."

Lazarus shot a look to Tanner as he asked Faolan, "A light in her eyes you say. What kind of light?"

"I don't know. It all happened so fast, and we were in kind of a hurry. It was probably just a reflection from the lights in the park." Faolan frowned as he thought back.

"Now that I think of it, there were no lights where we were. Strange."

"And the injury?" Tanner asked feeling the vessel at his temple begin to pulse with his rising temper.

Their eyes locked. Neither one was willing to back down.

"She'd said it was just a nick, and I wasn't to worry about it."

A growl formed low in Tanner's throat as he took a menacing step towards the Scotsman. "A nick, like in knifed."

Faolan held up his hands to ward Tanner off and backed up a step. "You know how stubborn she can get. As soon as I'd realized it was worse than she had let on, I brought her back here. Honestly, Tanner, do you really think that I wanted her to get hurt again?"

Lazarus stepped between them.

"Tanner," he said, laying a restraining hand upon the trainer's chest.

"She is fine, Tanner," Faolan said. "You can Link with her and see."

"I will," Tanner said, somewhat mollified.

"Gentlemen," Lazarus said, "your concern over Sharra is commendable, but may I remind you of the bigger picture? We need to direct our energy into finding Katie and bringing her home before that madman does something more to her."

"Rule number fourteen: 'Never leave an agent behind,'" Faolan said low and compelling.

"Never leave an agent behind," Lazarus repeated.

The fight left Tanner as the real problem was brought back to their attention. He dropped his gaze from Faolan, releasing him.

"It doesn't mean that this is over between you and me. But you are right," Tanner said, sighing in frustration. "We need to find Katie. To do that we need a plan."

Though Tanner wanted to run down to the Ward to check on Sharra, he knew that finding Katie was a priority. All he allowed himself was a quick Link with her before following Lazarus and Faolan to the conference room. The rest of the Committee members were waiting: Maxum, Grimm, Tatiana, and Araylai.

Shutting the door, Lazarus directed them to sit as he took the head of the oval table, and called the meeting to order. One chair sat conspicuously empty. No one looked at it. They didn't need to. The small girl that it belonged to was on everyone's mind.

Chapter Eleven

Chicago, Illinois
1986

A cold wind whipped at Sharra's coat as she ran with Faolan to the first thing that they saw – the wall of the garage. Pressing their backs tight against it, they both peered around in that critical moment to see whether they had been spotted. They were in someone's backyard. Dried leaves skittered across the slightly overgrown lawn and gathered at the bottom of the fence. Something felt oddly familiar about the place.

"All clear," Faolan said.

Incoming clouds covered the sun. The trees danced above their heads. The few leaves left on them rustled angrily in the wind. Near by the swings of a rusting swing-set squeaked back and forth as if two invisible children sat on them. Sharra breathed in the air, feeling the familiar sting of the cold autumn wind that signaled the start of winter.

"Storm's brewing. Happens this time of year," she said.

Sharra guessed it to be midday, a school day, if they were lucky. Besides the wind and a bit of traffic noise coming from the distance, all was quiet.

"Which way now?" Sharra asked.

Faolan checked the readings on the receiver. The black arrow of the digital compass hovered inside the dense screen, pointing to the top right corner of the device. Near the corner floated the green blinking dot that was Greyson. Faolan swiveled his body until the arrow lined up with the dot.

"The dot puts Greyson about seven hundred and fifty feet away." Looking up, he studied the backyard, and said, "I wonder if we should stick to the back of the houses until we get closer. I don't like the idea of walking out onto the street in broad daylight. He might see us coming."

"No, he won't. He's not expecting anyone to know where he is, so he won't be looking. Come on," she said, grabbing his sleeve and pulling him away from their hiding place.

They quickly left for the street via the driveway. Once on the sidewalk, Faolan checked the direction, and started down the street. Sharra wrapped the coat around her and hurried to match her shorter steps to his long stride.

The neighborhood was not new to her. Though it'd been years since she had been there, she recognized the houses as soon as they were on the sidewalk. Robin Taylor, a girl two years older than she, lived in the two-story house they just passed. Mikey Pratt lived across the street. Robin and he were a big item back in the day, always together, like glue. They'd even kissed on the school bus in front of everyone. A few houses down were the Snyder's. She had loved the old couple. Mr. Snyder used to let her take his dog, Max, a large black Newfoundland, for a walk whenever she came by for a visit. Mrs. Snyder had made the best chocolate chip cookies, the kind that were crunchy on the outside, but soft in the middle. Then one day, she died. Mr. Snyder must have loved his wife very much because not long after her funeral they had found him in his bed dead. Sharra never did find out what had happened to the dog.

Sharra shook off the memories, and kept walking. Being back so close to her home unnerved her.

Back at Faolan's townhouse, the tagfinder had given them a preliminary address: timeline, date, and general location. She knew before they had left that they were going to Chicago, but it never entered her mind that Greyson would bring Katie here, back to their home neighborhood. The house where she grew up sat four houses away on the side they were on. She could see it from there.

"We're getting close," Faolan said.

A tight feeling gripped her stomach as she asked, "Where?"

Faolan pointed the receiver at a house three driveways down on the other side. "Over there. The white two-story with the red mailbox."

She sagged with relief. It wasn't their home. For some reason, it mattered to her.

"You said this was your old neighborhood. Do you recognize the house?"

"Yes. One of Greyson's old schoolmates used to live there. I mean, he does live there... now... in this timeline. Cade was his name. Greyson used to hang out with him all the time."

"Do you know where they'd hang out? Bedroom, living room, garage?"

She shrugged her shoulders. "Your guess is as good as mine. I was never allowed over there."

"We'll take it carefully then."

They ran down the driveway to the side of the house, and pressed their bodies flat against the white siding. Faolan took a quick peek into the window beside him.

"The living room," he whispered as he flattened back against the wall. "Empty."

A shout of anger came from the back of the house. Sharra sucked in her breath as the hair rose on the back of her neck.

"Greyson," Sharra whispered.

From his position, Faolan scanned down the driveway to where the double garage was partially hidden by the back of the house. A thunk sounded against the inside of the garage door, followed by another shout.

"Follow my lead," Faolan whispered.

They crept down the driveway, hugging the side of the house all the way down. When they came in full view of the garage, they slowed, ducking behind the low shrubs that lined the back porch. Both the garage doors were shut, along with the door on the side. The only other way in was through the double window that was partially blocked from inside. From their location behind the shrubs they could hear Greyson yelling at someone.

"Answer me, you bitch!" he yelled.

In the silence came the harsh sound of a slap.

Sharra's head jerked, feeling the slap as if it was she inside the garage.

"Come on," Faolan whispered.

Leaving the bushes, Faolan crept across the small strip of lawn that separated the garage from the house, pulling her with him. At the garage, Faolan hugged the side wall. Sharra did the same. Slowly they inched to the window, keeping their heads down.

"It's an easy question! You're all the same. Stupid bitches, all of you!" Greyson said. "Why won't you cooperate?"

As Greyson ranted inside, Faolan put a finger to his lips before pointing up. Sharra gave him a nod. Together they rose up inch by inch until they were high enough to peek into the garage.

The cars were gone. Old oil patches marred the paved floor where they had been. Boxes overflowing with sports gear and other household items were stacked against the far wall. There were also pieces of plywood and boards stacked upright, along with lawn equipment and other odds and ends that had been demoted to the garage for storage. Sharra hardly noticed those things, for her attention was on the girl tied to a wooden chair with duct tape in the center of the floor. Another piece of tape covered her mouth.

It was Katie.

Sharra saw the fire burning in her friend's eyes as Katie watched Greyson pace. All of a sudden he stopped, and swooped down upon her. Grabbing her shoulders, he shook her.

"Don't lie to me! I know that you're her friend. How did she get back to the Vault? How?" he demanded as he shook her.

Duct tape covered Katie's mouth. She glared at him, breathing heavily through her nose.

Faolan pulled Sharra back down to their haunches.

"Why doesn't she shift out?" Faolan said.

"Greyson must have already fused her agrylium patch," Sharra said. "Like he had done to me. We need to get her out of there."

"I don't see how. The only way in is through the doors, and they're all closed. Besides, he'll hear us way before he'll see us, and then he'll know."

Another slap resounded from the garage.

Sharra grabbed Faolan's arm. "I don't care how mad Lazarus will get. We can't leave her like this."

Faolan looked around for an answer.

"There may be another way in," he said. "If there is, we can ambush him from two sides. The surprise might be enough of a distraction for one of us to get to Katie, and shift out. Stay here while I go around the back of the garage. I'll Link if I find anything."

He left her under the window as he crouched low, and disappeared around the corner. As soon as he was out of sight, Sharra lifted up and peered through the window. Greyson's back was to her. With his hands on his hips, he was busy spewing hateful things at Katie's face while she stared defiantly out at nothing. As the tirade continued, Katie glanced at the window.

Their eyes met.

In that instant, Katie's face changed. Her eyes widened with hope. Her body calmed against her restraints as renewed determination filled her face.

Sharra shook her head, and whispered, "Don't."

As she watched, Greyson stopped in mid-thought to stare at Katie. Her eyes flew away from the window and down to the floor, but it was too late. Greyson flung his head around before Sharra had time to duck. His eyes locked with hers, and flared red.

"You!" he growled.

Before Sharra could move, he jumped for Katie.

"Faolan!" Sharra screamed as she lunged for the side door.

Flinging it open, she rushed inside, but it was too late.

They were gone.

Chapter Twelve

New York City, NY USA
2002

It was night in New York City. That was where the tag finder brought Sharra and Faolan the second time. With a half mile radius entry point, they could've shifted anywhere, on top of a building, or inside one of their many floors, or even underground in one of the lower levels of the city. All were preferable because it was easier to contain a target when they were inside... and safer, especially at night and in such a big city. But, no. They were in Central Park in the dark.

The ground under their feet was wet from an earlier shower as they headed to the south side. The sound of busy traffic filtered into the park. The skyscrapers of midtown Manhattan lighted the night sky over the trees. The compass led in that direction, to the thick clump of skyscrapers. They wouldn't know which one Greyson was in until they were upon it, or if the tagfinder would point downward, which was another problem in itself.

Sharra threw open her coat to let in a breeze. The change from cold to hot was hard to keep up with. She guessed it to be summer by the balminess of the night air. Just a few minutes ago it had been autumn and cold in Chicago.

"We should've changed while we were back at the Vault," she said.

"You were the one that wanted to keep going," Faolan reminded her.

"I know. I know. I sometimes forget that we have the time to slow down when at the Vault. It's just that I know Greyson, and I'm afraid for Katie."

"I don't like leaving the others out of this. Especially Lazarus. He needs to be told what we're doing."

"If we tell him now, he'll stop us. I can't do that. Not yet. Not until we have our sights on Greyson again," Sharra said.

"I don't like it."

"I know you don't. But I'm doing it with or without you. It's your choice."

"That doesn't give me a choice at all, now does it?"

She smiled sweetly at him.

"Stubborn wench."

She heard the capitulation in his voice, and inwardly sighed in relief. Leaning over, she gave him a quick kiss on the cheek.

"Thank you."

"Don't make me regret it."

"You won't."

Faolan checked the compass on the tagfinder as he unbuttoned his coat.

"This way," he said, taking them deeper into the trees, and away from the benches and wide brick walkways.

As they left the footpath and down a slope, Sharra's high heels sank into the dirt. She shifted her weight to her toes to keep up, and wished again that she had changed into her Vault uniform like Faolan had suggested.

The ground grew uneven as it dipped into a shallow gully. At the bottom was another pathway. Both sides were thick with trees, covering the path in a canopy of darkness. Sharra looked down the path with trepidation.

"I don't like this. Too dark," she said. "We should go back to the other path."

"I thought you were in a hurry."

"I am."

"This is the most direct route."

"Just because it is the most direct route doesn't mean it is the fastest. It won't do us any good if we get ourselves killed before we can find them."

His teeth flashed brightly in his face as he sent her a smile. "I'll protect you."

"I can protect myself. It's you I'm worrying about," she said.

Faolan wrapped an arm around her waist, and pulled her body to his side.

"Thanks for caring. I love you too."

Mimicking her, he planted a quick kiss on her cheek, and let her go.

Unappeased, she grumbled, "Just don't feel like getting mugged again, especially wearing these shoes."

He heard her.

"We won't get mugged," he said.

Keeping a sharp eye on the shadows, she kept pace with Faolan, staying close to his side. Darkness sank in as they followed the gully south for another few minutes. They moved quietly through the night. Only the sound of the rustling of their coat sleeves and the soft tap of her shoes marked their presence.

A stone footbridge loomed ahead as a dark shadow against the backdrop of city lights. As they approached it, an uneasy feeling fell over Sharra. Warning bells went off in her head.

Too quiet, Sharra thought as her steps faltered.

Grabbing Faolan's sleeve, she pulled him to a stop, saying, "I have a bad feeling about this."

He studied the dark of the underpass. "I think you're right."

But they were too late.

Two bodies emerged out of the dark tunnel. They swaggered forward clothed in confidence with arms held deceptively loose at their sides. Their faces were all hard lines and shadows.

"Stay close," Faolan said to Sharra. To the men he said, "We're just passing through. We don't want any trouble."

"Trouble? Did you hear the way he said that?" One of them asked the other, and laughed. "Trouble. Trouble," he said over and over as he tried to roll his r's, mocking Faolan's Scottish accent.

"Cut it out, Dex." The taller one said, as he gave Dex a playful punch in the arm. "This fine gentleman has a legitimate concern. We should answer him. Right, guys?"

From behind Sharra came a new voice, another male, and young by the sound of him.

"Wha'ever you say, Chief," he said as he and two more emerged from out of the shadows of the trees.

They settled behind Sharra and Faolan. Sharra moved to press her back against Faolan's. A flash of teeth shined in the young man's dark face as he watched her. Sharra shivered at the sight of it, knowing that it meant no good. A flick of a knife hit her ears. And then another.

"Knives. Why does it always have to be knives," she mumbled.

Faolan held out his hands to the one called Chief, and said, "Chief, is it? You look like an interesting fellow. You must be full of entertaining stories. But, we just don't have the time. I'm sure you understand. So, if you don't mind, we'll be on our way…"

Laughter broke out among the gang members.

"Did you hear him?" said one.

"Where do you think you are? Disney World?" said another.

They laughed again until Chief silenced them with a hand.

Chief studied Faolan for a bit. "I guess I am an interesting fellow. Yes, interesting. I like that word. Interesting. Why don't we make me more interesting by telling you to hand over your wallets."

"Sorry, but we're not carrying any money on this trip. Come to think of it, we're not carrying anything at all. How about it, Sharra, you have anything to give?"

"Are you deliberately trying to aggravate them? There's five of them and two of us," Sharra whispered harshly over her shoulder to him.

"Nope. She has nothing either," he said with a shrug of his shoulders. Then, his voice turned to granite. "Let us pass, or you will have trouble, all of you."

A flash of anger changed the harsh angle of Chief's face.

"Are you threatening us?" He took a menacing step closer.

The others took their cue from their leader, tightening the circle.

Sharra remained back-to-back with Faolan, and prepared for the inevitable.

"Don't worry, we can do this," he said.

"They've got knives. I hate knives."

"Would you prefer guns?" Faolan whispered.

"I'd prefer neither."

"Remember what you've been taught."

As the circle shrank, her anxiety increased, stirring the sleeping threads in her head. They began to swarm within the confines of their ball, pushing against her mental shield. It wasn't hard, but it was enough. It gave her an idea.

Holding tight to the ball of threads, she dropped her shield, and quickly read the minds of the gang members. Each had something she could use. Though it wasn't a knife, it was something, and right now, she needed any help she could get. So did Faolan, even if he didn't want to admit it. She wasn't about to let pride get in her way.

Taking the risk of exposing her hidden ability, she whispered over her shoulder, "Watch the big one. He's got two knives. Can't aim worth anything though. That's a bonus. And Chief is nursing a recent injury, though he's hiding it well. On his left side."

"How do you know that?" Faolan whispered back.

"Just trust me."

Chief gave the signal to two of his friends, stopping all conversation as Sharra and Faolan readied for the fight. The two thugs sized them up. Faolan kept his back to Sharra as he drew one his way. The younger one went for Sharra. A cocky sneer was on his lips as he raised his knife, waving it threatening in the air at her face.

With a yell, he charged. The other one was right behind, going for Faolan with a vengeance.

Sharra's heart pounded as adrenaline pumped into her veins. Within the young man's mind she read his move and ducked the first swing, and went in for the kick to the gut before he knew what was happening. Leaving the man on the ground gasping for air, she swung around and knocked the knife out of the second one's hand with a clip of her high-heeled shoe. The knife sailed through the air and disappeared into the night.

The sneer was swept off his face with a look of surprise. He growled and charged her. Seeing it coming, she was ready.

At the last instant, she dropped to the side, and stuck a leg out. It tripped him. Caught unprepared he landed face down upon the paved walkway, hitting his forehead with a loud smack. His mind went blank.

There was no time to gloat. As the one went down, the first thug was back up and charging. With little time to think, she threw herself in front of him, rolling into a tight ball, flipping him over like a bowling pin. He flew through the air, all arms and legs and landed on the ground beside the path. Before he could get back to his feet, she grabbed a rock from the side and charged. With all the strength she could muster, she smacked the back of his head with the rock. The young man fell to the ground, unmoving.

Sharra looked over at Faolan who was busy with the big fellow with the two knives. What she saw was enough to know that he was holding his own. That was all the time she had, for the forth gang member had stepped over his fallen comrade and was eyeing her up.

As they stared at each other, she knew this one wouldn't be as easy to put down. His mind told her that. Where the other two were newly added to the gang, he was an experienced veteran for his youthful years.

She read the scorn in his mind for her, a mere female. She was nothing. She could see it. His thoughts were full of pride for all the other knifings he'd been involved in, knifings that were bloody and done with such zealousness that told her that he lived for it, craved it, even searched for it. She saw the faces of his victims, for they were burned into his head as they were now burnt into hers. They were faces of the injured, faces of the dying... faces of the dead.

Her stomach heaved.

His mind was confident as he studied her. He knew his reach was long, and that he was quick on his feet. And most importantly, he always returned to the gang the victor.

Yet, even with all his superiority, like the others he had a weakness: the fresh knife wound in his side.

It was the same fight where Chief had gotten injured too. Though his clothes hid it, the pain in his mind was tangible, pointing to it as if there were a laser directing the way. All she had to do was get to it.

A cry of pain came from the fight behind her. She spared another quick glance in time to see the man with the two knives go down. He landed on the wet ground with a thud and remained there, unmoving. Faolan leapt over his large body and went for Chief without breaking his stride.

With her attention averted, the man in front of Sharra thought to take her. Catching his move in his mind, she whipped around in time to sweep down to the side, just missing the jab of the dark knife in his hand. Her coat twirled around her as she came back up into a crouch.

"Come on, little girl," he said, goading her as they circled each other.

"You come here, puny man," she replied. "No, you're not a man at all. You're an evil little boy. You couldn't handle a real woman if you saw one."

"And you think you're a real woman? Hah. Let's see you say that after I have you on the ground begging me for mercy. Yes. I like the sound of that: you and your fancy man over there, begging for mercy."

Before the last of his threat left his mouth, he leaped forward with a swing of his arm. The sound of material ripping tore through the air, as the knife swept through her coat and across her side. She cried out, grabbing her side as she flung her body out of the way. The energy in her head leaped in response to the pain receptors so close to them in her brain. She squashed them down with a command as she turned to keep her sight on her assailant.

At the sound of her cry, a huge smile spread across his face as he strutted in front of her.

"See? I was right. Give up now, and I'll go easy on you."

He thought he had her. Sharra read it in his mind.

"Is that what you said to the last person you killed?" she said.

Letting go of her side, she readied her stance just as Tanner had taught her. When his next move showed up in his thoughts, Sharra was prepared. As his muscles bunched for the dive, she leapt to the side, missing the swing of his knife hand by inches. While his arm was up, it left his mid drift unprotected, just what she was hoping for. With all the force she could muster, she punched him in the ribs where the knife wound still oozed.

He yelled in pain, buckling in two as he grabbed the wound. Before he had a chance to recover, she swung her leg around like a dancer, and kicked the knife out of his hand. Another swing around brought her foot to his head. It connected with a snap, sending him to the ground. His head hit the walkway with a loud *thud*, stunning him into silence.

Breathing heavy with exertion, Sharra crouched low, and peered at the bodies around her, forgetting for a moment the wound in her side. The noise of fighting came to an end behind her. Whipping around, she saw Faolan standing over Chief's body, staring down at him with fists clenched. Like her, his chest heaved from the exertion.

"Hoodlums," Faolan said in disgust as he left Chief moaning on the ground to come to her.

At that moment, the young man who had been hit with the rock had recovered, and was struggling to stand. Before he could get fully to his feet, Faolan sent the young man back to the ground with a hard fist to the jaw. His eyes rolled back in his head before his body hit the dirt. He remained there, motionless.

Sharra read his mind. No thoughts transpired from him. She reached out to the four, and found only one, Chief, with any thought. None of it made sense, for his pain was too great.

With relief she slammed her mental shield back down, grateful for the silence of her own mind once again. Now that the danger was over, the adrenaline dissipated from her blood, leaving her feeling depleted.

"Are you okay?" Faolan asked when he saw her holding her side.

Sharra reached through her coat to the slit in her shirt and ran a tentative hand over the thin line of the knife wound. Warm wetness covered her fingers. She knew it was blood. Though long, it felt shallow to her exploratory touch, unlike the old injury that a Grex had given her on Ardus.

"Just a small nick," she said. "Nothing to worry about. We need to keep moving. We've wasted enough time already."

"All right, but when we get a chance, I want a look at it."

"After we find Greyson."

"We should move before they wake up," Faolan said, as he took her hand and dragged her away.

They fled through the underpass where the gang had been hiding. On the other side of the bridge, the walkway led them to a lit part of the park.

Faolan pulled out the tagfinder. The compass led them straight down the wide walkway and to the buildings ahead. The green dot blinked reassuringly on the screen. That meant that inside one of those tall buildings was Greyson... and Katie.

Chapter Thirteen

Midtown, like most of Manhattan, was abuzz with traffic that night. As they waited for the green light at the crosswalk of West Fifty-Eighth and Seventh Avenue, yellow taxis swarmed by like bright yellow bees. They were everywhere, beeping their horns, causing all sorts of commotion on the streets as they tried to outdo each other for fares. Sharra would've found it funny at any other time. Not this trip.

"How much further?" she asked.

Faolan waved the tagfinder in front of him. The needle of the compass remained pointing down Fifty-Eighth Street.

"Down this block in one of the buildings across the street." He shook his head as he glanced around at all the people on the street. "It doesn't make sense."

"What are you talking about?"

"Why Greyson would risk shifting Katie here. Look at all the people, the traffic. The odds of being seen had to be high, and yet he took that chance. Why?"

Sharra shrugged. "I don't know. Maybe he's so full of himself that he thinks it won't matter. Or maybe he's a precise shifter, like me. Whatever the case, he's here, and close by."

The light changed. Sharra kept her hand inside her coat firmly pressed against her side as they moved with the crowd across the street and turned east away from Seventh Avenue. Halfway down, the compass turned to face the door of a tall building.

"This one," he said. "Luck is on our side. It looks like it's still open."

She looked inside. "There's a guard at the reception desk."

"I hadn't thought of that."

Backing up into the street, Sharra looked up and noticed a row of lit windows on the second floor. Horns honked as vehicles swerved to miss her, but Sharra paid them no mind as she studied the windows. Pasted across one of them was the sign: 'Rogers, Mariner, and Freid'.

"Can you see any monitors?" she called over.

Faolan peered into the main floor foyer. "None that I can see."

She joined him back on the sidewalk. "I have an idea. I just need to get my hands on some paper. Something official looking."

From out of his coat, he withdrew a packet of papers.

"Will this do?" he said as he handed them over.

The folded nineteenth century vellum paper felt heavy in her hand. Someone had written on the front in elegant scrolled writing. Though it was done with ink and quill, the beautiful calligraphy looked very official. It was just what she needed.

"It's for my lawyer," Faolan said. "I was supposed to have dropped it off earlier before all this."

"Perfect. Keep it for now," she said, handing it back, "and follow my lead."

The glass doors swished opened as she strode in and headed purposefully to the reception desk. At the counter, she smiled shyly at the stern-looking guard.

"Sorry that we're late," she said to him. "We've an appointment at the lawyers' office on the second floor." Resting a hand on Faolan's arm, she turned to him and asked, "Who was it with, dear?"

"I have the card here somewhere," he said as he fished around in his coat.

The guard frowned as he rechecked a monitor. "It must be Ms. Freid," he said. "She's the only one in tonight, though nothing was said about any clients coming in."

"It was kind of a last minute thing," Faolan said.

"That's right. We're supposed to be getting married tomorrow, and we've just discovered that we needed to get one more paper signed. I don't know how we forgot it. First time wedding jitters, I guess. We've brought the papers. Show him, honey." She nudged her make-believe fiancé, and smiled at the guard. "Show the papers to the man."

"The papers." Faolan gave her a look.

Reaching into his coat, he slowly withdrew the packet of papers as Sharra laid her head upon his shoulder, staring lovingly into his eyes. Before the fake papers were all the way out, the guard spoke, stilling Faolan's hand. A whimsical look came over the guards face, softening the hard lines from before, making him look years younger.

"I don't need to see them," he said as he eyed the two with a smile. "Just go up. And…good luck."

The papers quickly disappeared back into Faolan's coat.

"Thank you, Sir," Sharra said as she took Faolan's arm and pulled him away. "Thank you."

They kept up the act until they were well into the elevator corridor, and out of sight of the guard.

There were six elevators in the wide corridor, three on each side. Each was made of polished golden metal. Dropping the act, Faolan fished out the tagfinder to check the reading.

She leaned over to have a look at the handheld device. Inside the dense screen the 3D needle of the compass drifted up to a ninety-degree angle.

"We have to go up," he said.

"Does it tell us which floor he's on?" she asked.

"No. But don't worry. The needle will guide us to the right one."

Faolan pushed the up button on both sides, and then stood back to wait. As they waited, Sharra studied their reflection in the golden door in front of them.

No wonder they were getting such odd looks. Faolan was dressed in a full nineteenth century costume, looking every part the gentleman, yet so out of sorts with modern New York City.

She was no better.

Though her clothes were more acceptable, even if the coat was out of date, the bloodstains where she had touched her coat were not.

Lifting the edge of the coat, she peeked at her hand against her side. It was covered with blood. Underneath it the wound throbbed. She winced, quickly dropping the coat back in place.

One of the doors finally *dinged* and opened. Sharra settled against the back wall inside the elevator as Faolan pressed the top floor button. They followed the compass until the needle leveled, and then, swung down as they passed a floor. Though Faolan was ready, they passed two more floors before he got the elevator to stop.

"We'll take the stairs down," he said, getting out. "It will be quicker and silent."

Faolan took off down the hallway in the direction of the exit sign. Sharra followed, staying behind him as they entered the stairwell, and headed back down. Each step jarred her side. She stifled a groan, knowing that if Faolan found out that the injury was more than a scratch, he'd call the hunt off and make her go back to the Vault. Pressing her lips together, she kept in the pain, hoping he wouldn't notice.

Fortunately for her, his eye was on the tagfinder, and not on her.

Two flights down the needle leveled out again. Faolan swiped the compass away with the motion of his hand. The keypad appeared on the lower portion of the screen. Soon, a 3D schematic for the floor on the other side of the stairwell was inside the screen. The green dot was there, floating inside one of the rooms near the far outer corner of the floor.

"Got him," Faolan said. "We should inform Lazarus."

"Don't we need visuals on the office for a precise return trip? It will speed us up."

"We can do that after the Link."

His eyes turned inward as he made contact with the Head Director. The details of their mission were given with some backlash from Lazarus.

"You don't know how persuasive she can be," Faolan said into the wire.

"Hey," she said, hitting him in the arm. He frowned and shook his head at her, pointing to the Link behind his ear.

"I'm sorry, Lazarus. I figured that if I stayed close to Sharra, she wouldn't come to any harm."

Lazarus fired something back. Faolan's eyes turned stormy as he responded with harsh words.

"He's got Katie, for Christ sake! You didn't see him, Lazarus. If we don't do something quick, he's going to hurt her more, or worse."

Whatever Lazarus was saying made Faolan look uncomfortable.

"I can't go back, and change our timelines. You know that," he clipped back into the wire.

Sharra wished she were brave enough to connect in their link, but dare not. Instead she had to be satisfied with listening.

"I realize that it was reckless," Faolan was saying, followed with, "We can't leave now, not when we're this close to finding them. We just want to get a look at his exact location. As Sharra says: "for a precise shift back" with the team. Nothing more. I promise."

Before her eyes the tension left Faolan's posture.

"I understand." Faolan caught her eye, and gave her an intense look as he listened. "No more than a look, and then we're out of here."

The conversation ended.

"You heard. No more than a look," Faolan said.

"I heard," she said. "Let's go before Greyson shifts."

Sharra opened the door a crack and peeked through. A wide corridor of soft grey carpet was on the other side. What doors she could see were shut, same with the blinds that covered the glass partitions that separated the corridor from the offices. All was quiet except for the flicker of a dying fluorescent bulb in one of the overhead panels.

Though it was past working hours, she was taking no chances.

"Clear," she whispered.

Slipping silently into the hallway, they left the stairwell, following the tagfinder. They went down the corridor past several businesses, and turned right into another hallway, until they came to the double doors of the end suite. A large golden sign hung on the wall next to the door. It read 'RoeTech Corp.' in large black lettering.

Pressing an ear to the door, she listened for a few seconds before stepping away.

"The door's too thick," she whispered.

Faolan tried the handle. It stopped partway down.

"Locked," he whispered.

"What do we do now?"

Handing her the tagfinder, he smiled at her, and said, "Unlock it, silly."

"How? We don't have a key."

"There are other ways. Tried and tested ways."

From inside his coat, he withdrew a roll of leather tied with a strap. After unwrapping the strap, he squatted and unrolled the leather pouch onto the floor. Lined up inside, in their individual pockets were an assortment of tools. Some she recognized. Others she didn't have a clue what they were. From them he chose three slim metal picks, and went to work on the lock.

"You can pick locks?" she said surprised, and wondered what else he could do that she hadn't discovered yet.

"Live and learn, my dear," he said as he pressed an ear close to the lock and fiddled with the picks. "Live and learn."

Not soon after, a decisive click came from the lock as it gave into the picks. He tried the door handle again. This time it sank down and clicked open. A catlike smile of satisfaction covered his face as he put his tools away and back into his coat.

As he got to his feet, Sharra checked the tagfinder. When they had moved closer to the green dot, the dimensions on the screen changed, dropping what they'd passed, and expanding what was ahead of them. Now, the RoeTech office schematic's floated in full detail on the screen. Walls, doors, and partitions were all clearly rendered in the 3D model, along with all the furnishings.

THE VAULT

At the far end of the new schematics floated the green dot that was her brother.

"He's in the executive office against the far wall," she whispered as she passed the tagfinder back over.

Faolan studied it for a moment before tucking it away.

"Remember, just a look, and then we're out of here."

She frowned, but nodded. She'd given her word, so she must obey, though the urge to save Katie was strong.

"Follow my lead," he whispered.

With a finger to his lips, he pushed the door in a slit, and slipped inside. Sharra followed close on his heels.

The reception area beyond the door was empty save for a long curved desk and a couple of couches. They went through another set of doors, and into the main floor of the office. Faint light from the city came in through the wall of windows and fell upon the maze of low-rise cubicles. Stealth was in their steps as they crouched low against the wall of cubical partitions and cautiously worked their way across to the executive offices. Occasionally they passed an opening in the partitions. In the dim light Sharra made out compact offices. Some were tidy. Some were not. All had computers and telephones.

It reminded her of the place she had left before she had been recruited to Vault Agency. Just like that the stifling feelings came back, and all its ugliness. The cigar smoke, the condescending, the cheating, and lying: it washed over her like an overpowering stink. She shook her head. That was the past. Her past.

Feels like a lifetime ago, she thought.

And maybe it was. Shifting used time, but not in the way that most people used it. With every shift out, the time spent in that timeline was erased as soon as she returned to the Vault. Time racked up, but was never cashed in. Age meant nothing. She could be twenty-four forever as long as she kept shifting.

Is that what bothered Greyson? My living on and on?

As she was contemplating that question, a bang came from one of the executive offices. It sounded like hollow metal. The bang was followed by muffled shouting. Even through the wall of glass and sheet-rock, Sharra could tell that it was Greyson. She grabbed Faolan's arm. He took her hand and squeezed it, pulling her on.

At the edge of the partitions, he drew her down, and gestured for her to stay low, pointing to the corner office, to the wall of windows that separated them from Greyson. After giving her a hard stare, he crept across the floor to the wall of executive offices, pressing his body low as he followed Greyson's voice.

Holding her side, she left the safety of the partitions, copying Faolan's example as she hurried across the carpet, and to his back. The closer they got to the target, the clearer they could hear Greyson. Her heart began to race with fear for Katie, as his speech thundered in a storm of profanity.

They passed the closed door and crouched down below where the glass met the wall. The profanity was still raging.

"Argg! I can't take this!" Greyson yelled.

Another smash of metal brought Sharra up to peer over the edge of the wall. Greyson was pacing back and forth, talking to himself, to Katie, or maybe to no one. She couldn't tell. His eyes darted around looking at everything and nothing, as he complained about her and his life.

On the floor at his feet, Sharra saw Katie lying on her side. The chair was gone. The duct tape was still wrapped around her legs and over her mouth. Her hands were tied behind her back, pulling her shoulders painfully back. Over one eye was a new cut.

Sharra's breath hitched at the sight of her wee friend.

Oh, Katie. I'm so sorry, she thought, and then froze.

Though her reaction had been nearly silent, Greyson somehow had heard her.

"What the heck?" he said as he caught her peering through the glass and froze.

"He's seen me! Get her!" Sharra urged Faolan.

Faolan bolted for the door, but Greyson was quicker.

Diving for Katie, he landed on top of her body, and disappeared with her as Faolan charged into the room.

Sharra slammed her fists against the glass in despair.

"NO!" she cried. "No."

Katie was gone. Their cover was blown. And Lazarus was waiting back at the Vault for an update. What more could go wrong?

A wave of dizziness hit her. She leaned against the wall, and sank to the ground just as Faolan came around the door.

"Sharra!" he cried, spotting the blood on her blouse through the opening of her coat.

Dropping to the floor, he moved her coat aside and gasped. "You said it was just a scratch!"

"I think I need to see Cam," she said weakly.

Scooping her into his arms, he lifted her up as if she were a feather, and pressed her to his chest.

"Just hold on," he whispered as he began the shift.

Chapter Fourteen

The Vault

Faolan laid Sharra upon the mat of the medical chamber, and moved away. Cael pressed a pen to her neck. The drug spread quickly through her veins. Sharra breathed a sigh of relief as the pain vanished. The mat felt soothing under her body as she laid upon her back as Cael set to work on her.

"I thought my treating of knife wounds was over when I left Ardus," Cael said with a wry smile as he gently began cutting the blood-soaked blouse away.

"I wouldn't want you to get out of practice," Sharra teased.

"Do you go searching for the blade, or does it just come to you?" he asked.

"Trouble tends to find me."

"That's an understatement," Faolan said under his breath.

Cael put the scissors aside and carefully lifted the piece of blouse up, laying it over her breasts, exposing the long gaping cut in her side. Fresh blood oozed out of it and dripped down her side to the mat. Cael moved aside to get some gauze. With his body out of the way, Faolan got a good look at the wound, and glared at her.

"You said it was nothing," he said.

"Is it bad?" she asked Cael.

He dabbed the blood away, and after searching the cut with experienced hands, said, "It is long, I won't deny that. But it is quite shallow. And with some rest, it should heal up nicely. You are one fortunate human."

Sharra remained still as he cleaned up the rest of the blood. Drawing the flesh together he placed a thin bead of glue over the line of the cut, sealing it.

"There," Cael said as he patted a plasiseal bandage over the glue. "All done. Nature will do the rest."

Faolan helped her sit up. Grabbing the side of the bed, she eased her legs to the floor, and stood up. The damaged blouse hung uselessly over her shoulders. A hospital gown was passed to her. Shucking off the blouse, she tossed it aside, and put on the gown.

"Look at my costume. It's destroyed. Grimm is going to kill me."

"He won't kill you. Maybe bark and growl a little to keep up appearances. I bet he'll be more concerned than anything else," Faolan said as he helped her tie the gown at the back. "Will you be okay here, while I go up to Lazarus?"

Sharra lifted her head to search his eyes. "You're going to tell him that we screwed up, aren't you..."

"He needs to know."

"I know. It's just... I worry for Katie."

The fresh cut on Katie's face and her vacant stare scared Sharra. They had compromised her safety. Who knew what Greyson would do now? He had seen her twice in two separate timelines. By now he must have guessed that they have a means of finding him. Sharra feared that it would drive him to do something drastic.

Faolan must've seen the fear in her eyes. Taking her hands he squeezed them reassuringly as he said, "The marker is still there. We can find Greyson again, in any time, in any place. Remember that time is on our side while inside the Vault. I'm sure Lazarus will call the Committee together to set out a proper plan of attack. We'll catch him. I promise. We'll find Katie before he can harm her anymore, and bring her back."

"I hope you're right."

"You've been through enough. Let the rest of us work out the details while you rest. I'll come to your apartment later after Cael releases you."

"I will make sure she rests," Cael said.

Faolan leaned in and gave her a kiss. "Behave yourself," he whispered, and then he was gone out the door.

"Come, Sharra," Cael said, taking her arm. "A bed has been made up for you on the Ward. A good sleep, and you will feel much better."

Later on Sharra woke up to a noise. Turning her head, she saw Tanner sitting asleep in a chair next to the bed. His head was tilted back against the wall. A small snore came from his open mouth. It made her smile. One of his hands was holding hers in a loose grip. She looked at them, his large hand encompassing her much smaller one, and felt safe.

He was the first friend she'd had in a very long time. Ever since her arrival at the Agency, he had always been there for her, through the good and the bad, even when she didn't think she had needed him. He was there, like a rock: solid, strong, and dependable. And he loved her. His was a real love, from deep within his being, the kind that she thought she'd never find.

Relaxed in sleep, his face was smoothed of lines, looking younger, carefree, though the dark circles of worry were still there, left over from her abduction to Ardus. She studied his unguarded face, and memorized the curve of his nose, the fullness of his lips, the fine lines around the outer corners of his eyes, the faint dusting of freckles over his cheeks, all of him, even the faint scar at the edge of his hairline.

Something stirred in her heart, something more than friendship.

Raising his hand to her cheek, she laid it against her skin, holding it there. The warmth of his hand tantalized her. It was definitely not a brotherly feeling. The temptation to kiss his hand was strong. She stamped it down, thinking of Faolan. She set his hand back down on the bed beside her, letting the moment pass.

Tanner's fingers gently curled around her hand. Her eyes flew to his face to find him awake, and staring at her with an intensity that made her shiver. She dropped her gaze to the sheet as he moved to sit on the edge of the bed.

"How are you?" he said, cradling her hand.

"Been better," she said as she struggled to sit up.

Dropping her hand, Tanner slipped a strong arm under her back. With his help, she sat up, and grimaced, holding her side.

"You're in pain. Do you want me to get Cam?"

"Not yet. Did I tell you that I hate knives?" she said.

"Yes, repeatedly."

Neither one said anything. Finally, when she couldn't bear it any longer, she peeked up at him. His blue eyes were stormy, dark with unsaid emotions. He took her hand again. Sharra's womanly instincts told her where this was going.

"Tanner," she whispered, trying to stop him… them… before something happened that she couldn't take back.

"I love you," he said softly, squeezing her hand. "There. I've said it. I love you. I can't hold it in any longer. Life is too short. I meant to tell you months ago, and then Ardus took you away… And now things have gotten… well, complicated. Faolan…"

He looked away for a moment as if saying the name brought him pain. When his eyes returned to hers, there was renewed determination in them. He squeezed her hand again.

"I've never told you about my family, have I?"

She shook her head.

"There's a reason for that. Like you, I once had loved deeply… and lost. There were just my sister and me. She was two years younger than me. As long as I could remember she was frail and delicate. I never did find out what was wrong with her. My mother loved both of us equally, and did what she could to make our lives... happy. My father..." he paused, pressing his lips together as he struggled with the memory. He took a breath, and started again. "My father was an abusive man, a drunkard. It wore my mother out, the fear, not just for herself, but also for us. I tried to direct the force of my father's anger to me, and away from Mom, but she wouldn't have it."

"What happened to her?" she asked quietly.

"She died of breast cancer."

"I'm so sorry."

He pressed a kiss to her hand before continuing. "I think it was the impotency of her situation that had made her sick. After she died, things got worse at home. With Mom gone, it was left to me to protect my sister. I got an after school job at the local feed store, and started saving money. You see, I had planned on running away with Reys. Her real name was Rachel. I called her Reys because she was the sunshine in our dark lives. She could find the good even in the worst of things and make us laugh when all was grim. She was what kept me going, giving me purpose. I had to get her away from my father. But I was too late."

His eyes shined with unshed tears. Sharra couldn't stand it. Wrapping an arm around his back, she leaned into him, and gave him what comfort she could.

"You don't have to tell me," she said.

"No, I want to. I have to. One day, one of the guys at the feed store fell through a chute, and broke his leg. I had to stay late to help finish unloading the feedbags. Usually, I was home before dad returned from drinking, and could deflect his abuse my way. But that night, I was late. I knew it as soon as I walked in and saw her lying on the living room floor, that she was dead."

"Oh, Tanner."

"He killed her. My father killed my beautiful sister, beating her into a lifeless pile of bloody clothes. If I'd been home, I could've stopped him, and she'd still be alive. She was only fourteen."

"I was fourteen when my parents died. Everything changed after that," she said.

"What made it worse was that we had planned on running away that weekend. I had everything arranged. All I was waiting for was one more paycheck. Just one more. Why didn't I take her away earlier? We would've survived on the little I had. I know that now, and it kills me. If I could go back and change my past..." He shook his head and sighed.

She held him tight, feeling his pain through the slump of his shoulders.

"I wish that, too," she said, "with all my heart, for your sister, and for my parents. It'd be such an easy thing to go back and fix, but we can't. It's against the rules."

"Our timelines are set. I know that. Yet, I'd gladly exchange my life for hers, if I could." He took Sharra in his arms and turned her face up to his, and continued, "Now, do you understand why it kills me to see you in danger? Why I have to stop your brother from doing anything else to you? I can't bear the thought of losing you. I don't think I could survive it again."

Tanner lifted away to look at her. His eyes burned with love. The turmoil of feelings that swept through her was washed away with that look of devotion. Her breath caught in her chest.

"Tanner," she breathed, putting into his name all the feelings that she dared not speak. Not yet.

His hand was warm in hers. She closed her eyes, resting her head upon his shoulder, lending him comfort. Though she knew that he wanted more from her, that was all she dared to give.

The door swished opened, surprising Sharra out of the intimate moment.

"Is this what you meant when you said you were just going to check on Sharra?"

Standing in the entrance was Faolan. His arms were crossed over his chest as he pressed his lips together. Sharra pulled away from Tanner, and sat up against the headrest of the hospital bed, pulling the blanket back over her gown. Heat rose up her neck.

"I was just comforting him," Sharra said.

"Is that what you're calling it nowadays," he said.

"Back off, Faolan." Tanner said as he slowly got up from the bed. "This isn't Sharra's doing."

She could see the muscles of Faolan's jaw clench as he shot a piercing look at Tanner. Tanner folded his arms and stared back at the Scotsman, uncaring of the jealous anger in the other man's face. The air grew thick with tension as the two men glared at each other like fighting roosters.

Sharra gripped the blanket and said, "Tanner was just telling me about his family, if you must know."

"We've all suffered loss, and yet, you don't see me crying about it."

"Maybe you should," Tanner said with a leer of a smile. "Look what you've missed out on."

The goading words hit home. Black thunderclouds darkened Faolan's face. A low growl rumbled in his throat as he balled his fists and took a menacing step towards Tanner.

"Tanner!" Sharra scolded.

"Don't think that I'm not blind to what you're doing," Faolan growled at Tanner. "Sharra's mine. I'd mind you to remember."

"Faolan!" Sharra said.

A triumphant smile spread across Tanner's face. "See? I think Sharra is protesting your claim."

"Both of you! That's enough!" she chastised, as she swung her legs off the bed to stand.

The movement made her cringe with pain. She sucked in her breath, and grabbed her side. Both men saw it. Faolan dropped his angry pose and went to her.

"I'm sorry for getting upset," he said as he sat on the spot that Tanner had vacated. "What can I do?"

"I just need some more pain medication, and I'll be fine," she said as she sent a Link to Cael. "Cael is bringing a pen."

She met Tanner's gaze over Faolan's head, seeing the apology there, and knew that it'd take more than pain medication to fix the tangle inside her heart. They were both so handsome and with qualities that any woman would desire in a man. And they both loved her. She had done nothing to discourage it. She was such a fool.

Lying back down, she closed her eyes, feigning weakness. "I'm tired," she said. "Would you two mind leaving?"

"Sure," Faolan said. "We can talk later, when you're feeling better."

He laid his hand briefly on hers where they clasped the sheet. If he waited for a response, she gave him none. The warmth of his hand left hers. She felt the bed shift as he got up. Soon after the door swished closed. Peeking through her eyelids, she found the room empty and sighed with relief.

The relief didn't last long. With the men gone, the full force of the turmoil she found herself in came tumbling out of her heart. That they both wanted her was plain to see. And she had done nothing to discourage either one.

At first, it was flattering, having two such handsome men vying for her attention, especially when there'd been very little opportunity for relationships before. No thought of where it might lead had entered her mind. Nor had she thought of their feelings.

Love was new to her.

The emotions were so unfamiliar that she hardly recognized them for what they were. It wasn't until she stole into Tanner's mind that one time that it hit her, all those raw, heartfelt, stirring feelings, and knew how powerful they were. She felt it again with Faolan. In an unguarded moment of weakness she'd fallen into the same trap of curiosity, and had sneaked into his mind.

She had to know. That had been her excuse for breaking her own rule.

'With great power comes great responsibility.' She'd learned the meaning behind Voltaire's famous words when in Community Night School. But back then they had just been words. Now, though, the full impact of what Voltaire so wisely noted hit home. She had a gift, a powerful gift. And so far, she'd used it without thought to the consequences. And look where it had gotten her.

Not only was she a two-timing schemer, she was also a thief, breaking and entering where she didn't belong. They were private thoughts, stolen from them without their knowledge. How could she have stooped so low? Her mother had trained her better than that.

"I'm a terrible person," she moaned.

The door swished opened as Cael entered. The thick aura encompassing his body was blue with concern. It was another 'gift' that the double agrylium had given her, the ability to read electromagnetic energy, something that the Arderian race gave off in a thick halo around their body. Only Cael and Araylai knew that she had that skill. Why she hadn't told Cam as Chief Medic, or Lazarus, the Head Director, she didn't know.

Her head hurt with all the secrets she hid from the others. Yet, it was her heart that suffered the most. Nothing could be worse than being torn between two men.

She was a fool.

"You are distressed," Cael said reading her thin human aura. "Why did you not call me earlier?"

"I had company. I sent them away."

He pressed the pen to her neck. The instant relief was a welcoming distraction.

"Ahhh," he said as if discovering something interesting in her aura.

She tried to calm the turmoil in her heart, but not soon enough.

"Tanner and Faolan, was it?" he said, as he went on to check her vitals. "Two dominant males circling does not make for a good outcome."

"Excuse me?"

"On Ardus, if a female could not choose between her suitors, then a challenge was set to see who was the dominant male."

"I don't know what you're talking about."

She knew exactly what he was talking about, and cringed under his perceptive gaze.

"Okay, I lied," she said. "In my defense, I didn't realize it was happening until it was too late. Now I don't know how to fix it."

"May I suggest a knife challenge? They are both worthy opponents. It would be an interesting fight to watch."

"I hate knives," she grumbled. "Besides, we don't revert to violence to solve matters of the heart."

"What does your kind do?"

"We talk it through."

"Talk. And how is that working for you?"

She glared at him. At the sight of it, he grinned, showing off his perfect white teeth.

"I take that to mean not well. If you change your mind, you know where I can be found. I would be happy to arrange a proper challenge. It would be an honor."

"Thank you, Cael, for the offer, but I'm responsible for this mess, so I should be the one to clean it up, for my own honor."

Finished with the handheld diagnostic gear, he slipped them into his pockets, and said, "Everything looks good. There is no reason to keep you here any longer. Just take it easy with your side for a few days. The wound is still fresh."

"I'll be careful," Sharra said as she slipped her legs over the edge of the bed and stood up. "And thanks for the advice, too... about Tanner and Faolan. I'll... I'll keep it in mind."

She watched his aura turn green with goodwill as he turned to leave. At the doorway, he gave her a slow nod.

"Try to stay out of trouble this time," was his last admonition, and then he was gone.

"I try. Believe me, I try," she said to the empty room.

Wrapping the hospital gown around her thin frame, she followed Cael out the door. Trouble was everywhere. There was no hiding from it. And she was no coward.

Chapter Fifteen

Angry voices carried down the hallway. So loud was it that it reached Lazarus through the closed door of his office. His head popped up from his work as the yelling grew more intense. Slamming down the information plate that he was about to slide into the slot in his desk, he stood up and left the room. Out in the hallway, it was worse.

"What is it now," he grumbled as he stomped down the hallway.

A small crowd had gathered in the communal lounge. Though they stood off to the side, there was no hiding their curiosity. And he couldn't blame them, for Tony and Zoe were going at it like never before. Tony's face was getting redder and redder as his anger reached a boiling point.

As he gestured wildly in the air with nostrils flaring, Tony yelled, "You're like a god damn anchor around my neck! I should've cut you off years ago."

"Why didn't you? And good riddance to you! Go have your fun with your latest floozy, because I'm done!"

"Anyone's better than you! Brunettes, browns, redheads, hey, even grey, I'll have them all."

"God damn you! I hate you! I hate you!" Zoe screamed.

She flung her tiny body at him. Tony tried to duck away, but the petite blond was having none of that. With her small fists, she pummeled his head all the while repeating, "I hate you" with all the ferocity she could. A slew of profanity left Tony's mouth as he tried to hold her off with one arm while protecting his head with the other.

"Stop it!" he cried as he raised a fist in the air and aimed it at her face.

Lazarus had seen enough. It had gone too far already. Storming into the fight, he grabbed Tony's fist as it was about to descend.

"That's enough!" he said. "Both of you!"

As he held them apart, they glared at each other. Lazarus knew better than to give into either party. They were both strong-willed individuals, and stubborn to the core. That's what made them good agents. It also made them difficult to deal with. Yet, this tirade went beyond their usual fiery episodes.

This one was different. Uncontrolled. Violent. Something was very wrong.

The seconds dragged on as the onlookers waited to see what the two would do. Lazarus kept a grip on them as he waited for them to cool down. Both were breathing heavily as if they'd been in a race, a race that neither party had won.

It was Zoe who backed down first. She shook off Lazarus' hand from her arm, and dropped her gaze, but not before he caught the tears in her eyes.

Shaking her head, she said, "I can't do this anymore," and walked away.

Zoe's back and shoulders were stiff with tension as she passed the small group of colleagues who had the sense to look ashamed for their blatant curiosity.

"Good riddance to you, too," Tony said to her back.

A sob escaped her lips. She covered her mouth, and picked up her pace until she was running out of the lounge away from everyone.

"Tony!" Lazarus said.

"Not you too, Lazarus," Tony said, pulling away. "I've had about as much as I can take, of her, of you, of this God forsaken place. I'm out of here."

His angry stride took him in the opposite direction of Zoe. Lazarus went after him. Whatever was going on had to be fixed, not just for the long-time couple, but also for the others at the Vault.

In all the eons that had passed since he became an agent, never had there been such disharmony inside the Vault. Morale was already low because of the ongoing issues surrounding Sharra. Tempers flared on a regular basis, getting increasingly more violent. It wasn't just Tony and Zoe, but also other long-term partners, and between old friends. None of it made any sense.

It was as if the Vault itself was sick.

The thought scared him.

"Tony, wait," he said, catching him at the elevators.

At the elevator doors, Tony turned and snarled, "What do you want."

"Let me help. You and Zoe_"

Tony stopped him with a sharp cut of his hand. "I don't need your help. What I need is to get away, and stay away."

"You don't mean that."

"Can't you feel it? It's... it's this place. It's sucking us dry. That's what you should be fixing. Not us."

The elevator door shut, leaving Lazarus alone in the hallway. Dark questions began to fill his thoughts as he pondered Tony's words. Maybe Tony was onto something. Maybe he, Lazarus, Head Director and caretaker of the Vault, was too close to the Vault, and couldn't see it.

Back in the communal lounge, the mood was subdued. The whispered conversations stopped as soon as those that had witnessed the tirade saw him. Their faces turned to him in expectation. He was no miracle worker. The sooner they remembered that, the better.

"The show is over, folks. There's nothing more to see here. I'll be in my office... if you need to talk."

Soon after he had returned to his office the first knock sounded on his door. Rubbing his face, he sighed, and wondered who was the first to come and complain.

Bracing for it, he pasted a business smile on his face, and called out, "Enter."

The door opened. Around the corner popped a blond head. Expecting it to be someone from the lounge, he was surprised to find it was another person altogether.

"Are you busy?" Araylai asked.

"No, come in. Come in," he said.

She was not alone. Cael, another Arderian, and the newest member of their elite group followed Araylai through the door. The door clicked as she shut it. Joining Cael at the desk, she stood side by side with her fellow Arderian. They were both ethereal, with their pearl-like skin, blond hair, and perfect faces; it almost hurt to look upon them.

"So what brings you to my office this fine day?" he said.

The two Arderians shared a look. Cael gave a nod to Araylai. She blinked, one slow blink that was their way, and turned to Lazarus.

"There is something that has been playing on our minds…"

"Go on," he encouraged.

"We have never talked about how we are different from humans."

"And this has now become relevant?"

"Yes."

"I see," he said, though he did not. "You're inclusion into our family was under unusual circumstances. Where all others had been recruited, you, and now Immari, were brought here for protection. Who you were was never an issue, and I've never been one to pry, unless it was for the greater good. And you've never given me a reason to doubt your abilities, or your commitment to the Vault. So I left it alone. I figured you'd tell me if it were important."

"Your trust has been a gift that I can never thank you enough for. I will always be honor-bound to you for saving my life. But that is not why we are here," Araylai said.

"I take it that it has something to do with you being an Arderian."

She gave him a slow nod, like the one Cael had given her before. "For many years I was afraid to reveal my true self, hiding behind the assumption that it would not hurt anyone to remain as I was… alone. I was wrong. If Sharra had not reached out as a friend, and I had not decided to tell her about myself when I had, who I really was, and where I came from, she would not have survived on Ardus for long. This made me consider that remaining silent is not always the right thing to do."

"And there is something you wish to say now that you felt unsafe to say before…" Lazarus prompted.

"In a way. It is because I was afraid to reveal how different we are from you. But that has all changed, and I know I cannot hold back any longer, not with Cael and Immari here to confirm my suspicions."

"Suspicions about what?"

"First I need to explain something. It has to do with the manner in which we communicate. We are not limited to our voice as most of your kind are."

"Most of our kind?"

"Yes, most of your kind."

Though Lazarus wanted her to elaborate on that point, she refused to move in that direction. Instead, she kept to her purpose.

"Living under the waters of Ardus, speech, which takes air, comes second place in the order of the nature of things. Our main means of communication is through the electromagnetic energy that we give off in abundance. It surrounds our bodies in an aura that we can read as easily as if someone were speaking. This electromagnetic energy also produces a charged wavelength that we can connect to if we are in close proximity to one another. It is a more direct way of speaking than even speech itself. It is similar to the way the Link works, but without the agrylium."

Lazarus sat silently behind his desk, absorbing this news with the aplomb that comes with years of experience, having witnessed countless strange things in his life. He was not surprised to learn that the Arderians could communicate under water. In fact, it made perfect sense. What concerned him, though, was where this was leading.

"Electromagnetic energy," he repeated. "I take it that this has something to do with what you want to talk to me about."

"Because of our sensitivity to it, I have known for a long time that the nine pylons use a form of the same electromagnetic energy. You can visibly see it in the patterns of sparks that travel between them, and also inside the metal spirals. Lately those sparks have become more agitated as if something has upset the balance inside of them. Then all these problems have started."

"What problems are you referring to?"

"People problems. J.D. Dash, Viktor, Sharra, Tony, and Zoe. Those are just a few. Everyone is off. We can see it," she said, pointing to Cael and herself, "in the thin electromagnetic aura that humans give off. It got me thinking about the agrylium metal in our heads. It is, after all, a highly sensitive substance, and is, by the nature of our profession, connected to the pylons. I have conferred with Cael and Immari on this subject, and we feel that there may be a connection between the disturbance within the electromagnetic field surrounding the pylons and the recent disturbance among the Vault agents."

Lazarus held back his surprise at Araylai's astuteness. The news gave him new worries, not only for the same reasons that Araylai presented him, but also for the reasons that they might see the truth, and know what he's done.

This damn secret!

He shut off the thought as quickly as it came, not knowing how much the two in front of him could pick up from his 'aura'. The Arderians were sensitive to electromagnetic energy. Not just to each other, but to humans, too, and most disturbingly, to the Vault. Could it get any worse?

"Are you saying that there's something wrong with the pylons?" Lazarus asked.

Cael, who had stood silently by, now came forward.

"We are not sure," he said. "That is why we came to you to ask permission to run a few tests. Nothing intrusive. Just a few measurements gaging the fluxes and patterns within the pylons and the particle cloud. Things like that."

"Won't that interfere with your studies?"

"I have already discussed it with Cam, and he feels that it would be a good opportunity for me to put some of my newly learned skills to use in a practical setting. The Medical Ward is right next door, so it will be no bother at all."

"I see that you've thought this through."

"Yes, Sir," Cael said. "It would be my honor to help. Sharra is my friend. And the Vault is now my home. How can I not want but to help make things right?"

Lazarus had no choice but to agree. "I will want regular updates on your progress."

"Yes, Sir."

"When the results are finished, I want to be the first to review them – even before Cam."

"That should not be a problem."

"Good. And if for any reason you should come across anything… unusual, I want to know about it right away."

Araylai stared at him with her knowing eyes, but said nothing about the odd request. With permission granted, they left, shutting the door behind them.

Sitting back in his chair, he rested his chin on the steeple of his fingers as he thought about their observations. His secret was no longer safe. He knew what the test results would show. Once they figured it out there was no stopping the truth from coming out. Things were spinning out of control, and he had no way of stopping it.

"My timeline is set," he reminded himself.

He rubbed his face, and sighed.

The bottle of scotch sitting on the sidebar called his name. He checked the time on the antique clock that hung on the wall, and decided it was too early in the day.

"Too bad, my friend," he said to the bottle.

Picking up the discarded plate from before, he dropped it into the slot and watched the information pop up in the air above the plasitop of his desk. The work must go on... until it ends. And by the look of things that may just happen.

Chapter Sixteen

Things were going all wrong.

It had never been his plan to take a hostage, and yet, here he was dragging the dead weight of a girl back to his hiding place. It was all Sharra's fault. He had been forced to do it. And now his cover was blown. They had seen him inside the Vault and knew.

Damn them!

It was probably through Viktor, the stupid lug. He should've gotten rid of him properly after he had dumped Sharra in the waters of Ardus. Yet, he hadn't. Maybe it was because Viktor befriended him. He hadn't had a friend in… he couldn't remember the last time he had a friend. It didn't matter. Look where it got him.

Friends make you weak, he thought.

Maybe he was getting soft.

No! That's not allowed!

Greyson knew that he was smarter than them, especially his sister. And yet, they had found him twice now. Once might have been a fluke. But twice? No. That was deliberate. And he knew someone who might have the answer.

Peeking his head through the door, he checked the hallway on the other side. Finding it empty, he pushed through with the girl. Halfway down, he stopped, and propped her against the wall while he fiddled with a wall panel. Prying it free, he pushed it in, and stepped inside the landing, bringing the girl with him. The panel was put back in place, blocking off the only source of light, hiding the forgotten stairwell from any passerby.

Greyson took the stairs down, one floor, then two. His feet were confident in the darkness. At the bottom he pushed through the doors, and in the darkness headed to the secret utility room. Above his head he heard the hum of the inner belly of the Vault, and felt safe for the first time since the surprise ambush.

Once inside the utility room, he dumped his burden onto the floor, and shut the door. Without a pause, he reached down and ripped the tape from the girl's mouth.

Before he stepped back, she was yelling at the top of her lungs.

"Help! Help!" she cried as she fought to get out of her bonds.

"Shut up!" he yelled. "Do you think that I'm stupid? No one can hear you down here."

The electrical panels blinked in the dim light. He saw her eyes flash in anger in her elvish face.

"Let me go," she said through her teeth as she struggled to free her hands from the bonds.

"Give it up. I'm not letting you go… not yet."

"What do you want?"

"What do I want? What do I want?" He felt the blood pounding in his temples, and knew another headache was coming on. "I want to know how they are following me. That's what I want to know."

She pressed her lips together, and glared at him, saying nothing.

Gritting his teeth he growled, and slapped her, demanding, "Tell me!"

Her head jerked to the side with the force of the slap. The tresses of her brown hair hung around her face, hiding her as she breathed heavily. He pressed his lips together and frowned. She was wasting precious time. Time that he didn't have. His patience gave. As he reached to grab a handful of her hair, her head turned slowly up to him. Her hair fell back from her face. He never noticed how big her eyes were until now. No longer was she a hardened agent. The face below him looked like a young child. In those eyes, he saw the innocence of youth staring back at him.

The fear and anger were gone.

She tilted her face and looked at him with curiosity. "What's your name? Mine is Katie."

Her voice sounded out of place in the dim light. It reminded him of a little kitten, innocent and carefree. Taken aback by the change, he answered, not knowing what else to do.

"Greyson, but you already knew that."

"Greyson," she repeated as her tongue played with the name. "I like it. It's different. My brothers had all boring names. Like George, and William, and Henry. I just had to give them nicknames, for how can you go around being called George all your life. Disgusting."

"You had brothers? I thought you're an orphan."

She nodded her head. "Mmmhmm. When my parents died…plague," she whispered the dreadful word with a cringe of her elvish face as if it were a curse word. "I was left on the street to die for fear that I was a carrier. I was picked up by a gang of thieves not much older than me. They taught me how to survive, stealing and such, just to eat, mind you. They taught me other useful things to. We were a family, those boys and I. So, yes, I had brothers."

"I wished I had a brother. Instead, I got a stupid sister."

"Sisters can be real stupid. Girls, and all their girlie stuff. All emotional. I hope I don't grow up to be like that. Yuck."

"I know exactly what you mean. My sister was so spoiled. She got everything. All she had to do was bat her eyelashes at Mom and Dad, and she got whatever she wanted. And did she get disciplined? Hah! I was the one who got blamed for everything. Their little darling could do no wrong. It made me sick."

"There's always one in the family like that. Percy… who names a boy Percy?" She shrugged her shoulders in disgust. "Anyway, Percy was like that. He was one of my brothers. All he had to do was whine and whinge, and everyone believed him. They couldn't see what he really was - a conniving liar. I tried to tell them, but he always had an answer. Always! I hated him."

"My sister was like that, too. Got all the attention, at home, and at school. "Your sister is so pretty. Your sister is so cool." That's from my classmates. Can you imagine putting up with that crap in high school?"

She nodded her head. "When Percy left the gang, I was so happy."

"I bet you were. I tried to leave my sister too. Yet for some reason, she keeps showing up..."

He stopped, and narrowed his eyes. Her eyes were wide with fascination as she looked expectantly up at him.

There was something wrong with this.

Then he remembered who she was and why she was there at his feet. He'd been taken in by her innocent act. Duped! Scammed! How could he have been so stupid? Not any more. She was one of Sharra's friends, and that was enough to make her the enemy.

"You bitch!" he said as he slapped her in his anger. "What do think I am? Stupid?"

Another slap followed. So hard was it that she toppled over and landed on her side. That wasn't enough for him. Grabbing a fistful of her hair, he dragged her back up, screaming in pain.

With her tight in his grasp he shook her, demanding, "How is she finding me? I know that you know. Tell me!"

Jerking her head up, he forced her to look at him. Tears ran down her face as she stared defiantly back. His headache grew worse as he felt his anger flare up, driving him over the edge.

Greyson's hands found their way around Katie's throat. He began to squeeze. The defiance vanished. A new look appeared, one that he liked better. Her body stiffened under his hands. Her eyes popped out in terror. He squeezed a little tighter and watched the paleness of her skin turn red as she fought for air. A rush of pleasure surged through him. He smiled.

"Do I have your attention?"

A small nod of her head was all she managed.

"Good. Now, I have a simple question, and if you answer it correctly, I just might let you live. You understand that? Live."

Her lips moved in her purple face like a fish sucking water, but no sound came out. It fascinated him.

She gave him another nod as she grappled for air.

"Listen carefully. Here's the question. And I'll know if you're having me on, so don't try anything." He let his fingers relax just enough to give her hope. "Tell me, how did they find me? I know that you know the answer."

She nodded her head again. Her eyes were frantic for air. It made him feel powerful. A strong desire to squeeze until he couldn't squeeze anymore almost overwhelmed him, but good sense won over. She'd be no good to him dead.

He let her go. She dropped to the ground at his feet, gasping for air. After five heaving breaths from the girl, his patience ran out.

"That's enough air," he said. Again, he grabbed her by the hair and pulled her onto her knees. Holding her tight by the hair, he said, "You want to live, right? So, answer me."

"You were tagged with a transmitter chip," she gasped out. "It's under your skin somewhere. They can track you with a receiver."

"Tagged? When was I tagged?"

"In the Vault... during the fight."

He remembered a sting, but had been too busy trying to get away to worry about it. Fighting did that to a man. It had been forgotten in the shifts back and forth through time with his hostage. He reached for the spot where he had felt the sting on his back, and touched a small hard lump.

"Sharra," he growled as he pressed all around it.

None of his prodding and poking moved the capsule. It remained under his skin, beaming his location even as he hid underneath the Vault chamber. He couldn't stay there, not while the chip was still in his body. They'd find him for sure.

A plan began to formulate in his mind. He'd have to be quick about it. The girl was a nuisance, but a necessary one. He still had one more job for her to do. And then, well, then he might get some real pleasure out of her before he got rid of her.

Looking down at the girl at his feet, he offered a smile of gratitude.

"Thank you, for your honesty," he said as he lifted his fist, punching her hard across the jaw. Her eyes rolled back into her head, and she slumped to the floor unconscious.

He smiled down at her limp body. "There. I spared you... for now."

Chapter Seventeen

Sharra knew that she couldn't put Lazarus off much longer. It wasn't as if she'd done anything wrong, not this time. It was her body, after all, and therefore her secrets. Not his, nor anyone else's. Though there'd been moments of weakness when she'd come close to revealing it to Faolan and Tanner. And yet, even then, with the two people she trusted the most, something had held her back.

The time had not been right for the truth. Her instincts had told her that.

So when the Link came in for a private 'talk' with the Head Director, she knew that something had changed, and her time was up.

Sitting in his office, she waited for him to bring it up. His steely eyes gave nothing away.

"With all that's happened in the last few months, I feel that I've been neglecting my duties to you, especially since the incident surrounding Dash's death."

Oh boy, here it comes, she thought.

"I'm fine, really," she said, buying for time.

He raised an eyebrow. It was a look that she knew all too well, a look that no one got away from. She squirmed in her chair.

"I see. Though in my experience, when someone goes through as many traumatic incidents as you've been through since your assimilation, there are bound to be... things... that need to be talked through."

He was right. It was a burden she needn't carry alone. Out of everyone at the Vault, he was the one with the most knowledge of the inner workings of the Vault. If anyone could answer her questions about the ball of energy that rested happily between the agrylium in her head, it would be him.

She opened her mouth to speak, ready to confess all. But, fate again decided differently.

A sharp knock on the door interrupted them. The timing couldn't have been better planned. Sharra was grateful for the reprise.

Faolan pushed through the door. The tagfinder was clutched in his hands.

"Greyson's at the Vault!" he said in a rush of air.

Sharra and Lazarus leaped out of their chairs at the pronouncement.

"He's here? Where?" Lazarus demanded.

As Faolan went to adjust the screen, Sharra saw the green dot inside the device disappear. A frown marred Faolan's face as he raised his head to look at them.

"He's gone," he said. "The green dot was there a moment ago. I swear."

"He had to come back in order to shift out again to some other timeline," Sharra said.

"Yes, but I would've thought that he had been and gone already since he shifted out of the New York office before us."

"Whatever the reason, he's gone now," Lazarus said, "probably heading to a new hiding place."

"How can you remain so calm?" Sharra said.

"As long as Greyson has taken Katie out of the Vault, we have time on our side. In those few moments that he's gone, we can have days to plan. It's that simple."

"He's back!" Faolan said.

He showed them the screen. The green dot blinked in the center.

"We must do something," Sharra said.

"Wait," Faolan said. "It's gone again. What's he doing?"

"Where's he now?"

"Give it a minute. It's coming. There it is." Holding it up, he read the screen, "Alexandria, Egypt, sixty-five B.C.E. Wow. That's going a long way back."

"That's what I'd do if I didn't want to be found... disappear into time," Lazarus said. "Keep an eye on the readings. If he stays there for more than a few minutes, we have our new timeline."

The green dot stayed put on the screen. With the coordinates confirmed, Lazarus called the Committee in for an emergency meeting. The others arrived one at a time, and soon all the chairs in the conference room were full. After Sharra and Faolan reiterated their tag following of Greyson and the results to the group,

Lazarus calmed the Committee members down with a preliminary plan.

"We'll keep the party small," Lazarus said, after loading a copy of the specifications of the new timeline to their individual Com-Links. "Maxum, you will be in charge. Your fluency of the Greek language, and the customs of the period will be needed."

Maxum checked the specifications of the trip. After a moment, he frowned, shaking his head.

"Damn it! I thought so."

"What is it?"

"Sorry, Lazarus," he said, "I will have to sit this one out."

"Is there a problem?"

"I won't be able to shift because I'm already there in the vicinity. One of my past jobs."

"That does make it a little more difficult for us, but not impossible. We will go to plan B. Tanner, you will take Maxum's place."

"Yes, Sir," Tanner said.

"Faolan will be your second. Maxum, Grimm, and I will run things from here. The timeline makes it a bit tricky to blend in. Grimm, you have charge of the costumes."

"Shouldn't be a problem," Grimm said. "Simple togas, tunics, and loincloths will do, I think. And some sandals. Leather. Yes, I can do that."

"I draw the line at wearing a loincloth," Faolan said.

"Because you're a true Scotsman," Sharra said.

"No. Well, yes, why not. Grimm, you understand, being a fellow Scotsman."

"Don't drag me into this, laddie," Grim said, holding his hands up in defense. "I come from a different generation than you, and am not so keen to air the family jewels as our kin once did."

"Faolan, it's only fair that if I have to suffer bindings to do a job, then you can wear a loincloth," Sharra said. "Remember that it's for Katie."

"I'm sorry, Sharra, but you're staying here," Lazarus said, breaking them up.

"I can't stay here. Please."

"You're too close. You need to back away, and let those who aren't emotionally involved handle it."

"It's because I'm emotionally involved that I should go. He's my brother. You'd want to do the same if it was your family."

She looked at Tanner when she said this.

"This isn't the same thing," Tanner said.

"Maybe not to you, but to me it hurts just as bad. I know I can talk some sense into him. I won't do anything stupid. I promise. I can help you. Please, let me go."

Her eyes pleaded with Lazarus as strongly as her words pleaded to the group. He stared at her for what seemed like eternity before his face softened, and she knew that her pleading had worked.

"Fine," he said, "but it's against my better judgment. I must have your word that you'll do whatever Tanner tells you to do, and nothing more."

"I promise." And she meant it.

Lazarus turned back to the job at hand. "I'll be asking Araylai and Cael to join the mission. Their perceptive abilities will give you an added advantage that might come in handy especially now that Maxum will not be there to help. I think you all realize how important it is that this mission doesn't fail. We're all counting on you. I'm counting on you."

All present what he meant, especially Sharra. Katie's beat up face and tied up body was always there in the front of her mind. Of everyone there, Sharra knew that she was the most desperate to see her brother caught and be brought to justice.

With her Com-Link in her hand, she left the others to talk. The information in the file called out to be memorized. Though Lazarus said that time was on their side, it never felt right. The urgency was there, pounding with every beat of her heart. It was hard to ignore. The only way to fix it was to get out there, find Greyson, and bring Katie home.

Chapter Eighteen

One, maybe, two. That's how many other agents Sharra had shifted with in the past. The logistics of five in period costumes with extra gear, all crowded into the same shiftroom made for a cozy trip. The swords that the men wore strapped at their hips over knee-length togas clanked against the walls, as the woman joined them.

Knives, Sharra thought, *very big knives.*

Cael hefted the heavy pack of scrolls over his shoulder. The 'gift' for the Library was an important addition to their gear, for it gave a reason for their presence in the city.

"Now remember," Tanner was saying, "if our entry should land us in the public eye, I want everyone to scatter for shelter, and wait until it's safe, but not too long. We're on a time schedule. We'll regroup through a Link."

"Wouldn't it be better to shift out individually?" Cael asked.

"Normally, yes, but we need to move in on Greyson as quickly as possible. And the only way to conserve time is to go together as one unit. Otherwise, who knows how far apart we'd end up from each other? A mile? A half-mile? A quarter? It would take too much time for all of us to meet up again. The more time we spend in Alexandria, the chance that Greyson will get word that we are there will grow higher. Besides, we have to stay together if the parts we're to play are to work."

"I understand," Cael said with a slow nod.

"Everyone, remember your parts," Tanner said as he linked arms with Sharra and Araylai.

Cael and Faolan followed his example, creating an unbroken circle among the five agents.

"Ready?" Tanner asked them all.

One by one they all replied, "check."

With a nod of warning, Tanner sent the command to the mainframe.

"Shift."

The air in the room flashed white right before the Vault sent them back in time.

Chapter Nineteen

Alexandria, Egypt
63 B.C.E.

In those crucial seconds when her eyes struggled to adjust from one light source to another, Sharra knew that they were in the open, and exposed. It was the beating heat that gave it away. It hit her with her first breath.

Instinctively she ducked low with the others. Everyone quickly disengaged, and prepared to sprint for cover.

They were outside. That much was true. Although, it wasn't on one of the broad roadways, of which there were many in the hot Macedonian city, and what Tanner had prepared them for. Nor were they in an open courtyard, an architectural must for most of the homes and temples built during that period.

So when Sharra saw not only the open sky, but also the protective stone parapets of someone's sprawling

167

roof, it came as a surprise. A good surprise. It took her brain another second to register that they were alone. That was a bonus.

The hot sun beat down upon them as they squinted, shielding their eye as they scanned the rooftop. As Sharra went to stand, Tanner pressed her back to a crouch.

"Everyone stay down while I get a bearing," he ordered.

Leaving them crouched next to a stack of rolled canvases, he crept to the edge of the roof, and stuck his head above the stone parapet just enough to scan the skyline of buildings. While he was busy searching for landmarks, Faolan pulled out the tagfinder from his tunic, and stared at the screen.

"Well?" Sharra asked after a few nerve-wracking moments.

"Greyson is still here. He's moved to the Musaeum," he said.

A soft sigh of relief escaped her lips. He heard it.

"Don't worry. We'll get him. And Katie."

After a three hundred and sixty degree look, Tanner came back and squatted into the circle of agents.

"I've got good news and bad news. Which do you want first?"

"The good news," Cael said.

"We're inside the inner city wall, maybe two or three long blocks away from our target."

Faolan gave a nod of approval. "That solves that problem. What's the bad news?"

"There's no sign of a horse or a donkey in sight. Without one, we can't proceed with the mission."

"What do you want us to do?" Sharra said.

"First we need to get off this roof before the owner discovers us. Araylai, can your abilities tell us if anyone is home?"

"It does not work quite like that. Human electromagnetic energy is weak compared to ours, making it more difficult to read. We need to be in close range to sense your presence."

"How close?"

She shrugged her delicate shoulders. "Ten feet, maybe?"

"That'll have to do. I want you and Cael to take point. This is a big house. Hopefully you can get us down to the ground without us being seen. Faolan will bring up the rear. When we get outside the house, we'll split up. Faolan, you'll take the team and find a safe place to wait while I search out a ride for our foreign dignitary."

Faolan nodded again, and shifted to the back.

Araylai, their 'foreign dignitary' moved up front with Cael. Dressed in a flowing white toga of the finest of silks with a long under-tunic of pale blue, she looked every inch the part. Gold braided ropes were tied enticingly across her breast and around her waists, showing off the curves of her body. Her long blond hair was intricately braided and piled stylishly on her head. Matching blue ribbons studded with pearls had been woven into them and dangled down her back.

Cael, as Araylai's adviser and spokesperson, was also garbed in a fine white toga and matching blue tunic.

Draped over his shoulders was a circular cape of dark blue, held together by a silver clasp pinned at the shoulder. The parcel of scrolls was slung over his back. Belted at his waist was a sword.

The Macedonian people of Alexandria were going to be in for a shock when they saw the stunning blond pair with their porcelain skin and exotic looks. It was something that Sharra worried about. If talk got back to the Musaeum of the strange pair before they got to Greyson, the mission will surely fail, and Katie lost to them.

At the corner of the roof was a canvas-covered booth, hiding the stairwell down to the lower floor. Araylai led the way. Her body tensed with caution as she tilted her head to listen before waving them forward. One by one they followed her down the stairs and through the home, pressing against walls, ducking behind furniture, crouching to the floor, whatever it took not to be seen, until they were outside in the long narrow lane that ran between that home and the next, and all the others that were connected.

The lane was deserted. Tanner took off to the back, while Faolan led them the other way. The smell of exotic spices drifted out into the alleyway. It came from the many doorways that they passed as they headed to the light at the end of the lane. Every once in a while, Sharra heard a tidbit of a conversation as they passed an opening. Though she couldn't understand what they were saying, she knew from the mission briefing that it was Greek.

The lane merged with a broad roadway. At the edge, Faolan stopped them to consult the map in his memory.

After a moment he said, "There's a temple between us and the Musaeum."

"The Temple of Isis Plusia," Cael offered.

"That's it. We can hide in there, in one of the many anti-chambers. It'll get us off the street, and out of the sun, while we wait for Tanner."

Sharra frowned, as she pointed out an important fact. "Tanner said not to go too far. There's two blocks between here and that temple. That's a long way. People are going to notice," she said, pointing to Araylai and Cael.

"We're just as exposed here, and..."

Faolan's eyes went blank, signaling a Link coming in. As he raised one hand to the group, with the other he slipped the wire of his Link to his jawline.

"That was fast," he said to the person on the other side, and then mouthed to the group, "Tanner" before turning back to the conversation. "We're at the other end of the same lane you left us in."

A minute later the wire went back up. Faolan herded them off the main road, and back into the shadows of the lane.

"Tanner says to stay put," he informed them. "He's just around the block. Says he found something better than a horse."

Ten feet in from the entrance, they settled in to wait. Five minutes passed, and then ten, and still no sign of Tanner. The sun moved straight overhead and into the narrow passageway to beat down upon them. No hint of a breeze stirred the air. Soon the flies found them, smelling the sweat that began to bead on their foreheads, making their skin shine. Swatting them away became a useless gesture.

Sharra unwrapped the extra scarf from her waist and draped it over her head, covering her braided hair. The sheer material wasn't much of a protection against the sun, but it was enough to keep the pesky flies off her head and neck. Araylai quickly followed her example.

Sharra was about ready to link with Tanner, when Faolan who was keeping watch at the entrance signaled to them.

"He's coming," he said.

Sure enough, a few moments later Tanner was at the entrance. After a brief word with the trainer, Faolan beckoned the rest of them forward. On the street behind Tanner was a cushioned divan held up by two poles resting on the shoulders of four slaves. Tanner commanded them in Greek. The slaves immediately set the divan on the ground, and stepped aside, leaving the wooden poles in the brackets.

Turning back to Faolan, Tanner asked, "Has the target moved?"

Faolan rechecked the tagfinder. "No, Greyson is still in the Musaeum." He pulled up the 3D image inside the device. "He's in one of the scroll halls of the Library."

"Okay, people," Tanner said to the group. "We are on. Remember your roles." He extended a hand out to Araylai and bowed. "Your ride, my Lady."

Araylai set her hand upon his, and let him guide her to the divan. Her chin was up, her movements graceful as she transformed into the princess of a distant land. At the divan, Tanner lent his arm as she settled back against the seat of pillows. A flap of canvas was held above her head by four slim poles of bamboo, shading her against the harsh sun.

When Araylai was satisfied, Tanner bowed to the 'princess' and stepped back as he barked orders to the slaves. They rushed in, grabbing the poles of the divan. Their muscular arms lifted the divan, bracing the poles upon their shoulders. Cael set the parcel of scrolls at Araylai's feet, and moved to the other side of the divan to take up position on the right. Sharra moved in close to the left, while Faolan headed up the rear.

After a sharp command from Tanner, the slaves began to move. With Tanner in the lead the slaves lumbered forward, taking the small party west upon the broad roadway.

Up ahead and to the right, Sharra could see a large monolith structure sitting upon a rise. It was the Musaeum. From the research Lazarus had given them, Sharra had learned that it was one of the greatest research institutes of its time, a university of sorts where ancient scholars from all over came to study, and to discuss the sciences, mathematics, and philosophies of the day.

Sitting on the crest of the hill inside the fortress-like walls of the Musaeum was a large Parthenon temple. Its many graceful columns glowed white in the backdrop of the blue sky. At the back of the Parthenon temple was a large courtyard where fantastical gardens lay between it and another building, a smaller one whose shorter pillars held up a golden-domed roof.

Sharra went over the layout in her head, seeing the many terraced walkways, open gardens with ornamental pools, and statues that beautified the grounds. There were other buildings: lecture halls, dining rooms, and apartments for the scholars, to name a few.

Like her first trip into the past, the sight took her breath away. Never had she traveled so far back in time. The smell of the spices, the oddity of the clothing, even the feel of the sun on her skin felt unreal. And yet, this was history, real history, history so old that the day-to-day affairs of the time had been forgotten. Only the rulers and prominent scholars of the time had been worthy enough to be noted in history books.

Greyson was here. In the Library.

All they had to do was walk the next few blocks, up the main steps of the Musaeum, enter through the heavy fortress-like wall, and get to the Library, all without drawing attention to their odd little party.

As she walked beside the divan, Sharra pulled the scarf back from around her head, and gazed about at the splendor of the ancient buildings, and diversity of people on the street. She breathed in the hot air, smelling the sea hiding behind the hill.

"So, this is Alexandria, the city of Alexander the Great," Tanner said from the front.

Sharra heard him. Raising her voice, she answered him, saying, "A few years from now, one of the most powerful women that the world had ever seen will be born."

"Cleopatra," Araylai said from her perch.

"You know of her?" Sharra said, surprised.

"I have read of Cleopatra in your books. She may have been powerful, but there was little honor in her through life and through death. Queen Elizabeth the first of England is more deserving of said honor. She is a human worth studying."

"I didn't know that human history interested you."

Araylai swept a graceful hand over the landscape, as she said, "In this profession, it is a necessary thing."

"I guess you're right. I never thought of it that way. We take a lot for granted, including our own history."

The first block passed as they talked. The Temple of Isis came to be beside them, taking up the whole corner of the block. The Egyptian stone pylon gate of the temple jutted into the blue sky. Three massive doorways were cut out of it, each leading deeper into the temple. On the surface of the pylon were carved large Egyptian figures that were surrounded by rows of hieroglyphic writing. It was as alien to Sharra as it was grand. It bespoke of a time when the pagan gods ruled with an iron will, and when Christianity was nonexistent.

Sharra was so busy admiring the ancient structures that she didn't notice the small group of locals gathering around them until Araylai reached out and touched her mind. Feeling the electromagnetic impulse upon her shield, she opened it, and let Araylai in.

We have a following, Araylai said.

Sharra peered around at the faces of the gathering audience. Ten... no fifteen men she counted, young and old, some in tunics of rougher weave, others of beautifully dyed material under white togas, all staring with avid curiosity at the woman on the divan. Their language was strange to her ears as they spoke with one another, pointing brazenly at Araylai.

Should we be worried? Sharra said.

I feel their curiosity growing. Others will come soon. Could be a problem.

Put Cael on alert. I'll let Tanner know.

Sharra slipped the scarf back over her hair. With her hand hidden within the material, she drew the wire of the Link down to her jaw. Building a picture of Tanner in her mind, she sent it to the agrylium metal in her brain. When the Link reached the agrylium in Tanner's head, and he accepted the call, she sent him a warning, leaving him to pass it onto Faolan.

The murmuring grew louder. The men became bolder as they pressed in to ogle the fair beauty on the divan.

One man stood out among the crowd. They parted to let him and his attendants into the ring that was forming around the divan. As he walked forward, his calf-length cape that was clipped at his shoulder with a clasp of gold swished around the well-formed muscles of his exposed legs. Under the cape, he wore a toga of rich crimson over a white tunic of the finest of materials. The clasp that held his cloak wasn't the only piece of gold on his body. Around his neck was a heavy chain, which hung an amulet of some sort. It shined brightly against the proud jut of his crimson chest.

His fingers flashed with jeweled rings as he motioned one of his attendants to his side. As he spoke to the attendant, he pointed to Araylai. The attendant left his master and jogged to the front of the divan to where Tanner marched. After an exchange of words, Sharra watched Tanner shoo the attendant away with an angry gesture of his hand. When the attendant returned to his rich master, Sharra knew by the expression on the man's face that it wasn't over.

The man pushed his attendant aside and marched up to the divan, halting the slow moving carriers with a sharp word. The party came to an abrupt stop. Raising a hand to Araylai, he spoke to her in Greek.

From her perch, Araylai stared down at the man. On her face was a look of mild curiosity as she listened.

Do you know what he is saying? Sharra asked her friend.

He is asking why there are only three to guard me when there should be a legion, Araylai said. *He wants to know where I hail from.*

The sound of swords leaving their scabbards came from around the divan from Tanner, Faolan, and Cael. Tanner approached the man with his sword out front. A heavy frown marred his face as he barked at the man. Sharra assumed that he was telling the man to back off. It was times like this that she kicked herself for not using the language sleep plugs like Tanner had suggested. But time had been limited, for it had been critical to shift as soon as possible. If it weren't for her connection with Araylai, she wouldn't have a clue what was going on.

Sharra glanced back at Faolan. From his place behind the divan, he held his sword out to the growing crowd with casual ease. His body was deceptively relaxed, his knees loose, as he readied for battle. A warrior's glint was in his eyes. Cael was on the other side somewhere out of her sight. She had heard his sword leave its scabbard, too, and knew that he was ready, as they all were trained to be.

The rich man remained unfazed by the sword in Tanner's hand. The tension mounted within the crowd at the sight of the weapons. Silence fell over the tunic-clad mob as they backed out of Tanner's reach. As for the rich man, his eyes were glued onto the beauty on the divan as he demanded something from her.

Araylai froze. Sharra read the concern in her aura.

What is it?

He wants me, Araylai said, as Tanner raised his sword and pointed it at the man's chest. *That could be a problem.*

Do you think? Sharra said as she slowly backed away from Tanner and the rich man, ending between the two slaves on her side until her back hit the wooden frame of the divan where she could go no further.

Chapter Twenty

The tension in the crowd became palpable as they waited to see what the rich man would do. Sharra was stuck between the two slaves on her side. Her back was to the divan. She reached for the knife at her thigh, and then remembered she wasn't on Ardus. Though she felt the bulge of the laser hidden inside her gown, she dared not pull it out.

Sharra glared at the rich man, but he had eyes only for Araylai.

You could just say no to the man, that you are already taken, she said to Araylai through the electromagnetic connection.

It is more primal than that. The problem I am referring to is the one that resides within him. He is arrogant with power and greed. He does not take no for an answer. In his heart, I am chattel. He seriously thinks that I can be taken. What is worse is that he has a small army stationed outside the city. Right now he is considering sending one of his attendants to fetch them.

That is a problem, a problem we don't have time for. Shifting back to the Vault and trying again won't work, not this time. We need to be here now. Not later. Or earlier, or we miss Greyson, and subsequently, Katie.

I know. I have an idea, Araylai said.

What is it?

I know this type of male, and have dealt with it before. Just follow my lead.

What about our team?

I have filled Cael in already. He is linking with Faolan and Tanner. I have asked for Tanner to come and stand in front of you when I give him the cue. Look, the rich man dares to test out Tanner's sword. How arrogant. Time to act.

He's all yours, Sharra said.

With the grace born from the blood of queens, Araylai looked upon the rich man as if he were a mere worm on the ground.

"Julius Vetus," she said to the man, staring at him in her unblinking way.

Those two words, though nothing complicated, evoked a unified gasp from the ones who were in reach of her bell-like voice. It wasn't the fact that she knew the rich man's name that made them gasp. Unprepared for the power of her siren call, they gazed up in wonder. When she spoke again in their native tongue, they were caught in her spell.

Sharra's eyes widened in surprise as her friend handled the language as though it was her native tongue. Araylai commanded something to Tanner. He tilted his head in a bow of respect, and slowly backed away from the rich man until he was standing directly in front of Sharra, and close to the divan.

I have told Tanner to let the man approach, Araylai said to her.

The rich man, Julius Vetus, gazed upon Araylai with undisguised longing as he took a step, and then another until he came to the point of Tanner's sword. He raised his head to say something, but was stopped by a harsh command from Araylai.

Proud and beautiful, Araylai stiffened in her seat, and became the Queen that she was born to be. Disdain colored her voice as she spoke to the man.

"What's she saying?" Sharra whispered to Tanner.

Keeping his sword to the man's chest, he interpreted the conversation for her over his shoulder.

"Araylai has told him that he is a brave man to dare to think that he could own her."

Julius put a hand to his heart and replied. By his soulful tone and lovesick eyes Sharra knew what was going on. It didn't matter the century. It was the same reaction that most men had whenever Araylai walked into the room.

Tanner snorted, and said, "He's saying that he couldn't help himself, for her beauty is like a rare treasure, more precious than gold, or jewels, or… you get the point. Now, he's telling her that he only wishes to know who she is and where she hails from, so that he may visit this place where the gods have created such a creature as herself."

Araylai's eyes flashed as she gave him an answer, her voice both musical and harsh.

"Araylai isn't happy with him. She's saying that her name is too great to be spoken out loud to a mere man such as himself. She belongs to the gods, and the gods are displeased with him, for they have read his thoughts, and now she knows them, too." Araylai waived a hand to the distant wall of the city. "She's pointing to where his army is stationed, and telling him that if he does not desist from his thoughts of taking her, then the wrath of the gods will not only destroy him and his two young sons, but also, his army."

Julius stared up at her, taken aback by her words. Araylai wasn't done. Leaning down from her perch above their heads, she lowered her voice so that only the rich man and those standing close by could hear her. Tanner said nothing as he listened.

All went quiet.

The rich man's eyes went wide as he sucked in his breath. He whispered something. From his look, Sharra guessed it was a vulgar word or a shocked exclamation. Whatever the case, the man dropped his gaze to the ground, and bowed deep before the divan as if a stone weight was tied to his neck. His tone of voice changed. No longer was it haughty. When he next addressed her, his voice shook with fear.

Sharra knocked Tanner's back. He shot her a look over his shoulder.

"Not now," he whispered.

From over Sharra's head, Araylai answered Julius Vetus with a firmness that Sharra rarely heard come from her friend. The man remained with his head bent low as he backed away into the crowd, saying a phrase over and over again, until he was a safe distance away.

"Tanner, get us moving," Araylai said in English as she sat gracefully back upon the pillows of the divan.

Tanner barked a command to the slaves. The divan began to move as the slaves shuffled forward. The crowd parted, letting the divan through as Tanner strode to the front with his sword in hand.

Sharra looked back into the crowd. The crowd's voices started and gained strength as they talked excitably among themselves as they watched the party move away. Julius Vetus stood staring at the divan. The arrogance that he wore like armor was gone. Fear and uncertainty were in his posture. It sat uncomfortably on his face as if it was a new experience for the man. Sharra knew that the man never had a chance once Araylai got started. Even death did not scare the Arderian agent. Sharra had seen that firsthand in the throne room of Araylai's family castle.

"You can put your swords away," Araylai said to the men. "It will draw less attention to us if we can continue on peacefully."

"You heard the Lady," Tanner said as he sheathed his sword.

Two more swishes of metal against leather told Sharra that Cael and Faolan had done the same.

The excitement of the crowd behind them began to disperse as the people went back to the business of the day.

The small party of agents left the Temple of Isis and made their way slowly to the next block. The face of the rich man stuck in Sharra's brain. She wished she knew what Araylai had said that scared him into submission. A Link with Tanner gave her the answer.

Tanner's voice filled her ear as he replied, "She told him that 'no' she belonged to no man, and 'yes' she was dangerous, and that the plan of taking us by surprise wouldn't work, for she could read it in his mind as clearly as she saw the affair he was having with Lydia, Marcus' wife. Who the heck are Marcus and Lydia?"

"I don't know."

"It sounded like Araylai was feeding him a bunch of bull, that is until I saw the color drain from Vetus' face. White as a ghost he was. I thought he was going to faint. And then, he was bowing and apologizing. 'Great Lady of Magic, the Divine One. Please forgive me. I did not know. Please forgive me. I did not know.' That's what he kept repeating. It was weird. How did she know what to say?"

Sharra thought of how to answer that without saying too much. It wasn't easy.

"You know those Arderians. They're quite intuitive as a species. I'm sure she has said some weird stuff to you, too, that had hit close to home."

There was a pause, as if he were thinking, and then he said, "Still weird, if you ask me. Whatever-the-case, it got us out of a tricky situation."

"Hopefully we don't draw anymore attention. If word of our presence gets to Greyson, we're screwed."

"Don't worry about what we can't control. The Musaeum steps are just ahead. And then, the Library inside. Besides a few hiccups, we're still on schedule."

THE VAULT

"Has Faolan checked the tagfinder recently?"

Sharra felt the connection go blank and knew that Tanner was checking in with Faolan. While she waited for an answer, she peered around the slave in front of her to look ahead.

Upon a rise of land was the large walled structure that housed the famous Alexandria Musaeum. The encounter with Julius Vetus was quickly forgotten as she stared at the impressive structure.

"Wow," she whispered.

The dimensions that had been given back at the Vault weren't enough to prepare her for the real thing. When she had studied the blueprints it had reminded her of a layout of a castle, complete with fortified walls too high to scale, and too thick to break through. It wasn't just a Library. It was a University, a place of great learning.

Now seeing it firsthand, it was grander than anything Sharra had ever seen before on earth. She marveled at the amazing feat of architecture that stood upon the hill as a monument of the achievability of mere men. No wonder it was still talked about in the twenty-first century as one of the great wonders of the ancient world.

On the street between the wide staircases that led up into the main gates of the fortress-like structure were two square towers four stories high. Large hieroglyphic symbols were carved upon their stonewalls, row upon row, all the way up to the shallow parapets that encircled the top. The hieroglyphics wrapped around the structure in one continuous work of art. No wall was left untouched. What story they told, Sharra could only guess at. Probably a tale of some Pharaoh's family, or some conquest against another people. Greed, power, and lust seemed to be the most common themes of the Egyptians. It was no different in her day, or any other time period. Mankind never seemed to learn.

Then, there were the gods.

Against each tower sat a pagan god upon a throne of stone. High above the mortals on the ground, their cold lifeless eyes stared out of stone faces of strange beasts that were perched upon human bodies clothed in ancient garments and heavy jewelry. So large were the carvings that if they were alive, a man could be crushed under the sole of a foot. They were fear-inspiring to behold. Like all the other timelines Sharra had visited, no picture could do them justice.

The saying was true: seeing was believing.

Somewhere past the stone gods that guarded the entrance, and inside the magnificent structure, was the Library…and Greyson with Katie.

Her mind fuzzed for a millisecond as Tanner came back online, interrupting the darkening path of her thoughts.

"Faolan has checked. Greyson hasn't moved, so you can rest easy," Tanner said. "This will work, Sharra."

"I hope so."

They came upon the stairs, passing the first tower of the two gods that guarded the way into the Musaeum. Sharra looked up at the towering god with the jackal's head and shivered, not from fear, well, maybe a little fear, but also from something more carnal - the power of man. It was not the kind of power that came with the advancement of technology. This was true power, power from the source, from within man himself, where there was no need for anything but the mind and the strength of will to accomplish whatever entered their hearts.

The divan stopped with a command from Tanner. In unison, the four slaves lowered the divan until it rested upon the ground. Stone steps ascended up the hill to the main entrance. On both sides of the staircase were rows of Grecian pillars that supported the rooftops of the thick stone barricades that enclosed the way into the Musaeum, keeping the unworthy from its hallowed grounds. If the entrance was meant to be intimidating, it was working, for Sharra felt a heavy weight push down upon her shoulders as the two gods stared down at her.

Cael came around to Sharra's side of the divan, and offered his hand to Araylai. With the grace of a ballet dancer, she gave him her hand and lifted to her feet. As the gossamer material of her gown settled around her golden sandals, the team moved into position. Cael grabbed the wrapped parcel off the divan and slid beside Araylai as Faolan led them to the first staircase.

"Everyone stick to the plan," Tanner said from behind the small group as they started to climb. "Especially you, Sharra."

"Me?" Sharra said, glancing back from the other side of Araylai. "Why me?"

"Because you are too close to the situation."

"And your track record has been, well, for a better word, crap," Faolan said from the front.

"Thanks, guys, for your vote of confidence." Sharra huffed, "Haven't I stuck with the plan so far? I won't muck it up. Too much is at stake."

Araylai's eye-rings flashed as her bell-like voice broke into the conversation.

"Boys," she said, "leave Sharra alone. She, more than any of us, knows what needs to be done. We are not through yet. The gates are up ahead."

The discussion ended with that sentence. The staircase leveled out onto a platform in front of the main gates into the University. A robed man saw them approach the open entranceway. Leaving the shade that the wall provided, he shuffled over. His aging balding head gleamed in the bright sunlight as he bowed to the party. When he raised his head, his eyes fell upon the beauty in the middle of their small circle, and remained speechless for a moment until he remembered himself. Though his eyes never left Araylai, he addressed a question to the group.

Tanner came to the front, and pointing to the parcel in Cael's arms, he spoke to him. Sharra assumed it was about the acquisition room. That was their way into the Library portion of the Musaeum, and to the blinking dot on the tagfinder.

The man bowed again, and asked them to follow him through the gates with a gesture of hands, all the while talking nonstop. After escorting them through the high archway of the entrance and beyond the fortified wall on a parade of words, he pointed past the courtyard of gardens to the left side of the temple-like building that rose above all the rest.

"Check the tagfinder again when you get a chance," Tanner said to Faolan. "In the meantime, we will head across the gardens to the Acquisition Department. We'll keep up appearances for the old man's sake until we're out of his line of vision. Just to play it safe. Then we will cut across to the Library."

The heady scent of manicured gardens full of exotic foliage floated in the air. Once they crossed the courtyard, Faolan veered the party to the right to the marble path that led to the lower level of the temple-like structure in the center of the University. They followed it under the gazebo arches full of flowering vines until they came to a set of arched doorways in the temple wall. Faolan didn't need to give directions, for they all knew the way inside. Only the tagfinder was needed to spot Greyson's exact location. From her last look, Sharra knew exactly which room in the vast archives underneath the temple he was hiding in, hopefully with Katie.

As soon as they entered the first division of rooms, the light lessened as they left the sun and the heat behind. The air cooled the further the agents moved inside the heavy stone structure.

Sharra's eyes widened as they adjusted to the dim light. She looked around expecting to find scrolls. The room was empty, save for the colorful murals painted upon the four walls of the vast outer chamber. The only other things in the room were six arched doorways, three in the long wall in front of them, and one in each of the other walls.

Faolan slowed the team as he brought the tagfinder out from the folds of his toga to fiddle with the screen.

Voices echoed from one of the inner archways, moving closer with every second. And then, they were no longer alone in the vast chamber. Sharra stiffened as two old men in long flowing white robes with dark brown over-tunics and heavy grey beards walked in through one of the arched doorways on their way to the outside. Faolan hid the tagfinder in the folds of his toga as soon as he had heard them. Deep in conversation, the aged scholars barely looked up at the small party as they passed by.

As soon as the men were gone, Faolan whipped out the tagfinder again.

Getting a fresh reading, he said, "This way," and led them through the same archway the scholars had come from.

A faint smell of dust and mustiness tickled Sharra's nose. It grew stronger the further the group moved into the belly of the Library. Soon, the smell became overpowering as they passed through room after room of scrolls too many to number. Occasionally she heard voices talking, or sometimes saw a figure or two bent over a table studying an opened document. Over all, for such an immense collection of precious scrolls, stone tablets, and other forms of preservation of words, the place felt deserted. Their passage remained undetected as the team walked like ghosts through the halls of stored knowledge, all the while following the tagfinder.

Finally, in a dark and deserted room, Faolan stopped them with a signal of his hand. They gathered around him against a wall filled with musty-smelling scrolls. The smell reminded Sharra of death – something she'd never forget.

THE VAULT

Faolan held the tagfinder up. On it was outlined in 3D the schematics of the surrounding rooms. A basement room complete with a staircase showed up on the other side of the wall where they now waited. The green dot blinked steadily within the basement compartment. Sharra worried her lower lip between her teeth. They were very close to the dot, to Greyson and Katie.

"He hasn't moved from the aisle," Faolan whispered.

"How many aisles is he from this entrance?" Tanner asked.

Faolan studied the diagram. "Thirteen."

"Figures," Sharra whispered.

Tanner looked at Araylai, and asked, "Can you or Cael 'sense' any electromagnetic energy from here?"

"No. They are too far away. We would need to get closer."

"We can't wait for that," Tanner whispered. The whites of his eyes glowed green from the light from the tagfinder as he pulled out a slim metal gun from inside his tunic. Checking the settings, he continued, "Faolan, you take Araylai and Cael, and head down the staircase and take the left side of the room. Sharra and I will take the right side. Whoever sees him first, shoot. Don't hesitate, or he'll be gone. We can ask questions later. Check your lasers. Remember, not a sound once we leave this spot. Understood?"

Everyone nodded as they reached for their weapons. Sharra checked the setting of her gun. In the quiet she heard a heart beating, and realized that it was her own. She took a cleansing breath as she prepared to follow Tanner.

He heard her, and asked, "You okay?"

"Yes," she whispered back.

He stared at her for a few seconds longer as if trying to gage her mood. She stared back, her face hard with determination. He rested a hand on her shoulder, and gave it a squeeze. Then it was back to the business at hand.

"We have to assume that Greyson has a view of the entrances into the room. So use the darkness. Keep low until you reach the bottom of the staircase. When you reach the twelfth aisle, stop, and wait for my signal," Tanner said.

He raised a finger to his lips. With the other hand he waved Faolan's team forward with two sharp fingers. They made no noise as they disappeared through the archway. Tanner sent Sharra a quick nod, and took off.

Left alone, Sharra raised her gun, and on silent feet, followed him into the basement.

The strong smell of decay hit her in the face as soon as they rounded the corner. From the landing of the staircase, the walls of the basement expanded in all directions, becoming one with the darkness. Aisle after aisle of wooden racks went as far as Sharra could see until they, too, were swallowed up by the darkness. The space was crowded not just with the huge treasure of musty scrolls, but with shadows and dark places.

Greyson had chosen well.

Sharra hugged the wall as she followed the team down the stone steps. Their footsteps made no sound as they crept to the bottom, and split apart. When they reached the first row of shelving, Tanner pulled her to the ground. They waited crouched against the smelly stack of scrolls as Faolan, Araylai, and Cael headed to the far wall. Once the second team made it to the end of the row, Tanner squeezed her arm as he signaled the other team forward.

Leaving their hiding spot, Tanner and Sharra started down the long line of racks, row after row, matching speed with the other team so that with each aisle they were synchronized, moving as one organism.

Sharra's pulse quickened with each passing aisle. The ball of energy in her head felt her anxiety, and pressed upon their prison. It wasn't the time for it to come forward, and she told it so. The threads hummed within the confine of the ball, but obeyed. By the time they reached the twelfth aisle, her heart was ready to explode from her chest.

Down the other end of aisle twelve, the three agents blended into the backdrop of the wooden dowels of the wall of scrolls, darker shadows within the shadows cast by the racks.

Tanner touched her arm, and pointed to his ear, and to the aisle beyond the wall of scrolls they hid behind. She listened for a few seconds with him, and shook her head. She knew that Katie was gagged, tied, and most likely drugged, and therefore, effectively made mute. And Greyson, if he was as smart as she was coming to realize… would make sure that Katie stayed that was.

No, there was no noise.

It felt… wrong.

Tanner positioned his laser as he raised his other hand to signal the others. Sharra gripped the handle of her laser. Her hand shook as her finger hovered over the trigger. With one quick movement, Tanner slashed the air. With the signal given, the team sprang into action.

The charge was quick as they shot around the rack from both ends, and into the thirteenth aisle.

With her gun at the ready, Sharra peered down the long stretch of shadows, and saw... nothing.

The two teams met in the middle. Greyson wasn't there. Neither was Katie.

Confusion filled everyone's faces. Tanner gestured to the device in Faolan's hand. The dot was there, a steady blinking blip in the center of the image. Encircling the green dot was another dot, the blue one of the tagfinder. Faolan did a full circle with the tagfinder, but the green dot remained inside the blue dot. He shook his head at Tanner, and shrugged his shoulders.

Tanner pointed up to the top of the racks.

Faolan frowned and shook his head again, and mouthed, "Not possible according to this." He showed him the diagram again.

Sharra touched Araylai's arm. *Can you detect anything?*

Nothing. He is not here.

"They're not here," Faolan spoke into the silence, coming to the same conclusion as Araylai's private answer.

Tanner grabbed the tagfinder out of Faolan's hand, and frowned at the overlapping dots.

"I don't get it," he growled. "How can that be when it says he's right here?"

A bad feeling came over Sharra. She moved in to get a closer look at the blinking dots, and stepped into something wet. Bending down, she touched the spot on the floor with a finger. Bringing it up close to her face, she studied the dark drop on the end of her fingertip with a frown. The frown deepened the longer she stared at it, creasing her brow. When she brought it to her nose to sniff it, she knew what it was.

"Blood," she said.

No one heard her small exclamation for they were busy with the tagfinder. Swiftly she rose to her feet, and frantically searched the shelf directly above the small puddle of blood. It wasn't long before her fingers fell upon a small metal object. She drew it out, and held it up between her thumb and forefinger in the light of the tagfinder.

The tagfinder hadn't lied after all. Only it wasn't Greyson that it had found.

The tiny capsule gleamed with wetness.

"Oh God, no," she said.

The team lifted their heads as one, and saw the distress on her face.

"Sharra... What's the matter?" Tanner said.

"Greyson's chip. It's Greyson's chip," she choked out.

She held it up for all to see. Her fingertips were dark with blood, Greyson's blood from where he had cut the capsule out of his neck. Sharra looked at her friends and saw the shock on their faces.

"Don't tell me he dug it out, and put it here just to taunt us?" Faolan said in disgust.

"He's gone, truly gone. How are we going to find Katie now?" Sharra moaned in despair.

In the silence that followed, Araylai dared to voice what was on the forefront of everyone's mind.

"What are we going to tell Lazarus?" Araylai said softly.

A tear fell down Sharra's cheek.

Oh, Katie, she thought.

What were they going to tell Lazarus?

Chapter Twenty-One

The Vault

A dark shadow hung over the Vault. Sharra knew why, and hated it, blaming herself. Lying in her bed, she turned over, resting a hand upon Amadeus. The cat was curled up in a ball next to her. Petting his soft warm body brought her some comfort in a world that had gone crazy. Her world. Her brother. Maybe even herself, if she cared to admit it.

The room was pitch-black, like her thoughts.

It was her fault. Though the others denied it, she knew it to be true. Ever since she had joined the Agency, people had gotten hurt either mentally or physically, or worse, killed. Before that, the Vault had been quiet. Maybe trouble did follow her. She had never wanted to believe it before. Yet now, after all that's happened… She had to admit that there was a pattern, and that she was at the center of it.

Since the team had come back with the bad news, things had gone from bad to worse. After a long heated discussion between the Committee and the agents involved, they were still no closer to coming up with a plan of attack.

Katie was lost to them.

Sad to say that was the only thing they could agree on. After the last meeting, Sharra left for her apartment, dejected, and hadn't come out since.

In the dark she thought about packing her bags and cat, and leaving the Vault. It didn't matter where she went, as long as the Vault was free from her and the baggage that followed her.

Maybe that was the answer. It's what Greyson wanted all along. With her gone, there'd be no reason to keep Katie as a hostage.

That thought gave her hope. Then she remembered the last time she saw Katie, the cut on her face, the drugged look in her eyes, and knew that there was no trusting Greyson.

"What time is it?" she asked the PVC.

"The time is ten thirty-two a.m.," replied the soft-spoken female program.

Amadeus woke up at the sound of the voice, and stretched under her hand. Sharra had to agree with him. Lying around was useless.

"Lights," she commanded.

Immediately the lights came on. Throwing the covers off, she swung her legs over the edge of the bed to the floor, and swiped the Link off the nightstand. It clipped reassuringly onto the agrylium patch behind her left ear.

She thought to contact Tanner, but stopped before the transmission went through. Biting her lip, she frowned at her mussed-up figure reflecting in the dresser mirror.

Tanner was the first person to enter her thoughts. Not Faolan. That was another problem that plagued her... a problem she never dreamed in her life would happen to her. She knew that something had to be done about it before they actually hurt each other fighting over her. She had too many other things on her conscience already that kept her up at night.

It was while she sat on the bed that a signal came in the Link. It wasn't Tanner or Faolan. Both she could handle. This signal felt new, which in itself should have warned her that something wasn't right.

"Sharra, my darling sister."

She froze as the voice of her brother filled her ear.

"Greyson." She swallowed hard as a feeling of trepidation crept into her soul.

"What's the matter? I thought you would be happy to hear from me, especially with all that's happened between us."

"How did you get a Com-Link?"

"Tsk, tsk. Someone that I happen to have with me right here is letting me... borrow... Yes, I like that word. I'm borrowing it."

"Where are you? Where's Katie?"

"Now, now. Where are your manners? Mother taught you better than that. Yes, I'm feeling quite well. Thank you for asking. And no, I am not having a good day. Hmmm... why do you think that is?"

"What do you want, Greyson."

His laughter echoed in her head. She cringed, and tried to block it out.

"That there is a million dollar question that I bet you know the answer to."

Sharra did know the answer, yet hesitated to say it. For once it was said, there was no going back. Finally, when she spoke her voice was soft as if in her heart she had given up. Maybe she had.

"You want me."

"Smart girl."

"You can't have me."

"I think I can. You know why? Because I have something that you want back."

"Katie."

"That's right. Sweet little Katie. And I bet you'd do anything to fix that itty-bitty problem, especially with the way I hear that you and the Head Director are tight. A little creepy, don't you think? You and Lazarus? Isn't he a bit old for you? Though, I guess you can't be picky with your track record."

"Shut up, Greyson. You know nothing. Bring Katie back alive, and I'll do whatever you want."

"There's the girl I remember. I knew I could count on you to see things my way. So, here's how it's going to happen."

His words clipped out with precision as he laid out his demands. She listened carefully. There was no room for arguing, no changing of his mind. It didn't matter. He was giving her a way to redeem herself, and they both knew it.

Chapter Twenty-Two

After Greyson broke the Link, Sharra sat on the edge of her bed contemplating his demands, what that meant for her future, and came to realize it didn't matter. With a sigh, she got up and started to dress. As she slipped the straps of her bra over her shoulders, her hand went up to the back of her neck to search for the tiny hard bump of the transmitter chip. The sensitive tips of her fingers soon found it, and paused over the raised bit of skin.

It had been useful, the chip.

In the mirror her hazel eyes stared back at her, wide and sad.

"This won't do at all," she said.

She turned away from the mirror, and finished dressing. As she headed out of the bedroom, she slipped the wire down and sent a Link to Lazarus. The Link bounced back unanswered.

Without waiting, for Sharra knew that time might eat away even the strongest of resolves, she left her apartment and headed down the hallway to the Administration offices. Her solid stride brought her to the Head Director's office in record time. After a quick knock, she waited for permission to enter. When it didn't come, she tried again. Pushing the door open, Sharra called his name.

"Lazarus?" she said as she popped her head in.

The tall leather chair behind the plasitop desk was unoccupied. On the desk was an empty whiskey bottle next to a glass tumbler. The office was silent except for the ticking of the antique clock on the wall.

Sharra got on the Link again. This time it was to Tanner.

"I'm looking for Lazarus," she said.

"Have you tried his office?"

"I'm standing in it. He's not here."

"I saw him briefly after our meeting, but that was yesterday."

Sharra walked over to the other side of the desk to see whether there might be a clue left on the monitor. As she got close, something crunched under her foot. It was a work chip, the kind that agents left on his desk for review. Looking around, there were more scattered on the floor behind the desk as if they'd been swiped off the surface. Her eyes returned to the empty bottle.

"Tanner, I'm worried about him."

"Hold on! I'll be right there!" he said, and broke the Link.

Not long after, Tanner strode through the door.

"I've tried Lazarus on the Link," he said. "I couldn't get him either. Grimm and Maxum haven't seen him all day. I told them it was nothing when they asked why."

"I'm worried about him. He seemed so... I don't know... unfazed when we told him about the chip. He must know that finding Katie is next to impossible now. It's his daughter! He should be upset."

"Not everyone shows their emotions on the outside like you or me. He was probably working up a plan in his head. You know how he gets – all Vault business-like. I'm sure he's okay."

"I'm not so sure. There's an empty bottle of liquor left on his desk and a stack of work chips thrown on the floor. For a man that likes everything in its place, they are signs that scream that he's not okay."

Tanner stared at the bottle on the desk with a frown. "Maybe you're right. We'll try his apartment. After that..." He shrugged. "He could be anywhere. It's a big complex."

On the ground floor of the complex, after exiting the elevator, Tanner turned left in the ornate foyer and led her down another residential block, one that she had not visited before. Stopping in front of a door a few down from the foyer, Tanner asked the PVC permission to enter.

"Permission denied," said the female voice of Lazarus' PVC.

"So, he's home," Sharra said. "Try again."

"Didn't you hear the PVC? Lazarus doesn't want to be disturbed," Tanner said.

"But it doesn't answer whether he's okay. The whiskey... If he's been drinking... Katie is his daughter. You know that he loves her more than life itself. And I know how I was after I lost my parents. I'm worried about him. Isn't there some way we can override his PVC to check on him?"

"You're asking me to invade his privacy. We're talking about the Head Director, the most powerful man this side of time."

"He is still just a man, and can break like the rest of us."

"You do realize that it will mean violating the Vault protocols on privacy."

"I'll take full responsibility. Please, Tanner."

He sighed, a big sigh from low in his chest as he stared down into her big eyes. When his shoulders sagged, Sharra knew that she had won before he said anything.

"Thank you. Thank you." Standing on her tippy-toes, she gave him a quick kiss on the cheek.

"The things I do for you," he mumbled as he pressed his hand upon the pad next to the door. The pad lighted red under his hand. To the PVC he said, "Tanner Holmes, three-one-eight-four-seven VPT requesting override of locks."

"Code, please," the PVC said.

"Systems Personal Lock Lazarus Maitland, code L-one-four-one-nine-four-one," Tanner said, rattling off the numbers from mote.

The pad under Tanner's hand turned green.

The PVC responded, "Code accepted. The lock is disengaged."

The door swished open as Tanner removed his hand from the pad.

"After you, madam," Tanner said with a bow and a sweep of his arm.

Sharra hesitated at the threshold as she struggled for a moment with the breach of privacy. Yet, her concern for Lazarus was stronger. And so, she stepped into the apartment, taking all the responsibility with her that went with that decision.

Expecting to find a more spacious apartment than the rest of them, she was mildly surprised, for it was the same size as hers. Where hers was decorated very simply, this apartment was like walking into a museum. Not like the Musaeum of ancient Alexandria of their last mission. This was newer than that, maybe eighteen century new. Though she had very little knowledge about the Head Director's former life, his apartment told her much about him that he kept hidden from the outside world.

Like her, it looked as though he also couldn't leave his past behind. Gilded mirrors along with framed paintings of all sorts and sizes filled every space of wall that wasn't taken up by the three ornate china hutches. Behind the glass of the china hutches, and crowding the shelving, were antiques of crystal, bone china, and other odds and ends. Some had jewels like the collection of weaponry in his office. All were worth a king's ransom. A Persian carpet of reds, greens, and gold, covered the floor. A two-seater couch of dark wood and upholstered in deep burgundy and greens was placed between matching chairs and small rounded tables.

What stood out the most was the ceiling-high bookcase stuffed with books that ranged from classic literature brittle with age to modern works, some that even she was surprised to recognize. A nature book lay open on the couch as if Lazarus had just left it.

A suit jacket had been flung over one of the chairs. It was the one he had worn yesterday before the mission.

"Lazarus?" Sharra called out. "It's Sharra and Tanner."

As Tanner came to stand beside her, a muffled sound came from the bedroom.

"Did you hear that?" she said to Tanner.

"Yes. This way."

He took off into the bedroom. Sharra followed close on his heels.

"Lazarus?" she called again. "Are you okay?"

An angry voice yelled from behind the bathroom door on the other side of the walk-in closet.

"Didn't you hear me? I said go away!"

The words were slurred and angry, yet it was unmistakable that it was Lazarus.

Sharra plowed ahead of Tanner, racing through the walk-in closet to the bathroom door. At the door, she stopped. It was cracked open. The bathroom light was off. She heard movement in the darkness.

"Lazarus," she said softly into the crack. "I'm coming in."

"No," he moaned.

Her heart broke at the sound as that one syllable said more than a thousand words.

"Can you command the lights?" she whispered to Tanner.

He nodded and gave the command to the PVC.

As she opened the door, the lights in the bathroom flicked on, eliciting another moan from the man curled pathetically on the floor between the wall and the toilet. Lazarus covered his eyes from the light with one hand while the other clutched a half-empty bottle of alcohol to his chest.

"Leave me alone," he said as he wiped at his eyes with a slack hand.

Tears sprang into Sharra's eyes at the sight of him. Blinking them away, she ran to him, and dropped to her knees at his feet. His shoes and tie were gone. His dress shirt had come untucked from his pants and had been partially unbuttoned. It hung loosely open as he struggled to rise. But the effort was too much, and he gave up, falling back to the floor with the bottle still clutched to his chest.

Resting his head against the bowl of the toilet, he said, "Why are you here? Can't a man grieve in the privacy of his own home?"

Sharra wanted to gather the man into her arms like a mother comforting a child, but had to settle for a hand on his shoulder. He flinched at the gentle pressure, but didn't push her away.

"You shouldn't be alone," she said.

"Why not? She was everything to me. And now, she's lost... gone. Is this it then? The great pain and loss that I would experience because I recruited you? I should have taken that warning more seriously when I had the chance. Why didn't I tell myself that it was Katie... my Katie. Why?"

A sob fell noisily from his lips as he began to weep against the lid of the toilet seat. The tears returned to Sharra and fell unbidden down her cheeks as she sat helplessly beside him.

His babbling made no sense. Turning to Tanner, she looked beseechingly at him for help. Tanner's blue eyes were bright with unshed tears as he stood stiffly inside the doorway.

After a few horrible moments when Lazarus' grief filled the air of the bathroom, the sobbing finally slowed down. With a sigh that shook his whole body, Lazarus brought his grief under control. The bottle was lifted to his lips for a quick swig. Wiping his nose on his sleeve, he moved his head so that his red-rimmed eyes fell upon Sharra.

"Tell me, Sharra, are you worth this?" He sniffed, and swung the bottle around in the air, precariously swishing the golden liquid close to spilling out. "Because, right now, I can't see it."

Fresh tears dripped down her cheeks as the hurt of his words hit home. She had to agree with him. Since her recruitment, she'd caused nothing but worry and pain for the dear man.

Her lips wobbled as she whispered, "I'm sorry, Lazarus. I'm so sorry."

"What does the Vault want you for anyway?" He tried to shake his head, and almost fell over. Tanner swooped down and caught him before his head hit the toilet. Slipping the bottle from his friend's hand, he lifted Lazarus off the floor and sat him on the seat of the toilet.

Sharra remained on her knees at his feet. Her eyes hurt from crying. Her heart felt worse. A headache began to form at her temples.

His question burned in her head. The Vault wanted her for something? That was news to her. What did it want? And why her? She had caused nothing but trouble for the Vault since her recruitment. And now, Katie.

"I can make it right, if you give me a chance. I can get Katie back for you," she said, breaking the patch of silence.

Lazarus snorted. "It will take more than chance to make this right, Sharra. You and I both know that."

"Well, isn't it lucky then, that I have brought something more than chance with me."

Tanner frowned at her, and said, "Don't play with us."

"I'm not playing. It's real. I got a Link from Greyson just before. He has offered us a deal. Me for Katie. An even exchange. If we agree with his offer and comply to his conditions, then he promises to leave the Vault for good."

"No," Tanner said, shaking his head.

"Tanner's right. We'd be sacrificing one life for another. Where's the justice in that?" Lazarus said, dropping his head into his hands as if its weight were too much for him.

Sharra rested a hand on the poor man's knee, and softly said, "Katie shouldn't have to suffer because of my problems. Neither should you, nor the Vault."

"He'll kill you. You know that," Tanner said.

"Not if you find me first."

Lazarus lifted his head from his hands, and stared at her with dawning comprehension. "You're still tagged."

"Yes."

"Are you hoping for another Ardus?" Tanner said. "Greyson is obviously not stupid. He found his tag. He'll find yours too. And then what?"

"It doesn't matter. I've already accepted his terms. Look at what Greyson's done already, the pattern of violence. He's unstable – a psychopath. Katie is just the beginning. He will not be satisfied until he has me. I'm not willing to sacrifice Katie, or anyone else if there is a way to avoid it."

The two men stared hard at her. Raising her chin, she pressed her lips together and stared right back. Lazarus raised an eyebrow as he slowly shook his head at her. The action was too much. He sighed, and rubbed his face with tired hands.

"How can I fight you when I can't even think clearly," he said. "Tanner, help me to the kitchen. I'm going to need some coffee."

Once in the kitchen, the silence returned as Sharra went about making coffee for everyone. Lazarus downed the first in a few gulps, and handed his mug back for another. By the time he reached his third cup, he was looking sharper around the eyes, though his face was still flushed. Looking down at his body, he humphed when he saw the condition of his shirt, that it was open to his bellybutton.

"I'm sorry that you had to find me this way," he said, fumbling with one button after another until only a portion of the shirt was left open at his neck.

"We are family, and we're here for each other, good and bad. So don't apologize for being human," Tanner said.

Sharra reached over, briefly setting her hand over Lazarus' hand where he clutched the mug.

"Family," she repeated, squeezing his hand before letting go. "That's why I have to do this. You can argue until the end of time, but it will do you no good."

"Sharra…"

"No," she said, cutting off the Head Director. "Let me explain. When I left my timeline, I never dreamed I'd have a family again. All of us at the Vault may come from different timelines, have different upbringings, and social statuses, but the one thing we have in common is the need to belong, to be cherished, to be a part of something intimate and long-lasting. That's what makes our eclectic group a family. It is a great treasure worth more than all the gold, jewels, and money that have ever been, or will ever be. Katie is my sister, more so than Greyson has ever been a brother to me. And so, yes, I will do anything for her. Anything."

"Stubborn woman," Tanner muttered under his breath.

"That's me. You can add it to my name: Sharra Stubborn Trouble Lane. Try to say that three times fast."

Lazarus' lips cracked into a smile. Sharra's heart did a thunk at the sight of it.

"Okay, stubborn woman that you are, so you say we can get Katie back, tell us Greyson's conditions," he said.

And so she told them all of the conditions, except for one pertinent piece of information, understanding that, if they knew about it, the deal would be off. Though neither Lazarus or Tanner were happy about the matter, they finally agreed to it. To Sharra, there was no agreeing or disagreeing. She had already made up her mind as soon as Greyson had laid out the conditions. She only told them of her plan out of respect for them.

"So when is this to happen?" Lazarus finally asked.

"This afternoon, our time."

Lazarus checked the antique clock on the kitchen counter. "That only gives me a few hours to sober up, and to get you ready."

"Right... Ready."

Was she ready?

No.

Tanner walked her back to her apartment, leaving Lazarus to clean himself up before they met again to discuss matters with the team in an hour. Amadeus came running at the sound of the door. Sharra swooped him up, settling him into the crook of her arm, and kissed the top of his head.

"Will you keep an eye on Amadeus for me?" she asked Tanner.

"Sure, but you'll be back before he can say meow."

She hid her face against the cat's neck, and let the statement pass by.

"We will find you, Sharra. I won't let him win."

Tears threatened to spill from her eyes again. This time it was for Tanner. If only he knew what she knew, he wouldn't be so confident. It broke her heart not to tell him. Blinking back the tears, she lifted her head and gave him a wobbly smile.

"You have always been there for me, my constant strength, my rock, through the good times, and the bad times. What would I have done without you?" she said.

Love for this man swelled in her heart. It shook her to the core.

Taking the cat from her arms, and setting him on the floor, he said, "Come here," as he drew her into his arms.

She went willingly, needing the comfort he offered. Before she knew it, his lips were on hers, kissing her with a need that she understood, for she needed him too.

Her arms went around his neck as she sank into the kiss. Pressing her body against him fueled him on. Passion rose up, and filled her senses, blocking the pain of the future. Their lips parted for air, but not for long. She pulled him back down for she didn't want this moment to end. There was no time for words. So with her lips and her body, she tried to tell him what she couldn't say out loud.

She loved him.

Cocooned in his muscular arms, she felt safe from the outside world. Yet even through the passion that coursed through her body, she knew this was a delusion, though a pleasant one. And still she let him kiss her, knowing this was it. There'd be no other chance. She was leaving, most likely for good, and it broke her heart.

Finally, she pulled away as the need for oxygen grew overpowering. Resting her head against Tanner's chest, her starving lungs worked hard to replenish the oxygen in her blood. Tanner's heart pounded under her ear as his chest moved with each great breath he took. As she leaned against him feeling the comfort of his arms around her and the strength of his heartbeat under her ear, reason slowly returned.

Her body stiffened within his arms. While she had been lost in the emotional upheaval since the Link with her brother, she had forgotten all about the other person in her life.

Faolan!

Now that she remembered, guilt crept into her bones. It couldn't get any worse than to love two men who loved her in return, and then to lead them both on.

She pulled out of Tanner's arms, and backed away.

"I've got to get ready," she said.

She looked at him, and wished that she hadn't. Tanner's eyes were hooded with lingering passion. His lips were red from her kisses. She groaned inside.

As she backed away, the cloud of passion in his eyes cleared as confusion set in.

His brow furrowed as he said, "Have I done something wrong?"

"No. No. It's not you. It's…"

His face hardened. "Faolan," he finished for her.

"Don't make me do this now. I can't. Not until this thing with Greyson is over."

"You've said that before, and yet you kissed me. How am I to take that?"

"I'm sorry," she whispered.

He rubbed his face in frustration. And then sighed. "I'm sorry, too. Sorry to have put you in this position. You're right. This isn't the time to talk about it. I should go."

Tanner left her apartment without a backward glance. The room felt empty without him. Amadeus meowed from the couch. She sank down beside him as the turmoil of emotions she tried hard to hide started to bubble out of her heart. Amadeus rubbed against her, but she hardly noticed.

"Oh, Tanner," she whispered. "What have I done?"

Chapter Twenty-Three

Tanner held his emotions in check as he headed down the hall to the lifts. Passing the communal lounge, he allowed only a quick wave and a hello to the few agents relaxing on the couches. They called him over, but he ignored them. The way he was feeling he couldn't stomach putting on a show of cocky assurance for anyone. He felt far from it. In fact, he was doing his damnedest to keep it together. If he was rude that was too bad. For once he didn't care. Let them think he was having a bad day. It was the truth.

The lift swished closed on his heels.

"Ground floor," he commanded as he leaned against the wall.

The lift dropped to the next floor in a matter of a few seconds, hardly enough time for him to formulate a thought. On the ground floor he peered down the hallway that housed Lazarus' apartment, but saw no movement. With the condition they had found Lazarus in, Tanner doubted that his friend was up and going yet. Instead, he turned and went down the opposite hallway.

Once inside his apartment, he threw himself upon the couch. Grabbing the first pillow he came to, he flung it across the room, and growled in frustration.

"Arggg!"

The pillow hit the wall with a *thunk* before falling to the floor. Another pillow followed soon after. Yet, he felt no better. Giving up, he settled back onto the armrest, crossing his long legs, and thought about where he had gone wrong. It wasn't hard to figure out. He should have claimed Sharra right away before anyone else had come into the picture. And here he was forcing her to choose when he had no right to. He was a bloody idiot.

Propped on the back of the couch was Sharra's teddy bear. She had given it to him to hold onto when he'd left her at Faolan's house after the test trip to her old timeline. She must have forgotten about it, for she hadn't asked for it back. He was glad. He knew it was silly, but it felt like it was a little piece of her that was his own.

He reached for it. Its worn body flopped in his hands. Its coal button eyes looked warm and inviting to his tortured heart.

"You've known her longer than I have," he said to the teddy bear. "What do you suggest I do?"

The pleasant face stared back at him, saying nothing.

"I see how it is. Not giving away any of your secrets. I don't blame you. If she were mine, I'd do the same."

He stared at the bear as he thought about the kiss. The way she had wrapped her arms around his neck and pressed her breasts against his chest gave him a boost of confidence. And the way the kiss went on and on... it nearly drove him to his knees.

"I'll tell you this though," he said to the bear, "she definitely has feelings for me, even if she doesn't want to admit it. You can't kiss someone like that, and not have feelings. The body doesn't lie. If only Faolan weren't in the way."

What was he to do about that? The two of them go back a long time. And though Faolan had been in exile for god knows how long, he was still part of the Vault, and a friend. Their community was a tight knit group. What happened to one affected them all. This thing with Sharra went beyond Faolan and him. He needed to remember that. She was right when she asked him to wait until after this ordeal with Greyson was done.

"I'm being selfish, am I not?"

He moved the bear's head up and down.

"Thanks. But that doesn't answer what I'm to do about Faolan."

It had been so long since he had allowed himself to love again. And now, there's a good chance that he was too late to claim her as his own.

When the teddy bear had nothing else to offer, Tanner propped it back on its spot, and got up from the couch. At his desk, he pressed his thumb to the screen of his monitor to wake it up. If Sharra was going ahead with Greyson's plan then he wanted to be ready.

"Rule number nine: Always be prepared for the unexpected," he quoted.

Experience had taught him this. And in Sharra's case, it had proven true too many times not to think that it wouldn't happen again. Greyson was unpredictable, conditions or no conditions. Tanner didn't trust him. The only way to outsmart a madman was to think like a madman. At this point, Tanner was dammed if he were going to let Greyson win.

Chapter Twenty-Four

Sharra waited in the Terminus with the others while Lazarus gave out final instructions. Biting her lip, she half-listened, for her mind was on Greyson and what he would do to her after he had her away from the Vault.

"Are you sure you don't want one of the men to come in with you for the exchange?" Lazarus asked her, bringing her back to the present. Though his eyes were still red-rimmed, he was in full control again, missing nothing.

"Let me go with you," Grimm piped in.

"Thank you, Grimm, but Greyson will feel less threatened if he sees a woman with me. Plus, Araylai might be able to get a read of him if she can get close enough," Sharra said.

Sharra held her emotions in check as the Arderian searched her aura.

"It is a sound plan," Araylai said to the group as she reached across the breach of space between them to ask, *Are you okay?*

THE VAULT

You must be in the Vault with me. You must!

What is it that you are not saying?

I can't tell you yet.

"Well, I don't like the whole blasted thing," Faolan said.

"None of us like it," Tanner said. "Yet, it's the only way to guarantee that Katie gets back to us safely."

"And what about Sharra? Who's going to guarantee her safety?"

"Guys!" Sharra said. "Can you try to get along for my sake? The plan is going ahead, whether you like it or not. Lazarus has agreed. And that should be good enough for you."

Lazarus touched her arm. "You don't have to do this."

"You know I do."

"We'll find you. I promise." He gave her a hug, and whispered, "Thank you," and let her go.

She nodded as tears welled up behind her eyes. Swallowing hard, she forced them back before turning to the two men who were standing side by side. As she hugged each of them in turn, she pressed a soft kiss to their cheek, and said goodbye. Though she wanted to say more, goodbye was all she could manage.

Grimm was the last. Though he stood like a red-bearded avenging angel, his eyes glistened with unshed tears. He wrapped her in his burly arms and gave her a huge hug.

"We'll find you, lassie," he said. His voice growled with emotion. She hugged him back as fiercely as he hugged her.

"Take care of Tanner and Faolan for me," she said. "Try to keep them from killing each other."

"I'll try," he said as she stepped away.

Her mind fuzzed as a Link came in.

"Are you at the Vault yet?" Greyson asked.

"I'm ready."

"You and one other person. That's it. If I see anyone else, the deal is off. Understood?"

"Understood."

Greyson broke the Link, cutting her off like a switch.

"He's on his way," she said to the group. "Remember the conditions of the deal. Don't do anything, or it's off."

Taking a deep breath, Sharra entered the Vault chamber with Araylai by her side. Their footsteps echoed off the curved walls as they headed to the bright lights of the shiftrooms on the left side. The threads of energy that were balled inside her head grew excited with the stirring of the partical cloud. She was ready for it, and quickly clamped them down.

Once out of earshot of the others, Sharra quickly revealed the last of her plan to Araylai. Time was of the essence, and she needed Araylai desperately for it to work.

"I don't have time to explain, but I need you to do something for me."

"Anything," Araylai said.

"I need you to connect with me, and stay connected."

"Easy. What else? Your aura says that you want more from me."

"At some point I'm going to enter Greyson's mind, and I need you there to see what I see. It's imperative that you do this, otherwise, I am lost for good."

"You want me to use you as a bridge."

"Yes. I have to drop my shield to do this. When I do, I need you to keep me from the pylons."

In the center of the chamber, the pylons rotated gently inside the waking cloud of particles. She knew that they had sensed her presence long before she had entered the vaulted chamber just as she had sensed them. The hallway walls no longer protected her. Neither did the Terminus. Only the strength of her mental shield kept the overwhelming power of the pylons from consuming her mind. Yet, her plan required that she drop her shield. There was no other way around it. It was a risk she was willing to take.

Araylai turned her unblinking gaze upon Sharra. Though, Sharra tried to control her emotions, she was sure the blue of her aura was bright with fear.

Before Araylai could say anything, a shiftroom close by flashed bright. Sharra threw out a thread of electromagnetic energy to her friend. Araylai opened her mind, connecting Sharra's electromagnetic energy to hers, creating a bridge of communication.

Sharra swallowed hard.

He comes, she said.

Araylai touched her arm. *You are not alone, my sister.*

The pylons stirred upon their axis, growing more agitated as Greyson strode out of the shiftroom with Katie clamped to his side. Tied and gagged, the petite girl was dragged along as if her legs were useless. In his arms, she mumbled angrily from behind the gag, fighting him with the little energy she had left.

"Shut up!" Greyson said, squeezing her in a death grip.

Through the gag, Katie yelped in pain, and sagged in his arms.

"Stop! I'm here. You don't need to hurt her," Sharra said as she hurried across the floor. *Stay with me,* she said to Araylai as they approached her brother.

They were almost upon him when he said, "Stop right there. That's close enough."

Ten feet of onyx floor separated them. Sharra stared at her brother, trying to remember him as a boy, and failed. It was a full-grown man that held Katie captive, a man who resembled her brother, yet was a stranger to her. They had the same parents, and had similar features, yet they were nothing alike. She was grateful for that, and also that her parents would never have to know how he had turned out. It would have broken her mother. She could barely believe it herself. Yet, there he was, standing in front of her, the evidence of his instability shining bright in his hazel eyes.

"My lovely sister, always ready for the rescue," he said with a scowl.

"You've got me. Now hand over Katie."

"Slow down, Sis." He looked over her head, searching the darkness of the Vault. "Where's Lazarus? When I said you were allowed one person with you, I had assumed that he would have been your first choice. Or at least one of your lover-boys." His gaze fell upon Araylai. At the sight of her, a tiny smile of contempt tickled the corner of his lips. "That would have made sense. But no, you had to bring a woman. Do you really think that she can help you? Haven't you seen what I do to women?

He shoved Katie in front of him. Holding her against his body with an arm of steel, he forced her head up. In the light shining from the shiftroom, Sharra could see the dark bruises that covered Katie's swollen face. The wound over her eye was scabbed over. The blood from it had dried where it had run down her face and onto her ripped blouse. Sharra cried inside for Katie. The bruises on the young-looking girl confirmed that she was doing the right thing.

Katie caught her eye. They flashed hot with anger and indignation.

He's trying to bait us, Araylai warned.

We need him to make the exchange.

When neither woman moved, Greyson pressed his lips together in disappointment and shook his head.

"Right then, to business. Did you bring what I asked you to bring?" he said over Katie's imprisoned head.

From the belt of her Vault uniform, Sharra pulled out a small jackknife, and held it up for him to see.

Araylai sent her a sharp look. *He asked you to bring a knife? Why?*

Greyson caught the slight movement. Peering through the dim light, he studied Araylai for a moment as he tried to figure out who she was.

Finally he said, "Araylai, is it?"

Araylai opened her mouth to answer, but before she got a sound out, Greyson shut her up with sharp words.

"Stop right there. You can shut your pretty mouth, and keep it that way. I've heard about your siren ways. We won't have any of that here. Not one word from you, or this deal is over."

Araylai snapped her mouth shut, and glared at him.

Don't get him riled up. He's already unstable enough. We need him to release Katie, Sharra reminded her.

"That's a good girl," Greyson said. "Now take the knife from Sharra, and remove her tracking chip."

No! Araylai said to Sharra.

Greyson studied the stern look on Araylai's face, and said, "Don't pretend that she doesn't have one. I'm not so stupid as to fall for that trick twice."

Sharra held out the knife to her, and pleaded with her eyes. *Don't argue. Just do as he says.*

The chip... How will we find you?

There is another way. Take the knife.

Araylai pressed her lips together as she swiped the knife from Sharra's hand. The blade snapped open with a flick of her finger. She tested the grip in her hand as she eyed Greyson. His eyes narrowed. From his pocket he whipped out a gun, and pressed it to Katie's temple. Katie went stiff under the prison of his arm. Sharra sucked in her breath, for his finger was on the trigger, and she had no doubt that he would pull it.

"Now, ladies, I suggest no funny business with that knife, or I will kill Katie before you can say boo. Remove the chip before my finger gets tired."

Araylai gave him one of her slow nods, and moved closer to Sharra.

"It's underneath the skin on the back slope of my neck," Sharra said, as she turned, and placed a finger over the tiny bump on the left side of her neck between her spinal cord and one of the large tendons. "Right here."

One hand went on her shoulder, as the other found the bump. Sharra held still as the cold steel touched her flesh, and sank into her skin with a sharp burst of pain.

I hate knives!

I am sorry, Araylai said.

Gritting her teeth against the pain, Sharra said, *Just hurry up and get it out!*

Araylai held her tight as she searched for the capsule with the tip of the knife. A familiar feeling of warmth ran down her shoulder and into the collar of her Vault uniform. She knew it was blood. Finally the pressure eased as the capsule was pushed out of the cut by the knife. Araylai passed the knife over to Sharra. On the tip in a bed of blood floated the tiny capsule.

"It's out," she said to Greyson, holding the blade out to him as Araylai held her steady while pressing the wound on her neck closed with a finger.

"Good. Now toss the knife with the chip into the cloud. That's right. Into the cloud where no one can get to it."

Without hesitating, she did what he asked. The knife clattered inside the cloud as it hit the floor. A breeze stirred the air as the pylons grew agitated. The cloud responded, building a charge as the particles within it protested the intrusion of the foreign object in its midst.

Greyson ignored the growing cloud. As soon as the knife had vanished into the cloud a smile appeared on his lips, transforming his face. Yet, Sharra wasn't fooled for one second.

"Come here, Sharra."

"Not until you let Katie go. That was the deal."

He rolled his eyes. "Of course, I'm going to let her go. She has served her purpose. She got me you."

As he spoke, the gun left Katie's temple and turned onto Sharra.

I can't wait any longer, Sharra said silently to Araylai. *I have to drop my shield now, while we are still together.*

Do it.

Dropping her mental shield, Sharra felt for Greyson's mind, finding it blocked.

As her shield released, the force of the pylons slammed into her, pressing her mind with its white energy, overpowering her senses. She stumbled where she stood. Araylai caught her before she fell to the floor, and held her steady. With the strength of her friend beside her, Sharra fought back the consuming white heat in her mind with all the mental power she could muster, until only the excited ball of threads was left. And still the pylons would not give up. In Araylai's arms, her body trembled as the effort grew harder. Yet, she couldn't let the pylons win.

With all the mental strength that she could spare, she reached out to Greyson again. Finding a crack in his mental shield, she slipped through.

"Feeling a bit dizzy, my dear sister? No need to stress out. It will be over soon. Stop procrastinating, and get over here," Greyson said, waving the gun at her.

Araylai stayed behind as Sharra took a tentative step forward. The power inside the cloud called out to her, to the ball of threads in her head, compelling her to join with it. Soft tendrils reached out from it to touch her skin, sending tiny spurts of energy through her. Fighting off the desire to obey, Sharra struggled to hold them off as she held on to the thin link between her and Greyson.

Araylai, Can you make the bridge? Sharra asked as she took another tentative step.

A precious moment passed before she got an answer.

Yes. I am inside his mind. It is… ugly.

I know. That can't be helped. I need you to be ready. I'm going to ask him a question. He won't answer it out loud, but I'm hoping the question will make him think about it. I need you to interpret what you see and remember it.

Sharra took another step. Each one was getting harder, yet she pressed forward. Katie's eyes were round like saucers as she watched from within the band of Greyson's arm. She was saying something, but the duct tape that covered her mouth made her words indistinct.

Greyson shoved Katie's head down until her chin rested on her chest. Pushing her hair to the side, he revealed a metal clamp on her neck below the base of her skull. When he unclipped it, Katie instantly came alive as if a switch had been turned on. She began to wriggle aggressively within the steel band of his arm.

Without warning Greyson shoved Katie towards Araylai. "She's all yours, well and truly paid for. I got what I came for."

Araylai caught the girl before she toppled to the ground. Katie sagged within her arms.

A wave of relief passed over Sharra, though it did not last long, for the will of the cloud beat relentlessly inside her mind. She pressed the side of her head with a hand. Her brain hurt as her hold on the bridge that connected the three of them grew more difficult to maintain against the pressure of the cloud. She had to ask soon before she lost the bridge completely.

"Hands down, and keep them down," Greyson growled.

She dropped her hand from her head as the cold end of the gun was pressed into her back. It dug into her flesh as her brother checked the utility belt around her waist. When he was happy that it was empty, he pushed her towards the closest shiftroom with the barrel of the gun. Her feet dragged across the onyx floor as she struggled to maintain the bridge. In desperation she pushed her mental gift harder. With the renewed force, the inside of Greyson's mind cleared, and she could see.

Looking over her shoulder, she asked him, "Where are you taking me?"

He smiled a secret smile, and said. "You'll see."

In the milliseconds that it took him to say those two words, a series of pictures popped inside his head: miles of unplowed fields, a blue car parked next to an old barn, a four-lane highway, a city in the skyline, a house, her parents. The odd scenes flashed by, one by one, too

quick for Sharra to think about what they meant, only
knowing that the answer was there.

Her body began to shake as the effort to hold onto the
bridge grew too much.

I can't hold it! she cried to Araylai.

The bridge wavered. Her strength was all but spent.
She had no choice but to let it go. The guillotine of her
mental shield slammed down around her brain. It
severed the connection with a finality that brought
instant relief, not just from her brother's mind, but also
from the constant pressure of the cloud. At the same
time, the ball of energy in her head beat against their
restraints in disappointment as the contact with their host
was lost.

Sharra's body slumped in exhaustion as a sob formed
in her throat. She quickly swallowed it before her
brother noticed.

Araylai? Did you get any of that?

I saw it.

*Tell the others. Use it to find me. It will give them
hope.*

What about you?

Too exhausted to answer, Sharra let their connection
slide away. There was no answer to that question. Hope
was for the living. And right now, her future was looking
pretty bleak.

Greyson had her inside the shiftroom before she knew
it. The bright air of the room assaulted her eyes. Sharra
blinked away the tears, refusing to admit that they were
there. She looked back into the darkness of the Vault
chamber. Against the wispy cloud stood Araylai and

Katie, two statues frozen in place. Sometime during her walk to the shiftroom, Katie's bindings had been removed. Her arms were wrapped around Araylai as the Arderian supported her boyish body. Though their faces were hidden in the shadows, their postures were stiff.

"Sharra!" Katie cried. "We'll find you! I promise!"

Greyson gripped Sharra's upper arm, and snorted. "Good luck with that."

Like the little spitfire that she was, Katie refused to give up, and screamed, "You hear that, you bastard? We're coming for her! And you! And when we find you, you'll be dead meat! You hear me? Dead meat!"

Greyson smiled, and whispered to Sharra, "She's a darling, isn't she. I'm going to miss her."

Exhausted and out of hope, Sharra stared out into the Vault as Greyson prepared for the shift. An instant later, his hand tightened on her arm, the telltale signal that he was ready.

"No!" Katie cried.

"Goodbye," Sharra said softly, and disappeared.

Chapter Twenty-Five

The shouting in the Vault died away with the last of the echoes. All that remained was the sound of the whooshing of the pylons. A breeze flowed out of the archway and into the Terminus where the four agents stood powerless to help the women inside the Vault.

Time ticked by as the silence grew.

Tanner shook his head, breaking the spell of worry that had fallen over him since Sharra and Araylai disappeared beyond the arched entrance into the Vault. Every muscle in his body screamed to do something, damning the conditions that Greyson had set.

"This is taking too long," he said. "I'm going in."

Lazarus grabbed his arm, halting Tanner. "No! We do what Greyson says."

Lines of desperation creased the folds around the Head Director's mouth and on his forehead, aging him greatly. Tanner warred within himself over the hurt for his friend, and the need to help Sharra. He glanced over to Faolan. The Scotsman had argued with Sharra over the fallacy of her plan until he was blue in the face. Tanner had to admire the man for trying to get past Sharra's stubborn streak. Not that he hadn't tried to convince her too. Sharra was, after all, Sharra.

A little smile touched his lips as he thought about her more endearing qualities. That brought him back to their last kiss, and the reality of what she was doing. Faolan understood it too. It was written in the stiff tension of his body. His face was tight with controlled emotion. Tanner knew exactly how he felt. He couldn't lose her, not now, when he needed her so much.

"It's killing me to just stand here and do nothing," Tanner said.

"I agree," Faolan said as he sided with Tanner. "It has gone quiet in there. At least let one of us investigate."

From the side Grimm grew excited as he pointed a beefy finger to the darkness inside the Vault.

"Look! I see them!" he shouted.

From the darkness appeared Araylai supporting another woman out of the Vault. The woman was holding her side and limping as they moved slowly into the light. Tanner's heart stopped for a brief second as he thought that something had gone wrong, and that it was Sharra hurt in Araylai's arms. And then the woman lifted her head, and he saw the bruised pixie face, and knew that Sharra was gone.

"Oh, lassie," Grimm said, his voice rough with shock.

"It's okay, Grimm," Katie said.

Hearing his daughter's voice broke Lazarus from his trance.

"Katie," he groaned, and ran to her.

Katie let go of Araylai as her father took her into his arms and pressed her to his chest in a hug that spoke volumes of the love that he had for her. Tears fell unabashed down his face as he tenderly cradled his daughter.

"I thought you were lost," he said, placing a kiss on the top of her head.

"Father..." was all Katie could manage.

A lump formed in Tanner's throat at the sight of the small family reunion. Though it was a small victory, getting Katie back, it came at a cost. Sorrow for the past, for the loss of his sister, surged up into Tanner's heart. He would've done anything to save her. Anything. Even giving up his own life. And that's what Sharra was doing for Katie. He knew it even if the others didn't want to admit it.

Unless they found Sharra first.

Tanner swallowed the lump in his throat as his mind churned to get on with finding Sharra before Greyson killed her. Faolan had the same idea.

"I'm sorry to interrupt, Lazarus, but we need to ask Katie some questions," Faolan said.

"You're right," Lazarus said as he looked down into the bruised face of his daughter. "But first, Katie needs medical attention."

He pulled her hair away to check the spot behind her left ear. Finding the metal tattoo intact, he dropped her hair, and hugged her again.

Pulling away, she said, "Father, I'm all right. Really."

"You'll do as you're told, spoiled thing. Or do I have to ground you?"

"You wouldn't."

"A father will do anything to keep his child safe," he said as he kissed her head again.

Katie wobbled on her feet. Lazarus gently scooped her up into his arms, and settled her against his chest.

"You don't have to carry me," Katie said.

Though she denied she needed help, she settled into her father's arms and closed her eyes in exhaustion.

Lazarus looked down at his daughter, at her peaceful face. All the anxiety from before was wiped away by the look of love that he gave her. Yet, it was short-lived. When his eyes returned to the group, they turned hard with anger.

"We have Katie back. Now let's go find Sharra. Araylai can fill you in with what happened in the Vault," he said as he turned to leave.

"Don't you want to know?" Araylai said.

"I need to take my daughter to the Ward. We can talk later."

Lazarus carried his daughter through the arched entranceway of the Vault. A minute later they heard the swish of the Medical doors on the far side. Tanner felt a prickle at his neck. He turned to find Araylai staring at him in that strange manner of hers. He saw sadness in their amber depths, and knew that something wasn't right.

"What is it?" he asked her.

"Greyson knew about Sharra's chip."

"No." Tanner shook his head as despair rose up and choked his throat.

"No," echoed Grimm.

Araylai's eyes darkened as she continued, "He had me remove it. It was thrown into the particle cloud before he took her away."

"How are we going to find her now?" Faolan said in dismay.

Tanner looked hopelessly around at his fellow agents. "This can't be the way it ends. I had promised that I'd find her."

Faolan's face clouded as his dismay turned to anger.

"We all made the same promise," he said. "But that's when we knew we could use the tagfinder. Without it…" He snapped his jaw shut, unable to say what they were all thinking.

Araylai set her hand upon Faolan's arm, a gesture that Tanner had never seen her do before to any agent.

"Do not give up hope," she said softly in her bell-like voice. "Sharra knew that this would happen and has left us another way."

Araylai went on to tell them about how Sharra had braved facing the compelling power of the pylons, and dropped her shield to make the bridge between Araylai and Greyson. How she had felt Sharra struggled to control that powerful draw while keeping the bridge open. And how, when Sharra had asked where he was taking her, that it was through that bridge that Araylai had been able to see a series of images in Greyson's head, images that inadvertently gave the answer.

"If we can figure out what the images mean, we can find her," she said.

"For Christ sake, why would she drop her shield? Didn't she remember what happened the last time she had dropped her shield that close to the cloud?" Tanner said.

"What's this about a bridge?" Faolan said, picking up on the odd statement when Tanner was too busy ranting.

"It is like looking through one mind into the next, seeing the third person's thoughts as the second person sees them, kind of like watching another TV inside a TV."

"And she did this bridge thing," Grimm said.

"Sharra has an unusual mind…"

"That's an understatement," Tanner grumbled. "Still, it's no excuse for putting herself in such danger. It almost killed her the last time."

"Wait a minute," Faolan said. "Are you saying that Sharra can read minds?"

Araylai gaze never wavered as she said, "It is not my place to say. You must ask her yourself."

"I just might do that," Faolan said. He pursed his lips as he thought about it. "It would explain a lot of things."

That Sharra could read minds shook Tanner to the core. Had she read his? He didn't know what to make of it. Though right now, they had bigger issues to think about. So, he pushed it aside, and drew them back to the obvious.

"If you want to ask her, we have to find her first," he said. "Otherwise, what does it matter? Araylai, you said that you 'saw' images in Greyson's head. What were they?"

She listed them off in the same order that she had seen them. Grimm and Faolan asked her to repeat them, for it seemed an odd collection. Not to Tanner. The more he thought about it the more confident he became.

"Greyson would've thought of the pictures in order of execution," he said, growing more excited as he explained. "If that's the case, and I hope it is, then that would make the fields their entry point within the half-mile radius dictated by the shift, and the car, his target. We need to talk to Katie."

Tanner wanted to rush over to the Medical Facilities, but Araylai stopped him with a shake of her head.

"We have time on this side. Our questions can wait until later. Right now, Lazarus needs to be alone with his daughter," she advised.

Later didn't happen until the next day, after Cam released Katie from the Ward. Tanner received a Link from Lazarus and dropped everything, not that he was doing much to begin with. After they split up yesterday, he had gone back to his apartment to think about the images that Araylai had relayed to them. All of them had been vague which had slowed down his research. He knew that he needed more information.

So when the Link came, he transferred the research to his Com-Link, and ran to the lifts. It was there that a thought came to his head – a hunch. Instead of heading to the conference room, he went to Sharra's apartment. Fortunately, he was still programmed into Sharra's PVC, and it let him in. On the coffee table was the item he was looking for. He swiped it up, and without breaking stride, took off for the conference room.

Pushing through the conference room door, he paused, breathing heavily as he scanned the agents that were already there. Faolan, Grimm, Araylai, and Lazarus were sitting at the oval table. So was Katie. In the light of the conference room, her bruised and swollen face looked worse. At the sight of Tanner, her eyes brightened. She tried to smile and winced. So she dropped it until only the ends of her lips curled. Yet, the light was still in her eyes. He pressed his anger down, as he sent her a genuine smile. If he ever got a hold of Greyson, he'd kill him for the animal that he was. No man who beats up women deserved to live.

"Tanner," she said, getting up, and drawing him to the empty chair next to her. "We were just wondering where you were."

"Sorry, I had to get something. Welcome back," he said as he sat down.

"It's good to be back, but I wish Sharra hadn't done it. Her brother is a psycho. I don't know how else to describe him. It's as if he's obsessed with Sharra, and not in a good way."

Katie paused as her eyes turned inward. Deep furrows creased her forehead as her body shrank into the chair. As she sat silent in her thoughts, a darkness fell over her like a heavy thundercloud. Tanner had never seen her like this; the girl who was always the bright spot in the room, the one full of optimism, and love of life. This new Katie scared him, and his fear for Sharra grew tenfold.

"Katie?" Lazarus said, his voice rich with worry.

Her eyes came back to the room, clouded with fear. "He's going to kill her. I overheard him talking about it.

He thought I was still drugged up, but I heard him. We have to stop him before it's too late."

Grimm shook his head, confused, and said, "Why doesn't she just shift back?"

"Don't you remember what happened the last time Greyson had her? He fused her agrylium," Faolan said.

"He won't need to do that this time. He's found something a lot easier to use," Katie said as she rubbed the back of her neck. "It's some kind of device that when it's clamped onto your body it stops you from doing things... like shifting, or even moving."

Araylai who had remained quiet, spoke up. "I saw him remove a clamp-like device from the back of your neck right before he threw you to me."

As Araylai described the clamp, Lazarus activated the table. Soon there was a 3D hologram of a claw-like device floating in the center.

"A Neuro Inhibitor," Lazarus said.

"I have never heard of it," Faolan said.

"I have, but not in a long time," Grimm said. "Nasty little bugger, that's what it is."

While the image rotated slowly in the air above the table, Lazarus explained, "Grimm is right. These are nasty devices. Inside them are hairlike wires. When it is clamped onto the back of the neck and activated, those wires then find their way past the vertebra and into the spinal cord where the controller can directly block signals to and from the brain. They were invented in the early twenty-second century as a means for controlling the more criminal-minded of the masses. It was a way of reducing the cost to the public by integrating convicts back into society, thus eliminating the need for prisons. The idea was good, but as humans do, the technology got into the wrong hands, and was quickly banned."

"And he's got one of these things," Tanner spat out in disgust.

"I guarantee that it's already on Sharra," Katie said, rubbing her neck. "She won't be able to shift as long as it's there."

"Then, we have to find another way," Lazarus said. "Any information you can tell us will help."

"I was out of it for most of the time."

Lazarus patted her shoulder. "It's okay. Just do your best. Maybe we can start with the images Araylai extracted from Greyson's head. See if they mean anything to you."

Turning to Araylai, Katie said, "Describe them for me."

"The first one was of flat farmland as far as the eye could see, recently harvested judging by the stubby yellow stalks left behind. Corn, I think. Next was a blue car parked beside a weathered building, the kind used to store machinery. The ground was flat there, too. And I know you are going to ask, but no, I could not see the license plate of the car. It was the wrong angle."

"Damn," Tanner said. "That would've made it so much easier."

Katie perked up as Araylai spoke of what she saw.

"Wait. We were at a spot just like that right before Greyson shifted us back to the Vault. It was in the middle of nowhere. If there were a house, I couldn't see one, not that he'd given me much of a chance to look around after he pulled me out of the boot of the car."

"If that's the case, then I wonder if you were on the same four-lane highway pictured in the third image," Tanner said.

"Was it flat and straight?" she asked. "Because lying in the dark, I kept thinking it went on forever with hardly a hill or a turn, just the endless thunk-de-thunk of the wheels hitting the cracks in the pavement."

All eyes turned to Araylai for the answer. "Yes, it was. Also, I've been researching makes and models of cars to try to match the image to a vehicle to help narrow our timeline. I didn't have much to go by. The angle of the car was wrong. All I could come up with is that it was made somewhere between late 1970's to mid 1990's."

"Great work, Araylai. That helps narrow down our timelines. Yet we still don't know where the images originated from," Faolan said.

"I do recall that the traffic was moving on the right side of the road, if that helps," Katie said.

"That rules out Great Britain, Australia, New Zealand, and a few other countries," Grimm said.

"Leaving about sixty-five percent of the rest of the world," Faolan said. "We need to narrow it down more. What about the land references? Can we cross-reference the two, and come up with something more useful?"

"Maybe the other images will help," Lazarus said. "Araylai, you said that you saw a house…"

"It was two-stories, the kind that had windows jutting out of the roof, with white clapboard siding and picture windows. There were gardens in the front of the house, and along the sidewalk that went to the wide front porch. I think the view was from the street because I could also see part of the neighboring houses and their driveways."

"Were there any cars parked in the driveway of the house?" Tanner asked.

"No, but it could have been in the garage. Or the owners could have been gone. I can only tell you what I saw, as he had thought it. No more, no less."

Lazarus turned to Katie, and asked, "Do you remember seeing this house?"

She shook her head. "I was kept chained to a couch in a basement. Most of the windows were covered. The one that wasn't let me see a bit of overgrown lawn and some sky, and not much else. He didn't let me out until he moved me to the car, and that was parked inside the attached garage."

"Sharra once told me that Greyson is a creature of habit," Tanner said. "If that is the case, then he'd be taking Sharra back to where he had held Katie. That would make the field his entry point, the road his way back, and the house his hiding place. So, I asked myself, if I were Greyson, what house would I keep returning to, and it hit me. Sharra had the answer all along. Because like her brother, she also is a creature of habit and has been unknowingly doing the same thing."

"What are you getting at?" Faolan said.

"It's home. Her home. Have a look at what I've come up with so far."

Tanner pulled out his Com-Link and set it on the conference table. With a few swipes of his fingers, the

Com-Link was soon talking with the inner workings of the table, drawing up a 3D picture of the world. Standing up, Tanner worked the image with his hands, touching the landmass that was the United States. The rest of the world fell away until only the fifty states filled the image. Illinois was touched next. Just out of Chicago on the southwest side of the city was a blinking red dot.

Pointing to the dot, he said, "This is the Lanes' home." He turned to Katie, and asked, "How long do you estimate that you were on the road?"

"I don't know… long enough to put permanent welts in my back from lying on the spare tire."

"So, let's say three hours," he said as he touched a spot on a highway due south of Chicago in the central part of the State. "This is State Highway Fifty-Seven. It meets all our criteria: four-lanes, straight, and right through corn country."

"Even if that's true, do you know how many corn fields are in Illinois? It'd be like looking for a needle in a haystack," Faolan said.

"What about the man and the woman that Araylai saw? What do they have to do with all this?" Grimm asked.

"I think I know." From his uniform Tanner pulled out the picture frame that he had taken from Sharra's coffee table. As he handed it to Araylai, he asked her, "Is this the couple from Greyson's head?"

The rings around her pupils flashed bright as she stared at the photo.

"Where did you get this?" she asked.

"Off Sharra's coffee table."

"Then you know who they are?"

He nodded. "They are the parents of Sharra and Greyson. I've seen her mother once before when Sharra had used her old home for a training exercise."

Araylai passed the picture to Faolan who, after a quick study, passed it on to Lazarus. After handing it to Grimm, Lazarus turned to the map that hovered above the conference table.

"If you're right, then he's taken her home," Lazarus said as he touched the red dot.

The image changed under his finger, turning into a street map of the suburb. The red dot blinked midway down one of the streets. He touched it again. Soon a picture of a two-story clapboard house with gabled windows and a wide front porch filled the 3D image.

"That's the house from Greyson's head!" Araylai confirmed.

"We have our where. Now, we need a 'when,'" Lazarus said.

Tanner sat back in his chair as silent as the rest, for that was the ultimate question. 'When' was a long time. Faolan had been right. It was like looking for a needle in a haystack. For as long as Sharra's parent's timeline ran, through each passing year, each month, each day, each hour to each second, Greyson could have Sharra hidden anywhere in the 'when'.

Yet, Tanner refused to give up. He loved her. And it was love that gave him hope, fueling his resolve.

"So," he said to Lazarus, "which 'when' do you want us to start looking in?"

Chapter Twenty-Six

Joliet, Illinois, U.S.A
1986

It took only a few seconds to leave the Vault for another place… another timeline. And this time was no different. If the pictures in Greyson's head were any indication, Sharra had a good idea where he was taking her. Hopefully with the pictures stolen from her brother's head, Araylai could help the others figure it out too. That wasn't so much the problem. The 'when' was the bigger question.

The smooth floor of the shiftroom was gone. Exhausted and unprepared, Sharra stumbled over a stub of corn stalk as they landed on a harvested cornfield. Greyson pulled her back to him with an iron grip, and pressed the gun into her side.

"Where do you think you're going," he said.

"Nowhere," she said as her knees trembled to hold her body upright.

"That's right. Nowhere. Now put your hands behind your back."

An autumn sun hung low over the curve of the earth. Slowly it began to rise into the velvety-blue sky, signaling a new day. A cool wind brushed her skin as it swept across the open fields. Not a tree, nor a house was to be seen, only endless rows of corn stubs left behind by the combines.

Midwest. Probably somewhere in central Illinois, she thought as she did what he demanded.

With a gun in her side, what choice did she have but to obey, unless she wanted to be left for dead in the middle of the field. He knew it. She knew it, too.

After pushing the gun into the back of his pants, he pulled her wrists together, and zipped an electrical tie around them, leaving no space for movement. Before she had a chance to test them, he grabbed her by the neck. His fingers dug into her flesh as he pulled her close.

"Hey! You don't have to be so rough. I said I'd cooperate," she said.

"I'm not taking any chances, not with you're track record."

Something hard pinched the back of her neck. A moment later a burning sensation spread into her head and down her spine. Fear stifled her breath as her brain went cloudy. She tried to move her legs, but they refused to budge. Her arms were the same.

"What did you do to me?" Her voice shook as she struggled to think.

"Taking away your ability to shift. Can't have you disappearing on me. I see that you don't believe me. Go ahead, and try."

She closed her eyes and thought of the shiftroom, but no blocks would form in the cloud. Even the ball of energy that rested in her head was subdued as if drugged. She tried again, this time pushing her brain even harder, and still her mind remained blank. Her mental shield had dropped. His brain was right there for the reading, but when she tried to penetrate his mind, there was nothing. For the first time since her assimilation, it didn't work.

She was blind to his thoughts.

She opened her eyes and found her brother watching her. Her face must have shown her shock, for a smile came to his lips.

"See?" he said. "Don't you just love technology."

The burning continued in her limbs. She went to shake her leg. It didn't respond. Neither did the other one when she tried, nor her arms. Panic set in.

"My arms! My legs! I can't move them!"

"Oops."

He did something to the clamp on her neck. The burning sensation eased, though not the cloud in her head. She tested her foot and was relieved to find it lifted off the ground. Her fingers made fists within their bindings.

"Thank you," she said begrudgingly.

"Don't thank me. I would have left you that way if circumstances were different. Now, get moving." He turned her around, and pointed to the structure at the end of the field. "That way."

The gun was back out and pressed to her spine. Her legs began to move. The dirt crunched under her boots as she worked her way across the rows of stubble, ever aware of the man behind her. Though she tried to get Greyson to talk as they walked, he refused to be baited into telling her anything.

She knew before they came to the structure that it was the barn from the series of images she stole from Greyson's brain, and that the car would be there.

Sure enough, when they came around the side of the barn, the blue car, a Nissan sedan, was parked beside the wall in the tall grass.

Greyson nudged her to the back of the car. Pulling out a set of keys, he unlocked the trunk.

As he lifted it, he jammed the gun into her back, and said, "Get in."

A dirty spare tire stuck up from the well in the floor of the trunk as if someone had been in too much of a hurry to put it in properly.

Sharra stared at it, and thought of Katie.

"Can't I ride with you in the front? I promise to be good."

"No. Get in."

Without waiting, he shoved her into the trunk. She tumbled in, hitting the tire with her shoulder. She cried out as pain shot down her arms where they were pinned between her back and the tire. Before she could move, her legs were thrown in. Tucking her legs in, she scooted awkwardly off the tire and onto her side to the back of the trunk before he smashed her legs with the trunk lid.

Greyson stared down at her from the opening. Behind him the sky was turning lighter.

"Comfy?" he said.

He snorted and reached in to grab her neck again. She tried to move away, yet his fingers easily found the clamp. Her heart began to race as the burning sensation returned. Soon after her body went limp. As he reached for a roll of duct tape, he dropped her head. It hit the floor of the trunk with a thud. She cried out, but he ignored her as he ripped off a piece of tape.

"Can't have you making any noise," he said as he stretched it over her mouth.

Her eyes were wide, her breath uneven as she watched the trunk slam down, leaving her in the dark. Her shoulders and arms hurt from the bindings. Besides that, a headache was beginning to form in the back of her head where the clamp pulled upon her skin. But they were nothing compared to the loss of the control of her body, coupled with the growing fear of what was to come after they reached their destination.

The engine of the car roared to life. Sharra's body bumped around in the trunk as the tires worked their way over the rough ground until they hit the smooth pavement of the road. Stuck in the dark, Sharra could do nothing but think until the sway of the car lulled her into a restless sleep.

It was the silence of the engine that woke Sharra with a start. Her body ached where she lay twisted around the spare tire. She tried to stretch, and then remembered the clamp on the back of her neck. The feeling had left her arms and hands from the weight of her body.

The lock of the trunk clicked, releasing the lid. She heard the car door slam, and footsteps clipping upon pavement as Greyson moved to the back of the car. The lid was flung open, and there he was.

"Hello again," he said with a smile as if he were happy to see her.

It scared her, for it told her how much he was not right in the head. She began to pant through her nose as his hand came in to adjust the clamp again. When he was done, the burning melted away, and the movement returned to her limbs.

She looked beyond him to the tidy garage. A washer and dryer stood in a bay to the side of a door that she assumed went into the house. A basket of dirty towels sat on top of the washer.

"I'm going to remove the duct tape, only because I'm not a cruel person. It won't help to scream. No one will be able to hear you," he said.

The duct tape was snatched off her mouth.

As soon as it was ripped off, she yelled, "You bastard!"

"Now, now. Don't make me put it back on."

She held her tongue at the threat, knowing she was beat. A light gleamed in his eyes as he watched her sag in defeat.

The pleasant smile was back on his face.

"Now let's get you out of there, and to somewhere a little more comfortable, shall we?" he said.

He hauled her out of the trunk and onto her feet. The muscles in her legs refused to cooperate, and she wobbled where she stood. Pins and needles burned through her limbs. Her shoulders throbbed as the weight of her arms dragged them painfully back. When her legs refused to work, Greyson threw her under his arm like a sack of potatoes, and half-dragged her into the house, through the kitchen, and to a door under the stairway.

"This isn't our home," she said as she craned her neck to see the unfamiliar dining room across the way.

"Why would you think that I'd bring you there?" he said as he hauled her down into the basement.

The image of their childhood home taken from his mind popped into her head.

"I don't know. Guess I'm stupid."

"Not so stupid."

A bit of light came from a squat basement window, casting dim shadows everywhere. One corner of the basement was sectioned off. It looked like a hangout spot with its mismatched furniture and posters taped to the painted cement block walls. There were posters of rock bands, cars, and hot women, just like in Greyson's bedroom. An old shaggy orange rug covered the concrete floor in front of a wooden-framed brown couch, both remnants from the seventies. Sheets had been strung across the beams, but were now pushed to the walls, letting in a patch of light from the one window that wasn't boarded up like the rest.

Greyson dragged her past a pingpong table, and over to the window, pushing her face to the glass. Through the shrubs, she could see the front porch of the house across the driveway.

"Recognize anything?" Greyson said.

Seeing it, Sharra knew where she was, and frowned.

"That's our front porch," she said.

"You get an A plus."

Making that point, he hauled her away from the window to the hangout side of the basement. When they crossed the carpet, something crunched under her foot. She looked down to see pieces of electrical ties, and knew this is where he had brought Katie after he found out about his chip. A blanket was thrown to one side of the couch. There was a plastic cup sitting on a scuffed-up end table beside the couch. Next to the cup was another roll of duct tape.

Turning her around, he cut the electrical ties with a knife. They fell to the floor and joined the others on the carpet. She rubbed her wrists where they had dug into her flesh, but he didn't give her long to ease her pain.

"If you are wondering, this is Matt's house," he said as he pushed her down onto the couch.

"I figured that."

Bicycle chains had been looped and locked around the wooden frame of the back of the couch and the armrest. He grabbed her wrist before she knew what he intended, and, with another electrical tie, attached it to the bicycle chain around the armrest. As he tied her up, he continued to explain, as if she didn't know.

"Cade and I used to hang out here with Matt all the time. Just the three of us. You can't imagine the trouble we'd think up while down here..." He chuckled at the memories. "Yeah, good times. Too bad they had to turn into boring grownups."

"You're not a kid anymore either."

He zipped the second tie around her other hand to the back chain, and stood up. She moved her arm and found that she could reach the cup, yet the other kept her from going any further. She went for the clamp at her neck, but he was smart, and had worked out the distance, giving her only so much leeway as to function on the couch, and not enough to escape.

After a few minutes of twisting this way and that, Sharra gave up, and glared at him.

"What are Matt's parents going to say when they come home to find us in their house?"

"They're not going to say anything because they are on vacation this week. You don't remember, do you? Of course not. You haven't figured out 'when' we are yet. Let me give you a hint, today is a very special day."

"What day is it? Tell me!"

A glint appeared in his eyes as he smiled down at her. She waited for an answer. All she got was a smile of amusement. Her anger grew the longer he smiled at her.

"Why are you doing this?" she said.

The anger in her voice cut the smirk from his face. He turned dark and stormy as if a switch were flicked in his head. It scared her.

"Don't you get it?" he said slamming his hands on the beam above his head. "Everything comes easy for you – school, friends, our parent's love. That's all I ever wanted. And I had it, too, for four years until you came along. Then everything changed. I became the 'bad one.' I was the one who always got in trouble. Not you."

"That's not true. I was always in trouble."

"No, you weren't. I was there. And what's more, Mom and Dad never looked at me the way that they looked at you. Don't deny it! I've watched them for years. You were always the favorite. Little miss princess who could do no wrong. Well, I'm going to show them just what I think of them."

"What are you talking about? When in the stream of time are we? Are they still alive?"

He didn't hear her, for as she watched, his eyes turned glassy as he started to talk to himself.

"I can do it. I can. They are already dead. That gives me the perfect alibi."

He laughed at his own joke. Sharra didn't get it. The laughter stopped as quickly as it started.

Greyson shot her a calculated look.

"If I do it, then my younger self is stuck with you. I didn't think of that. Four years I had to lug you around, the one person I hated the most. Four years! Do you know how hard that was?"

"I was there, Greyson, the whole time. I knew exactly how you felt because you let me know every single day. I thought it was just your way of grieving for Mom and Dad. I didn't think_"

He cut her off with a sharp laugh. "Grieving for Mom and Dad? Ha-ha. Isn't that funny. You're so stupid. Do you know what day it is today? It's Tuesday, October fourteenth, nineteen eighty-six, the day of the accident. That's right. I thought since they meant so much to you that I'd give you one last opportunity to spend some time with them, for nostalgia sake... before they die... again. Again! Get it? It's the perfect crime. I just love this time travel stuff. Don't look so horrified."

Her body went still as shock set in. Slowly his babbling began to make sense. When it did, her mind reeled with the implications.

"It was you? You killed them?"

"I was home with you when it had happened. Remember?"

"Not your younger you. This you, the you that's standing their gloating at me like a pretentious pig."

"If it was me or not, it won't matter to you soon anyway. So, you should enjoy the view while you can," he said, pointing to the window and the bit of porch of their old house. "I've got to go and get things ready before they depart for the city. That means leaving you alone for a bit."

He ripped a piece of duct tape off the roll, and came to her.

"No! No!" she screamed as he roughly grabbed her head and jammed the tape over her mouth.

He threw her back against the couch and stalked across the basement floor.

At the stairs he turned around, and said, "While I'm gone I want you to sit there quietly, and think about all that you've done wrong."

With that parting admonition, he turned and flew up the stairs, leaving her fuming on the couch. A soon as he was gone, she went to work on her bindings. Rattling the chains, she twisted and turned as she struggled to find a way to get her hands free, but Greyson had been too thorough.

The clamp pinched her neck as she rested her head against the back of the couch in defeat. The headache that it gave her was a constant reminder that it was there, blocking her way home. Desperation set in as she thought of her parents. Somehow she had to warn them.

Uncaring of what damage it might do, she beat the clamp against the armrest again and again, ignoring the jabs of pain that came with each blow as desperation turned to despair. Like the chains and the electrical ties, it remained fast. After a few minutes, she stopped, and fell back onto the couch exhausted, for the pain in her head had become unbearable, making her stomach roll with nausea.

Tears of frustration fell down her cheeks as she lay staring out at the bit of porch of her childhood home that she could see through the window.

Somebody, please help me!

But, she knew no one would come in time. Her timeline had been set. Her parents had died this day, and so they will die, no matter what happened next. Even with the clues that she had extracted from Greyson's head, it was more than likely that her friends would not find her in time, for Greyson meant to kill her too.

For once, time was not her friend.

She was truly lost.

Chapter Twenty-Seven

Though Lazarus wanted to be part of the field team, he was quickly overruled by the rest of the group.

"We will need someone here to coordinate our shifts," Tanner said. "Out of all of us, you have the most experience for this complex of an undertaking."

Grimm nodded. "I have to agree with Tanner. Besides, you just got Katie back. It wouldn't be right to take you away from her."

"I'm fine," Katie said.

"You may be okay, little one," Grimm said to Katie, "but your father is not. He needs to stay with you."

Lazarus looked around the conference table at his friends before resting on Katie's bruised face. Faolan, Araylai, and Tanner all nodded in agreement with Grimm.

"If that is how it is…" he said.

"It is," Tanner said.

Lazarus smiled at his daughter. "Then, I guess I should get to work."

His fingers flew over the top of the table in front of him, typing out new instructions to the 3D imaging. A graph appeared, breaking down the Lanes' timeline by years, months, days, hours, and even minutes.

"We will have to do this systematically," he said. "There is no way around that. Start with a year each. Be thorough. We can't let one hour slip by."

Taking a year each, Faolan, Tanner, Grimm, and Araylai left for the Vault to get to work.

Splitting the years between them did nothing to take away the tediousness of the search for Sharra. Each day that the Lanes' had lived in that house had to be visited, and each hour scoured for clues. Sharra's parents had been together for twenty-four years, twenty-two of them in the house in the Joliet suburb of Chicago. All of it had to be covered – shift after shift.

After finishing their first year, they stopped to regroup in the conference room. Lazarus and Katie were still there, for it had been only a few hours for them. Yet for the team, time had become a blur as they shifted back and forth, day in and day out for more times than any of them cared to count.

Tanner looked around at the team, and saw the wear on their faces, feeling the same, like being stretched too thin.

"We need more help," Tanner said as he plopped down next to Katie, exhausted.

"What about Viktor," Katie suggested. "He's the only one who's been with Greyson, and may know 'when' to look."

"It wouldn't hurt to add him to the team," Faolan agreed. "Maybe he can tell us how Greyson thinks."

Araylai frowned. "I have seen Greyson's psyche. He definitely has a plan. Though we should not expect Viktor to know anything. Greyson will not have made that mistake again."

"The extra body will be help enough, if Viktor is willing," Tanner said.

Viktor was called to the conference. After Lazarus filled him in on the situation, he readily joined the team.

"This whole thing is my fault anyway," he said.

"Don't beat yourself up," Katie said. "It could have happened to any one of us."

"Yes, but it happened to me. I have to make it right, if it's the last thing I do."

Viktor brought the team to five agents. They split the eighteen years left between them with Tanner, Faolan, and Viktor, taking an extra year each.

Tanner chose the timeline closest to the time of the Lanes' deaths, hoping that was where Greyson would have gone. Spread between the timeline, their goal had been to find Sharra as quickly as possible. But so far, Tanner's luck had turned up nothing.

Until now.

Tanner quickly learned that four years was a very long time to search. On a hunch, he had skipped ahead and brought his search closer to the time of their deaths. He didn't know why he had felt compelled to deviate from the plan. But, he had learned through trial and error to listen to his gut. And he was glad because this time it had paid off.

After adjusting the ceiling fan box between his arm and hip, Tanner knocked on the Lanes' front door, and checked his watch again. The door swung open. Mrs. Lane smiled at him.

"Good afternoon, Mrs. Lane," Tanner said as Sharra's mother let him inside.

"Please, you've been here all week. Call me Lilly. Mrs. Lane makes me feel so old," Lilly said.

The smell of home baking wafted through the house, and made his mouth water.

"Mmmm...something smells good," he said.

"Chocolate chip cookies, my daughter's favorite."

"Mine, too."

"Then, you must have one before they disappear when the others come home," she said as they walked to the kitchen.

Her heart-shaped face lit up with a smile, creating tiny laugh lines around her eyes.

The first time Tanner had come face to face with Lilly Lane, he almost had mistaken her for Sharra. They had the same face, the same hair color, and the same body shape. But after the initial shock he quickly realized his mistake, and caught himself before he blurted out her name. And it was a good thing, because it would have been difficult to explain how he knew Lilly's daughter when Sharra was only a fourteen-year-old girl in this timeline (and not twenty-four), as he was a thirty-three-year old man.

Time had been kind to the forty-two-year old woman. The first time he had gotten a glimpse of her, she was eight years younger. It was the time when Sharra had shifted him to her childhood bedroom on one of her trial shifts. If he hadn't known better, she could have passed for that younger woman.

Her large almond-shaped eyes sparkled in her heart-shape face as she passed him the plate of cookies. He took one.

"Thank you, Mam." It was still warm in his hand. "You're a great mother."

He raised the cookie to his lips, ready to bite into it when his eye fell on the calendar tacked to the corkboard next to the refrigerator. The cookie stopped in the air as he stared at the calendar. For a few moments he had forgotten what day it was, that it was the day before the car accident. That tomorrow, this lovely woman would be dead, along with Sharra's father.

"Is everything all right?" Lilly asked.

He looked away from the calendar, and shot her a sad smile. "Sorry, I got lost in a memory."

She held up the plate again. "Have another cookie. It will help dull the pain."

"Then, I'm going to need the whole plate," he said with a cheeky smile as he shook the future off, and took another cookie, stuffing it into his mouth.

Lilly Lane's timeline was governed by Sharra's timeline, and so it was set no matter how much Tanner wanted to change it for her. He wasn't about to create a paradox. His mission was to find Sharra. And to find her, he needed to find that blue car.

"Well, I'd better get started," he said around the cookie in his mouth.

"I'll be here in the kitchen if you need anything," she said as he went to the living room.

New electrical wires with red plastic caps hung out of a hole in the center of the living room ceiling. Setting the box on the floor, he went to the corner and got the ladder. He opened it underneath the wires. The wiring job that they had contracted him for was almost finished. When it was done, his excuse to be in their house would be gone. He had dragged it out as long as he could without causing suspicion. And still he found no evidence that Greyson had brought Sharra here in this section of time. None-the-less he held onto his gut feeling.

He sliced the box open and pulled out the new fixture, and set it aside.

Back in the kitchen, he said, "I need to shut off the power to install the fan. Is this a good time, or should I go work upstairs?"

"Go ahead and turn it off. I need to run to the store before the kids get home, anyway. I may as well go now, unless you need me to stick around."

"All the big stuff is done so I should be fine on my own."

Tanner followed Lily into the garage, and stood fiddling with the power box by the door as she got into her car and backed down the driveway. Once she was out of sight, he ran back into the kitchen to the basement door. Taking the flashlight from his toolbelt, he flicked it on and headed quietly down the basement stairs. At the bottom, he flashed the light around to see if anything had changed from the day before.

The brown couch was there, tucked against a wall just as Katie had described it. The posters were there, too. If Greyson were to take Sharra anywhere, he was sure it was here. Dark and full of boxes and covered antique furniture, it was an easy place to stash a person. Like the day before, he searched the basement.

"Nothing," he sighed in disappointment.

Everyday it had been the same, and still nothing. There was only one day left. He didn't want to think about tomorrow.

It was while he was standing at one of the basement windows that he heard the sound of the neighbor's garage door opening. Curiosity made him look. That's when he saw the blue car, and the man sitting behind the wheel.

It was Greyson. He was sure of it.

His heart froze as he watched the car back out of the neighbor's driveway, and drive down the street.

Tanner's eyes flew to the house next door.

"We've been looking in the wrong house!"

The flashlight shook in his hand as he took the basement stairs two at a time. He flew out the back of the house only slowing down when he came to the tall fence that separated the two properties. Ducking behind the tree that grew beside the fence, he held his breath to listen as his heart raced in his chest. Hearing nothing in the neighbor's backyard, he grabbed a lower branch of the tree and launched his body over the fence, landing into a crouch among the leaves on the other side.

After scanning the yard, Tanner took off for the back door, hugging the fence until he was forced to cross the yard. Crouching low at the back door, he peered around as he took two slim picks out of his tool-belt, and went to work on the lock. After a few attempts, it finally clicked, and he was in.

The sleek gun hidden among the tools in his tool belt was in his hand before he stepped into the house. He went straight for the basement door in the hallway under the staircase. The door was closed. Taking a calming breath, he inched the door open. Shining the flashlight in the crack, he checked for trip wires. Finding it clear, Tanner opened the door and moved inside.

A faded patch of light came from below. He guessed it was from a window, but couldn't tell from where he stood at the top of the stairs. Though there was a light switch on the wall, he didn't trust it. For all he knew Greyson could have tampered with it.

"Sharra?" he called softly as he beamed the flashlight down the stairs into the faded darkness.

No one answered.

With the flashlight as a guide and the gun trained ahead, he started down the stairs. The boards under his feet creaked as he crept down one by one.

At the bottom he called again, "Sharra? Are you there?"

What windows there were had been covered except for one. From it came a patch of afternoon light. It fell upon a wall of posters. Tanner spared them a quick glance as he swept the flashlight around the basement before returning to the posters. Below them was a brown couch similar to the one in the Lane's basement. A bicycle chain dangled from the wooden frame down the back cushions. Another one was wrapped around the armrest. A blanket lay crumpled at one end. He went over, and picked up the blanket. It still felt warm.

Disappointment washed over him as he put the gun away. Slipping the wire down to his jaw, he linked with Lazarus.

"I found Greyson's lair!" he said as he held the blanket.

"'When' are you?" Lazarus said.

"A day before Sharra's parents were killed. It's in the next door neighbor's basement."

"Not in the Lanes' house?"

"No. It was pure luck that I saw Greyson drive away. Otherwise, I would have missed it altogether."

"Did he have anyone with him in the car?"

"I couldn't see anyone. That doesn't mean that there wasn't. He definitely had someone here in the last half-hour."

"Sharra?"

Tanner pressed the blanket to his nose, and sniffed, hoping for a familiar scent. A lingering smell of fabric softener was all he got from it.

"That's the million dollar question. Am I early, or am I late? Was it Katie? Sharra? Or someone else we don't know about? I have nothing but a warm blanket in my hand to go by, and a sighting of Greyson."

There was a pause on the other end. Tanner threw the blanket back on the couch. As he turned something crunched underneath his foot. Shining the light on it, he could see broken bits of electrical ties.

Lazarus came back onto the Link just as Tanner was about to interrupt him. "Katie has asked what time of day it is there."

"Mid-afternoon."

He heard Lazarus repeat it to Katie.

"Tell her I just found some cut electrical ties," Tanner said.

The conversation on the other side was short. Lazarus came back sounding more confident.

"Katie said that it was mid-afternoon when he stuffed her into the trunk of the car. The sun was low over the horizon by the time she was taken out and shifted back to us. He had cut her initial ties before he had tied her to the couch. I think we can safely say that it was Katie who was there last."

Tanner ran his fingers through his short hair in frustration. "So where does that leave Sharra?"

"We have to trust what Sharra knew, that he is a creature of habit. You say that you are a day before the accident. I wonder…" Lazarus paused as the thought caught his attention. "No, it can't be…"

"Can't be what?"

"Nothing. It's nothing, just a thought. If Greyson just left, then he won't be back for at least another six hours: three hours to the field and three hours back. And when he does return, he'll have Sharra."

"How can you be so sure?"

"I think I know what is happening, but I can't explain it yet… not until I know for sure. Stay put. I'll call back the others and send them to you."

"Call them back to the Vault, but don't send them here yet. The basement is small, and there are too many of us. Anyway, I need to first tie up some loose ends over at the Lanes' residence. I can use the hours before he returns to come up with a plan. I'll Link when I have more to give you."

"I don't like it… you there alone."

"All the other times that it has been a group of us, it has failed. Please, Lazarus, let me do this. The others can work on a strategy from the Vault just as well as from here."

"True."

"I'll come back to the basement as soon as I finish at the Lanes' place."

"I'll want regular updates," Lazarus said, and then he was gone.

Tanner breathed a sigh of relief. He wasn't ready to abandon this timeline, and was glad that Lazarus let him stay.

Back in the Lanes' house, he had the new fan fixture installed and the living room back in order by the time Lilly Lane returned from the store. The clock struck five. It was time for him to leave. The younger Sharra was due home any minute.

"Not much left to do. Just the lights in the upstairs bathroom. I'll come back tomorrow to finish it up," he said as he prepared to leave.

"Do you need a ride?"

"No, my workmate is just around the corner. I can catch a ride with him," he lied.

"Ah, that's right. You told me that already. Here." She held out the plate of cookies to him. "Take some for the road, for you and your friend."

"Thank you." He smiled at her as he took a handful, and tried not to think about tomorrow, her tomorrow. "I'll just leave my tools in the garage for tonight and see my way out."

In the garage, he took off his toolbelt, minus the gun, and set it on the floor. The gun went into the back of his pants. Pulling his shirt over it, he grabbed the cookies from the floor where he had set them, and headed out the side door. From the edge of the garage, he scanned the neighborhood before shooting across the neighbor's driveway to the back of the house. Once inside the basement, he searched for a place to hide. Finding it behind an old stuffed chair, he hunkered down to wait.

A car drove up the Lanes' driveway soon after. He heard the car doors slam followed by voices. It was Sharra, but not his Sharra. He knew because her voice was higher, younger sounding. She wasn't happy. She was arguing with Greyson, something about school by the sound of it. Their dad, James Lane told them to knock it off, yet the younger Greyson kept poking at her. His words were full of contempt for his sister, and something more sinister, something that the Lanes' should have investigated. But, no. That was now history, and couldn't be changed.

As Tanner listened he gritted his teeth, feeling for the younger Sharra, impotent to help her. The fighting soon faded away as they walked to the front door and entered the house, leaving him alone again.

The dinner hour came and went. So did the cookies. After another word with Lazarus it was decided that Tanner should wait where he was until Greyson reappeared.

"If he comes back…" Lazarus said, skeptical.

"He will. Trust me," Tanner said.

Lazarus gave in. "Where do you want to place the team?"

"One upstairs in the house with a view of the kitchen. One in the attached garage. And one down at the end of the street. That should be enough coverage without it being suspicious."

"I'll send them out immediately."

"Put Faolan in the house with me, for backup."

"I'll pass on the request. And Tanner."

"Yes?"

"If Greyson does show up… bring Sharra home."

Chapter Twenty-Eight

Night turned to dawn, and still there was no sign of Greyson or Sharra. Tanner shifted on the cold floor, shaking his leg as he tried to bring some life into the stiff limb. His head felt heavy from a lack of sleep. He slapped his cheeks in an attempt to wake up.

"I'm getting too old for this," he whispered.

The need to use the toilet grew stronger. The cold floor didn't help. He got up and linked with Faolan, warning him that he was coming upstairs. After he relieved himself in the half bath in the hallway, Faolan met him in the kitchen.

"Have you heard from Viktor recently?" Faolan asked.

"Only a red Ford pickup truck and a silver minivan to report. They left for the main street around a half-hour ago. Probably going to work. More will be leaving soon." Tanner checked the clock on the wall. "School traffic will be starting within the hour. None of that matters. We're looking for a vehicle entering the street."

"What if he dumps the car after Katie, and just shifts in with Sharra?"

"That's why we have to stay put. He's going to show up. He has to."

"I hope you're right."

"Me, too. I'd better get back into position."

Another three hours went by. During that time, Viktor kept a dialogue account of the stream of traffic through the Link. The monologue droned on and on. Tanner felt his eyelids grow heavy and drop. It was the change of pitch in Viktor's voice that brought him back from the brink of sleep.

"Greyson has just passed by!" Viktor exclaimed.

"Are you sure?"

"Yes! He's heading your way! What do you want me to do?"

"Stay out of sight. If he sees you, it's all over," Tanner whispered into the Link. "Can you get to the rental car without being seen?"

"Yes."

"Go there and wait until one of us contacts you."

Tanner dropped him, and quickly linked with Faolan in the house, and Araylai who was hiding in the garage. "Greyson is pulling in the driveway as we speak. If he has Sharra, let him bring her inside. Don't do anything until I give the word."

Tanner ducked behind the over-stuffed chair as the garage door thunked to the ground. Soon after there was the sound of the side door opening, and then footsteps crossing overhead.

"It's Sharra," Araylai whispered in the Link.

There was no time to answer her. The basement door opened. And that's when Tanner heard Sharra's voice. His heart jumped into his throat. He swallowed it as he peeped out from behind the armrest, hoping for a glimpse. The light from the upstairs shined on the steps, lighting their figures as Greyson hauled Sharra unceremoniously down the steps. Tanner's fists tightened as he watched Greyson drag her to the window, and gloat over his hiding place. Her wrists looked red where the electrical ties bit into her flesh. Her body was stiff with fear or pain, or both. He couldn't tell. When she turned her face away from the window, her eyes were hard.

From his hiding spot, Tanner saw that there was a clear shot at Greyson. Ever so slowly, Tanner lifted his gun and aimed it at Greyson. His finger was on the trigger ready to shoot. He breathed in and steadied his hand. In the seconds that it took to breathe, Greyson moved away with Sharra, and his view was blocked.

Damn! he thought as he lowered the gun and silently shifted to get a better view.

When he could see them again, Greyson had Sharra on the couch and tied to the chains in no time. Tanner lifted his gun to aim, finding a support pillar in his way. When Greyson moved again, Tanner still couldn't shoot without the risk of hitting Sharra. He pressed his lips together in frustration, and lowered his gun to wait.

Greyson was chatting to Sharra as if what he was doing was normal. Sharra had been right. There was something dreadfully wrong with her brother. When

Greyson started talking about what he was planning to do to her parents, Tanner's blood froze in his veins.

Yet, it was Sharra's scream of protest that almost had him on his feet. It took all his self-control to stay behind the comfy chair as he watched Greyson grab her head, slap the duct tape over her mouth, and throw her back down. Then, he was gone, flying up the basement stairs, and out of the house.

After hearing the kitchen door shut, Tanner decided it was safe to move, kicking himself for not taking the shot as Greyson ran up the stairs.

Slipping from his hiding place, he rushed across the basement to the couch. As he jumped from the shadows, Sharra's eyes widened in fear, then, as quickly, turned to relief as his face became visible. She cried out his name behind the tape. The chains attached to the ties around her wrists clunked as she struggled to sit up.

"Shhh," he said as he dropped to the floor beside the couch and gently removed the tape off her mouth.

"You found me. You found me," she whispered over and over as she burst into tears.

He cupped her cheeks, wiping the tears away with a finger. "I told you we would."

"We?"

"Faolan and Araylai are upstairs. Viktor is outside. You were never alone."

"Greyson... he's going to kill my parents... and me."

"I heard him. We need to get you out of here."

He slid a knife from his boot and cut the ties from her wrist, and helped her to stand. The desire to take her into his arms was killing him, yet he held back. But not

Sharra. As soon as she was up, she threw herself into his chest and hugged him hard. His arms came around her, and held her tight.

"I knew you would come," she whispered into his shirt.

Stroking her hair, he said softly, "We must go. The others are waiting for us." As he stroked her hair, he came to something hard at her neck. "What's this?"

He pushed her hair aside, and sucked in his breath.

"A Neuro Inhibitor," he said, staring at the device attached to the back of her neck.

Sharra reached up and touched it with a tentative hand. "Greyson put it there. Somehow it is stopping me from shifting. Can you get it off?"

Tanner looked at the small screen on the back of the clamp, and shook his head. "It's coded."

"Just unclasp it," she said as she went to do it.

"No!" He grabbed her hand. Lowering his voice again, he explained, "There are wires from it that are buried into your spinal cord. You'll risk serious damage if you take it off without unlocking it first. I'll shift you back to the Vault. Cam can sort it out there."

"I can't leave yet. Not with Greyson planning to kill my parents."

Tanner ran his hand through his hair, tousling it even more. "Sharra, you know that we cannot interfere. Rule number three of the Vault Handbook states that our timelines are permanently sealed once we become assimilated with the agrylium, or risk a paradox. Your parents died in that car accident. Though it hasn't happened yet today, it is set in your past, your timeline, this timeline. The coroner's report stated_"

"The coroner's report," she said, stopping him in her excitement. "That's it. It all makes sense now."

"What are you going on about?"

"The fireball from the explosion had left next to nothing for the coroner to identify, just a few burnt bones and a couple pieces of melted jewelry. They decided not to do expensive DNA testing because of us kids, not wanting to drag our grief out longer than necessary. The jewelry had been enough. I was too young at the time to understand what that meant, but now…"

"You're talking nonsense. Come on," he said, taking her arm. "Let's go. We can't change what's to happen. God, I wish I could for you. But we can't, Sharra, we can't."

She pulled her arm free, and backed away. "Don't you see? It doesn't have to be them. Just hear me out. I understand that the car crash has to happen, because it has already happened. But there's no concrete evidence to support that it was my parents in the car. So why not exchange them for…two others?"

"Two others. You want to sacrifice two other people, rip their lives away just to save your parents? No." He shook his head. "No. That would be murder. Not even you can think of doing that."

"What are you, crazy? I'm not talking about living people." Her eyes looked everywhere as Tanner watched her mind work. "If you think of it, there are plenty of dead bodies around. J.D. Dash is still sitting in the Vault morgue. We can use his body. No one will miss him anyway. And it would redeem him from what he had tried to do to me and to the Vault. A kind of poetic justice, you could say."

Tanner frowned and shook his head. She sounded crazy. Yet, something in her voice made him listen, really listen.

"Okay, so say we do save your parents, where would we put them afterwards? They can't stay here."

"No, they can't stay here. That's why we have to shift them to the Vault. They are dead in this timeline, or will be as of tonight. And they have to go somewhere... some 'when'. Why not the Vault? Isn't life elsewhere better then being dead? Please, Tanner! Please!"

Her eyes grew wide as they pleaded silently with him. He sighed, and knew that he was caught. He understood her desperation. He thought of his sister. If he were man enough to admit it, he'd be doing the same thing if their positions were reversed.

Giving in, he asked, "And where are we to get our hands on another body, a female one?"

Relief came into her eyes.

"The Vault is full of agents that would help us search for what we need," she explained. "I've got that photo of my parents in my apartment. They can use it as a reference to find a similar female body somewhere in time. I'm sure that there is a doppelganger somewhere out there. We do the impossible everyday. This should be a piece of cake. Besides, time may not be on our side here, but it is with them at the Vault."

"I'm starting to hate that saying. Okay, say we find a female body that closely fits your mother, then what? How do we make the switch without Greyson knowing?"

"I'm still working on that."

She was biting her lip. Tanner knew that was a telltale sign of trouble. Her next words confirmed it.

"You have to leave me here so that I can learn more of what Greyson is planning."

"Not on your life!"

"It's the only way. If I leave, he won't stop until I'm dead. You know that."

Tanner lifted his gun up for her to see. "We can take care of him right now. Problem solved."

"No! Not yet."

"Shouldn't you guys have shifted out by now?" Faolan said from the basement doorway.

Tanner spun around.

"I'm working on it. You know how stubborn Sharra can be."

Surprise made him speak a little sharper than he intended.

Faolan frowned at him. "Well, hurry it up. Greyson can come back at any time. You do have your gun, right? I would have had him stunned and disposed of by now if I had been allowed down there instead of you."

"I'm telling you, Tanner," Sharra said, ignoring Faolan, "it will work. I can feel it in my bones."

"Well, right now what you're feeling in your bones will not get you out of here." Tanner sighed and rubbed his head in frustration. "Okay. I can't make you come back with me. Stay."

"What are you doing?" Faolan said as he came down the stairs. "Greyson wants her dead. Or have you forgotten that part. No, Sharra, you need to leave now."

"I'm not going."

Sharra crossed her arms and glared at Faolan.

"She's not going," Tanner repeated.

With that Sharra explained her idea to Faolan, growing more confident the more she talked about it.

Faolan scowled at both of them. "You two are fools, you realize that."

"Are you going to help us, or not?" Tanner said.

"Do I really have a choice?"

"No," Sharra said. "Now, help me figure out how to deactivate this thing on my neck. We need to figure out Greyson's code, and quick."

Faolan pressed his lips together when he saw the Neuro Inhibitor attached to the back of Sharra's neck.

"Greyson is a creature of habit, right?" Faolan said as he studied the numbers on the screen. "That's why he came back here, because it was familiar. Could that also apply to the code? What do you think, Sharra? Do you know anything Greyson might use? A special event like a birthday? A year of significance? A pet's name?"

A certain notebook flashed inside Tanner's memory. It was Greyson's notebook full of obscene pictures of death. In it were the same numbers counting down to the final written 'boom.' His eyes flew to Sharra. He saw the same look on her face that mirrored his.

As their minds reached the same conclusion, they said in unison, "Four, three, two, one, BOOM!"

"That has to be it," Sharra said excitedly as she moved her hair away and bent her neck. "Try it: four, three, two, one."

"Here goes nothing," Tanner said as he entered the numbers into the device.

As soon as the last number was tapped in, she straightened, and touched her forehead. Tanner stood back with a frown.

"Well?"

"It worked!" she said after a moment.

"Are you sure?" Faolan asked.

The relief on her face was real as she said, "I can build the blocks again. I can... see..."

The Link came on in Tanner's ear. It was Araylai. He held up a hand as he listened.

"Greyson is doing something in the Lanes' garage. I can't see inside, but I can feel his intent through the wall, and it isn't good."

"What car was involved in the crash?" Tanner asked Sharra.

"Mom's. Why?"

"She mentioned to me yesterday that she was going to catch a ride into work today with a co-worker." To Araylai, he said, "Lilly's car is in that garage. He must be tampering with it. Get Viktor here, and have him stand by until it's clear to go in. We need to find out what Greyson's doing to it."

"What's going on?" Faolan said.

Tanner looked at Sharra, and saw the hope in her eyes.

"We're going to break the rules," he said.

Tanner knew that he was about to make a huge mistake. Yet, as he took in her beautiful face, there really was no choice. Making her happy was all that mattered. And if it meant breaking every rule in the Vault handbook, and causing a paradox, then so be it.

Chapter Twenty-Nine

It was late afternoon by the time Greyson ran down the basement steps. Sharra sat up as best as her bindings would let her. Greyson's face was alive with excitement. She glared at him over the tape that covered her mouth.

"Still here," he said with a genuine smile.

Sharra was not fooled by it.

"What a surprise. Then again, it's kind of hard... no, that's the wrong word..." He thought for a moment, and then brightened as the word came to him. "Impossible. That's the word I'm looking for. Yes, I like the sound of that... how it would be impossible to find you in the infinite streams of time that revolve around the Vault."

The bicycle chains rattled as she struggled in her bonds, glaring at him.

"Poor Lazarus. First, his daughter, and now you. Though you are not returning like his daughter did, and he knows it. It must be eating him alive knowing that you sacrificed yourself." He chuckled. "That will teach him to be more careful who he recruits next...if he recruits anyone else. He might have a heart attack over this. Who knows? He's not a young man anymore."

Sharra's muscles quivered as anger made her heart pound. Her nostrils flared as she struggled in her bindings, yelling at him through the tape. All that came out were muffled sounds.

"Tsk, tsk," Greyson said, shaking his head at her. "All that noise for nothing. You realize that all of this is your fault. If you were as smart as Lazarus thought you were, you should have turned around and gone home when the training contract was stolen from you. Then none of this would've happened. Tanner wouldn't have gotten hurt all those times, Dash would still be alive, and Lazarus... well, let's just say, he's the one who has suffered the most, except for Mom and Dad. But that will soon be in the past. No... the future. Ah, what does it matter?"

He shrugged his shoulders, and laughed as if he found the concept hilarious.

The talking was over. Sharra could see it in his face. When the knife came out of his pocket, she grew frightened, not knowing if this was the end. As he reached for her, she sank into the couch, ready to shift out. Yet the knife was not for her, not yet. Instead, the ties binding her to the chains were cut away. Before she could react, he had her arms twisted behind her back, and retied using the weight of his body to pin her down. Crushed between him and the couch, she was helpless to resist. When he was done, he hauled her to her feet.

Pulling her close, he smiled deep into her eyes, and sneered. "You're destiny awaits you, my dear sister. And it won't be at the Vault."

THE VAULT

With the tape over her mouth, she could do nothing but glare at him. In his eyes she saw a madman, and wondered how this person could be her brother.

"Up you go," he said as he pushed her to the stairs.

As she climbed, her feet stumbled on a step. Greyson caught her, and set her back on her feet, giving her no pause. At the top of the stairs, he grabbed her by the clamp at her neck and maneuvered her body through the house, out the kitchen, and into the backyard. It wasn't long before they were in their childhood garage next door.

Their mother's car, a silver sedan, was in its usual spot. It was just as Sharra remembered it. Even the tiny ding on the left side of the back bumper was there. She wanted to see inside the car, but Greyson held her fast as he fitted the key into the trunk of the car, and opened it. The smell of gasoline hit her as soon as the trunk popped up. When she looked, she knew why. Inside the deep trunk were several red plastic gas containers. They were pushed to the back, leaving a narrow stretch big enough to hold a small person. In that split second when her brain figured out what he was going to do, it was already too late.

"In you go," he said as he dumped her over the edge and into the cramped space as if she were a piece of luggage.

Her shoulders screamed in pain as the weight of her body fell upon her arms. Though she cried out, the tape over her mouth muffled the sound.

"Now, now, no noise, that's a good girl," he said, pressing the tape securely around her mouth.

Grabbing her legs, he tucked them into the tiny space left between her body and the back of the car. With legs crammed in and her back jammed against the sloshing gasoline containers, there was no room for movement.

"Not that any noise from you will matter. Everyone is inside the house. I checked. In fact, I can remember this day as if it was today. Get it? As if it were today?" He chuckled. "It never gets old, these time jokes. Anyway, I have something real special planned for you, Mom, and Dad."

Sharra's breathing grew labored over the tape as he withdrew something from his pocket. It was a black box no bigger than his hand. He held it up for her to see. There wasn't much to it. There didn't need to be. The short antenna protruding from the top, plus the single red button on the box told her it was a trigger. His smile grew as he watched her eyes widen as she put two and two together.

"Boom," he whispered, spreading his fingers to emulate the action.

Her heart raced in her chest as she struggled to get free.

"Bye bye, little sister. You might have the best seat in the house, but I'll be getting the greatest view of the show."

He laughed at his own joke as he slammed the trunk shut. Her world went dark. She heard the back door of the garage shut, and knew that she was alone.

Sharra waited. Though her ability to shift had been returned, she dared not use it.

Stick to the plan, she reminded herself. *For Mom and Dad.*

Dinnertime came and went. Her stomach grumbled just thinking about it. As she lay curled up in the dark, she tried to remember when she had last eaten, only realizing that thinking about it made her gut hurt worse.

Yesterday? Has it only been a day?

She took in another slow breath through her nose and pushed the thought of food aside. The fumes from the gasoline burned her lungs, giving her a headache. No matter the discomfort, Sharra knew that she had to remain strong and trust the team.

When the garage door opener was finally activated, she knew the time had come. She could hear her parents talking as they entered the garage from the kitchen door. Movement was made impossible. Greyson had seen to that. And though she frantically tried to be heard, the car doors were slammed shut, and the engine was started.

There was nothing to do but wait… and hope.

Please, if there is a God, let this work.

More time passed as her father drove them out of their suburb. The *thud-thunk* rhythm of the tires told her when they had reached the highway. Maybe ten to fifteen minutes later, she felt the car roll to a stop. The engine was turned off. With it off, she could hear her dad's muffled voice talking to someone. Though she couldn't understand what was being said, the rise and fall of his voice told her that he was getting anxious.

The locking mechanism of the trunk clicked, and the lid popped up.

Sharra looked up in time to catch the shock on her father's face as he found in his trunk a gagged and tied stranger tucked among the cans of gasoline. His face went pale as the implications of the situation hit him.

"Step away from the trunk, Mr. Lane," said the police officer.

The shock hit her father hard. His mouth worked as he tried to come up with words. It was only when the police officer took his arm to drag him away that words finally bubbled out.

"Officer, I knew nothing of this," he said, gesturing to the interior of the trunk. "I can't even explain it. My wife took the car out yesterday afternoon, but other than that, it has been locked in the garage."

The officer turned Sharra's father away from the trunk. The officer looked back at her, and winked.

Tanner.

Seeing those blue eyes twinkling down at her sent rivers of relief through her body.

The plan was working.

She relaxed back against the floor, and waited to be released.

As Tanner walked her father and mother to the police car parked behind them, Faolan, the other officer, reached in and helped her out of the trunk. The tape was removed from her mouth. She took a deep breath of fresh air into her burning lungs and exhaled, letting out the stink of the trunk in one big noisy gush.

"Are you okay?" Faolan asked gently as he turned her around to remove the bindings.

"Don't worry about me. What about Greyson? Did he follow us?"

"No, he left in his car soon after you were put in the trunk. Araylai is tracking him as we speak. Says that he's eating at a fast-food place."

A knife sliced through her bindings. They dropped to the ground at her feet. As soon as she was free, she rotated her shoulders, and groaned. The clamp on her neck pinched her vertebra with the movement of her muscles. Her hand automatically went to it.

"Let me," Faolan said.

Brushing her hair aside, she presented her neck to him. After a few taps on the screen, the pressure on her neck released, and the clamp came off. Faolan set it into her hand. Sharra studied it in horrid fascination for a few seconds before pushing it into her utility belt. Her hand went to the back of her neck and felt the deep impressions left behind. As she massaged her neck muscles, Faolan handed her a Com-Link. It went behind her ear with a swish of her hand.

"Greyson has put a tracker on Mom's car," she said.

"We know. There's also a detonator attached to the chassis. Both of them are the reason we need to keep moving. Araylai can scramble Greyson's tracker for only so long. We don't want him to get suspicious and come too early, and blow the whole operation."

"And the bodies? Did you get them?"

"They're in the trunk of the police car."

Tanner came back, and said, "Your parents are settled in the back of the cruiser. Do you feel like breaking another rule, and go have a talk with them while we drive on?"

"What will I say?"

"You haven't seen them in ten years. I'm sure you can find something to talk about."

"Guys, we need to move," Faolan said.

"Go," Tanner said as he gently nudged her in the direction of the police car. "They need you."

Through the windscreen she saw her parents sitting close to each other in the back seat, and knew that they must be frantic with worry. When they saw her, the woman from the trunk of their car open the front passenger door of the cruiser and slip in, their worry looks turned to confusion. Faolan got in the driver side and started the car. Sharra snapped her seatbelt on as Faolan turned on the siren, and pulled onto the road.

Behind her parents' heads, she saw Tanner maneuver her mother's car in behind the cruiser. Together they whizzed down the highway to their next destination.

"Talk to them," Faolan whispered.

While the scenery flew by, Sharra turned to her parents and drank in their faces like a starving child. It had been ten years since she saw them this close. Worry creases covered her father's forehead.

He looked at his wife and back at Sharra, and said, "I'm sorry you were in the trunk. We didn't know. Otherwise, we would've gotten you out and called the police."

Sharra sent her parents a tentative smile. "It wasn't your fault."

A puzzled look came over her father as his head swiveled back and forth between his wife's face and Sharra's.

When his eyes settled back onto Sharra, he asked, "Do we know you? You look… familiar…"

Sharra squirmed in her seat, dropping her gaze from her father's questioning look.

Under her breath she muttered, "This is so hard."

Faolan heard her. Reaching over, he squeezed her hand, lending her strength. It was just what she needed. Straightening her back, she lifted her head, and met her father's gaze.

"My name is Sharra," she finally said. "My partner here is Faolan. Following behind us in your car is my other partner Tanner. I know this is all a bit odd. You must be wondering what's going on."

At the sound of her name, her mother turned to look at her. Sharra dropped her eyes from her mother's questioning gaze.

"Sharra. Our daughter's name is Sharra."

"Yes, well…" Sharra paused as she tried to figure out where to start.

"Just tell them," Faolan said in the quiet that followed. "They're going to find out anyway."

"I'm trying. This isn't easy, you know."

Turning back to her parents, she took a breath in and went for it, not knowing how else to break the news.

"I don't have much time to explain, so I'll try to keep it to the point. I am your daughter. Not the daughter you left back at home, but your daughter from the future."

"What?" her father said.

"I know this is hard to believe. But we've come back to save you. You were to die in a terrible car accident tonight. You saw the gasoline cans in the trunk. That was meant for you and Mom. But we found out about it thanks to a fluke. That's why we are here, although we're not supposed to interfere in this timeline, my timeline. You see, you did die, ten years ago when I was fourteen. We've come to change that."

"Excuse me, but you're not making any sense. Are you saying that you're our daughter?"

"Yes, Dad, I'm your daughter. And it's Greyson, your son, my brother who has rigged Mom's car with a bomb, and then put me in the trunk to die with you."

"Greyson?"

"Not the Greyson sitting back home right now. This is the Greyson from the future, like me." Sharra saw the confusion on their faces. "I know it's a lot to take in. I'm sure that I had the same look on my face when it was first explained to me."

"I'm trying to understand..." her dad said.

"Let me explain. I belong to a secret agency that can travel through time. Normally, we don't get involved in our own timelines. In fact, we're breaking all the rules by our interfering in your lives. That's why the accident still has to happen, for it already had happened. Otherwise, it will cause ripples in the stream of time, and we don't want that."

"No, we don't want that, that's for sure," Faolan chimed in. "There'd be no explaining away a paradox to Lazarus."

"Time travel..." her mother said.

Sharra nodded, and repeated, "Time travel."

"And Greyson, is he a part of this time traveling business too?" her father asked skeptically.

Faolan met his eyes through the rearview mirror, and said, "Greyson doesn't fit the profile required for recruitment. So, the answer should be no. But it's not. He found a way in anyway, by secretly befriending one of us, and using him mercilessly to get inside the Agency. Our lives have been a living hell since, especially Sharra's."

"I know Greyson has been a bit of a handful since he was young, but this? Why would he want to kill us?"

"We barely understand it ourselves. Lazarus, the Head Director of Vault Agency has a theory about it. You see, through the recruiting process, the weak of mind are sifted out. Shifting through time takes a strong mind with the capacity to adapt instantly to any situation. Not only that, the brain has to be resilient enough to withstand the internal forces generated by the constant shifting that our job requires. Not everyone can handle that. We have a term for it: Brain Shifted. We think that's what happened to your son."

"He's crazy, Mom," Sharra said. "He's determined to kill me, and now, you and Dad, too. We can't let that happen."

Lilly reached over and set her hand upon Sharra's where she rested it on the back of her seat.

"How can Dad and I help?"

The relief Sharra felt was instant. Yet, before she could open her mouth to reply, Faolan said, "We're here," diverting the conversation.

Sometime while they had been talking, they had left the highway and were now pulling into an industrial park. Faolan parked the cruiser behind one of the warehouses, and after popping the trunk, got out. Tanner pulled up right next to them in Lilly's car. Leaving the car running, he jumped out and joined Faolan behind the cruiser.

Sharra unbuckled her seatbelt and turned around in the seat to face her parents square on.

"I'll need all your jewelry," she said, holding her hand out. "Also your wallet, Dad, and your purse, Mom. We need to plant them in your car."

Her parents looked at each other as they unclasped their watches, and passed them over. The watches were soon followed by her mother's dangling gold earrings, gold necklace, and her father's tie clip, and wedding ring.

"Your wedding ring, too, Mom," Sharra said holding her hand out for it.

Her mother played with the simple gold band, twirling it around on her finger as she worried her lip, a mannerism that Sharra knew all too well.

"I'm sorry, but it has to go with the rest... for the police report. I realize it's hard to give up. But we have to get this right. One thing left out, and we create a ripple in time."

Slipping it off her finger, Lilly set it slowly onto Sharra's palm. Sharra smiled gratefully at her mother as she wrapped her fingers around the warm band.

"Dad can get you another ring. I promise."

A *thunk* came from the back of the cruiser as Faolan and Tanner hefted something heavy out of the trunk. Sharra watched through the window as they came around the back carrying Dash's burnt body awkwardly between them. Sharra saw that the body had been thawed out, dressed in a suit and tie, and manipulated into a sitting position. Yet it did not hide all of his burnt flesh. When Sharra got a close view of what was left of his face, she gagged, and turned away.

With a lot of huffing and cursing the two men maneuvered Dash into the back seat behind the driver's side. Once he was in, they slammed the door and ducked back to the open trunk of the cruiser, leaving the car running. With the men out of the way, Sharra's parents got their first good look at what the ruckus was all about.

"Oh my God! Is that what I think it is?" her father said as he stared pale-faced at the grotesque figure in the other car.

Sharra stole a look at what was left of Dash's face. His features were gone, burnt away, leaving bone and charred flesh behind. At one time she had blamed herself for his death, but she had grown up since then. Now, she had found purpose in his death. Her parents would live because of it, and that was something that eased the guilt in her heart.

"Yes, Dad, it's a dead body. He used to be an agent."

The worry lines on his forehead deepened even further. "Did you kill him?"

She looked away, and said, "No, we didn't kill him, or the woman, either."

If anyone were to blame for killing Dash, it was Greyson, but she wasn't about to tell them that either.

"Look, we can't leave the car empty. It's either you, or those bodies. And though it's an ugly business, I'd prefer you to be alive with me, than dead in that car."

She jumped out of the car, leaving her parents to fret inside, and went to help the men. Tanner had the second body in the front passenger seat. Wrapped in a sheet, the figure looked like a slim mummy. Faolan tugged on the sheet while Tanner held the body steady in the seat until the sheet slipped away, revealing a young woman with long brown hair. Her head slumped to the side as Tanner adjusted the seatbelt around her and snapped it in. She was wearing a dress like the one Sharra's mother had on. Her heart-shaped face was at peace, pale like the moon on a dark night. Her hands sat limp in her lap.

"I've got my parents' effects," Sharra said.

"Give me your mother's," Tanner said all businesslike as he held out a hand. "I'll do the woman. Faolan can plant your father's things on Dash."

Sharra handed Tanner her mother's wedding band. Tanner jammed it over the dead woman's knuckles of her ring finger, and set her hand back in her lap. He took the watch next.

"Is your mother right or left handed?" he asked.

"Right."

He picked up the dead woman's left hand and flung the watch around her slim wrist.

"Where did you get her from?" Sharra asked as she watched him struggle with the clasp.

"Faolan's timeline. She was from his clan. He remembered her dying when he was just a boy. Her parents had blamed a neighboring clan for stealing her body. Ironic, isn't it, that it had been Faolan all along."

"What did she die from?"

"They think it was food poisoning. Here, help me put the necklace on her."

He bundled up the dead woman's hair into his fist, and dropped her head forward while Sharra reached in to slip the necklace around her neck and clasp it together. As she laid it upon her neck, Sharra's hand touched her skin.

"She's still warm," she said, surprised.

"Warm is easier to work with than stiff," Faolan said from the back seat as he struggled to put the gold wedding band over Dash's big knuckles. "Don't look so worried. She won't be missed. My laird didn't believe me when my younger self had said I had found her dead in the woods. Said I had it wrong, and that she was just sleeping, waiting for her lover from a rival clan to come, and fetch her away." As he shoved the wallet into Dash's suit jacket, he said to Tanner, "I'll have a quick word with Sharra's parents about the shift to the Vault while you finish up. Don't take too long. Greyson is on his way."

Faolan shut the car door and went back to the cruiser. Sharra handed Tanner the earrings.

"This might be a problem," he said as he stared back and forth between the woman's earlobes and the thin metal hoops. "There are no holes."

"Just make a hole."

Taking out the knife from his boot, he jabbed the woman's earlobes and shoved the hoops through. "That will have to do. Pass me the purse."

Sharra handed it over. He tossed it onto the dead woman's lap, and shut the door.

"That's everything."

Tanner glanced over at the cruiser. Sharra followed the direction of his gaze and saw them land on Faolan who had his back turned to them as he talked quietly with her parents.

"Sharra, I need to talk to you." Tanner took her arms, and held her gently. Lowering his voice, he said. "I don't know how this next part will go. Timing is everything, and with Greyson…"

"I know. It scares me too. Please tell me that you'll be careful?"

"I will." As he stared down into her eyes, he drew her closer, and softly said, "I love you."

In his eyes she saw the depths of his soul as he laid his heart bare for her in those three simple words. But for Sharra it wasn't that simple.

"Did you hear me? I love you," he said again.

"Tanner. I can't."

"What is it? Is it Faolan?"

"Tanner not now. My parents… the bomb."

"Do you love him?"

She dropped her gaze. "Yes, I love him. But… I… I love you, too. And I can't bear the thought of losing you."

"You can't love both of us, not in that way. There can only be one."

He gave her a tiny shake. She raised her eyes and saw the hurt and frustration in the lines around his mouth. His eyes pleaded with her to give him something more, yet she couldn't.

"Don't make me decide now. I can't. I just can't."

"What about the kisses we shared. Didn't they mean anything to you?"

"Yes, ohh... I don't know. Don't make me do this."

"There can only be one, Sharra, one!" Dropping her arms, he shook his head. "Your right, I can't do this either."

"Tanner!"

She reached for him, but he dodged her hands as he slipped into the driver seat and slammed the door. He refused to look at her as he jammed the car into reverse, and started to back up.

"Don't leave like this," she said to him through the glass of his window as the car rolled away.

Giving up, she backed out of the way as he spun the car around, and took off in a squeal of tires. Faolan left her parents who had gotten out of the car, and joined her at the back of the cruiser.

"What was that all about?" Faolan asked as they watched the car disappear around the corner of the warehouse.

"He's in a hurry to get it over with," she said, not knowing what else to say.

They followed the sound of the engine as the car moved further and further away, until it was gone.

"Tanner knows what he's doing," Faolan said.

"I sure hope so."

Tanner's final words burned in her mind. Why couldn't he have waited until this was all over? They were so close to fixing everything.

Except us.

Her head ached with pent up emotions. She rubbed her temples to ease the tension gathering there. It wasn't just Tanner that troubled her. It was also her brother. Greyson was a loose wire, and he still had the detonator on him. If Tanner gave the game away, it would be all over for him. She didn't want to go there. Losing Tanner would kill her, especially the way that she had left things between them.

Faolan shut the trunk, and took Sharra's hand, drawing her eyes away from the corner of the warehouse.

"We've done all we can here," he said, reading the worry on her face. "Tanner will see it through. We must take care of your parents. They will need you now more than ever."

Sharra looked over at her parents where they stood silently holding each other. Lilly's finger kept returning to her ring finger where her wedding band had once sat. Sharra heard her father whisper words of comfort into her mother's ear. Their love was evident even in the uncertainty of the situation they found themselves in. Sharra knew how difficult it must be for them. It was difficult for her, too. Yet, having them alive was worth it. The other option was unthinkable. She couldn't bare to lose them again.

I'm doing the right thing.

Straightening her shoulders, she said, "You are right. They do need me, and I need them. Let's take them home."

Together Faolan and Sharra went to Lilly and James, and after a brief explanation, made a circle. Holding her mother's hand in one, and her father's in the other, and with Faolan connecting the circle, Sharra sent them a reassuring smile as she prepared for the shift.

"Get ready," she said, and with a lingering thought for Tanner shifted them back to the Vault.

The air whooshed into the vacuum caused by the abrupt shift of space and time. It stirred up the bit of dust and trash on the parking lot, brushing the debris against the abandoned police car until the vacuum was sated and the air stilled once again.

In the distance was the sound of a siren growing closer. Around the same corner where Tanner had disappeared a few minutes before sped another police car. Its lights flashed brightly in the darkening night air as its sirens blared. It stopped at a safe distance from the other cruiser. Two policemen with guns at the ready jumped out, using their doors for protection. One of them called out to the other car for the thieves to give up. But the car was empty, another mystery that was to remain unsolved.

Chapter Thirty

The Vault

Sharra's parents gasped as the bright light of the shiftroom hit them for the first time. Her mother swayed within the small circle that they had made as she struggled to get her bearings.

"I'm sorry. There was no time to explain," Sharra said. "The effect of the shift will wear off in a few seconds."

"I don't understand…" James said, shaking his head as if to clear the images away. "It has to be a dream."

"No, Dad, this is real."

Sharra took her mother's arm and helped her into the dark chamber of the Vault. Faolan followed with her father. Her mother pulled against Sharra's guiding hand as the pylons reached out to them. Holding her mother tight, Sharra drew her away from the center. Though Sharra had her shield firmly in place, she knew her parents were unprotected, for there had been no time to teach them to shield against the power of the Vault.

The row of majestic metal conductors rotated gracefully within the particle cloud, stirring their hair with a breeze of cool air. The flowing metal gleamed from within, sending bright flashes of silvery light down their spiral fins like liquid water. Whispery tendrils left the cloud at its feet, and reached out across the floor to the newcomers.

"Oh my," Lilly breathed.

"I had that same reaction the first time that I saw the pylons," Sharra said as she remembered the day Lazarus had brought her over from the Training Facility, and introduced her to the Vault. It was a day she'd never forget.

Lilly reached out to touch a questing tendril, just as she had done. Sharra quickly brushed it aside.

"Better if you don't touch the cloud," she said.

"It wants me to touch it." Her mothers voice was dreamy as her hand went up again.

"Yes, I know." Sharra pulled her mother away from the cloud. "But you need to fight it."

"How do I fight it? It's so… compelling."

"You must picture an invisible box and put it over your head every time you come into the Vault. That is your mental shield against it. The pylons are your friends. They are also your enemy. Thus, they must be respected. Don't wait to make the box. You, too, Dad."

Their voices carried across the Vault and out into the Terminus. Through the vaulted entrance came Lazarus and Katie. At the sight of Sharra, Katie broke into a huge grin, and ran forward.

"Sharra!" she cried.

Leaving her mother behind with Faolan, Sharra rushed to meet the girl. Together they hugged each other, each grateful to see the other, yet sad for what Greyson had done to both of them.

"I'm so sorry," Sharra said as she hugged the tiny girl.

Katie hugged her back just as fiercely. "Don't be sorry. We are all back safe."

"If I had never joined the Agency none of this would have happened."

She let go of Katie, and looked up at Lazarus who had come up behind his daughter. Dark circles were under his sharp eyes. New lines marred his gaunt face. Though he smiled at her, his eyes were shadowy with fatigue, and something more.

"If there is anyone to blame, it is I." He pulled Sharra into his arms, and hugged her. "Welcome back."

He released her, stepping back as Faolan brought her dazed parents over.

"I'm sure you are full of questions," Lazarus said to them. "But right now, we need to sort out your son. So if you don't mind going with Katie, she'll take you to somewhere more comfortable than the Vault chamber. I'll send Sharra to you as soon as we're finished."

"Sharra..." Lilly looked at her grown-up daughter in confusion.

"It's okay, Mom. Go with Katie. I won't be long."

Katie inserted her small body between her parents, and took them by the arm.

"Come with me. You can ask me anything you like," she said as she drew them away.

"What happened to your face?" Sharra heard her father ask.

"Just a little accident," Katie said. "Nothing to worry about. Would you like a hot drink? Or maybe something stiffer. I know that I am ready for something. I'll take you to our lounge upstairs and make you something. Did you know that Sharra has a cat?"

Katie chatted away, distracting Lilly and James as she towed them down the long hallway to the lifts. Sharra pressed her lips together in worry as she watched them go, knowing that it all had to be a bit shocking on their systems. Sharra understood it, for even now the pylons called out to her through her shield, stirring up the threads within her head. With an angry thought, they were pushed back into their ball and held there as Lazarus drew her and Faolan away from the cloud and closer to the wall.

When the others were out of earshot, Lazarus said, "Greyson has left the fast food place and is heading downtown."

"And Tanner?" Sharra said.

"Right on schedule."

"I sure hope this works," Faolan said.

"It has to," Lazarus said. "There's something that I haven't told you."

Sharra's heart skipped a beat as growing concern for Tanner surged through her veins.

"What is it?" she said.

"You must understand that this is just a theory, yet I cannot dismiss it."

"Go on," Faolan said.

Lazarus glanced at their expectant faces, and finally admitted, "I think that we're stuck in a loop."

"What do you mean?" Faolan asked.

"A time loop. I kept thinking, why Sharra? What does the Vault want with her? And that's when it hit me. Maybe it's trying to fix something… something that has to do particularly with her, and thus, her timeline. What was there to fix? Oh, there was much to choose from, but I realized that it had to be something special… a life-changing event. And then, I knew the answer."

"My parents' accident," Sharra said in dawning understanding.

Lazarus nodded. "Somehow the Vault is connected to that moment in time, as is Sharra. The loop will keep happening over and over if we don't break it."

"I know we can manipulate time, but to break a loop?" Faolan held up his hands, at a loss of how to help.

Lazarus rubbed his face in frustration. "I know. I know. I'm asking the impossible."

Sharra looked at both of them in surprise.

"We live in a world that defies all the rules," she said as she spread her arms out to encompass the Vault chamber. "Look at where you are standing, and then dare tell me that what we do is impossible. So what makes breaking a time loop any different?"

"It's not that simple," Lazarus said. "The fabric of time is a delicate thing. All our missions are carefully chosen and executed so as not to disrupt the flow of time, or cause a tear. A loop is a different entity altogether. To change it would mean to change everything connected to it. It could cause a paradox beyond anything that we could fix."

"Then, why fix the loop when the altered 'accident' solves everything? If the accident that changes my life never happens, then that creates a different timeline, not only for me, but for everyone connected to me. That is the grandest of paradoxes. I will not be responsible for ruining the fabric of time when we can solve this problem by keeping to the plan."

Lazarus opened his mouth to reply when a Link came into Sharra's mind. She raised a hand to Lazarus as she listened to the voice in her ear. It was Tanner. Lazarus nodded to her, letting her know that he was linked in.

"Araylai is somewhere behind me in the van," he said. "She says that Greyson is two cars ahead of her and is closing in on me."

"That doesn't make any sense," Sharra said to him. "He should be heading to the crash site. That's where the bomb is suppose to go off... did go off. What's he doing there?"

"He must have changed his mind. I can see him now. He's moved behind me. I'll try to lose him in the traffic."

"Can he see that it's you?"

"I can't tell." There was a pause, and then, "I'll try to shake him off."

"Stay linked with me," she said.

"Damn!"

"What?"

"He just slammed into my bumper! Damn! He did it again! My exit is coming up. I bet that's why your parents got off the highway where they did. He had given them no choice."

Her heart quickened as she thought of what they were attempting to do, and with her madman of a brother.

"Tanner, be careful. If Greyson sees you... he has the trigger to the bomb on him. I don't know what the range is, but he doesn't have to wait. He can do it at anytime."

Her eyes flew to Lazarus. Her voice grew insistent as she spoke her fears out loud.

"Greyson won't care about the rules of time," she said to the Head Director. "He only cares about himself. And if he sees that it's Tanner driving the car, he'll go ballistic. There will be nothing to stop him from detonating the bomb early, not even a paradox."

Lazarus took her arms, and stared hard into her eyes, willing her to believe his next words.

"You have to believe me. Your timeline is set. The 'accident' will happen where it did happen. Greyson can't change that."

"You don't know that for sure. And you don't know Greyson. If he sees Tanner, he will do it. He will!"

She twisted out of his hands, and turned her back to him.

"Sharra..."

Tanner's voice broke into their conversation, saying inside her ear. "Yep, he's pushing me to take the exit. Here I go."

"Has he seen you?" she asked.

There was another pause as she waited anxiously for Tanner's reply. The picture of the two cars barreling close together down the off ramp filled her mind. She just knew that they had to be close enough to see each other. If it hadn't happened already, it was bound to happen at any moment.

Sharra's gut cramped as she whipped around to face the Head Director. Heat burned in her eyes as anger made her voice harsh.

"Greyson is going to see Tanner," she said. "You know that. It's inevitable. We can't stand here and do nothing."

Faolan who had been silent finally spoke.

"What do you suggest we do?" he said, trying to calm her down.

"Let me shift into Greyson's car, and stop him before he can set the bomb off early."

"Into a moving car?" Lazarus said in shock. "No one can shift that precisely. Even if they were stationary, there is still the half-mile radius to contend with. But a moving vehicle?" He shook his head. "You're crazy. You would have to configure the rate of speed and direction... No, it's impossible."

"Lazarus is right," Faolan said. "You must listen to him. Besides, even if it did work, which it won't, your presence could push Greyson to set off the bomb early before Tanner is ready. Could you live with that?"

"I have to trust my gut, and right now, it's telling me to go."

"No, Sharra," Tanner said through the Link. "Don't do anything foolish. We just got you back. Lazarus, keep

her there." Before Sharra could protest, Tanner said,
"Damn! I think Greyson has seen me!"

"That's it. I'm going," Sharra said.

She took off to the closest shiftroom, taking the men
by surprise.

"Sharra!" Lazarus called. "Don't do it!"

Just as she reached the shiftroom, a hand stretched out
and grabbed her arm, pulling her to a stop at the
threshold.

"You won't make it," Faolan said.

"I have to try."

He pressed his lips together as his silvery eyes
searched her face. She wished she had the nerve to drop
her shield to read his mind, but did not dare. There was
no time. She had to go. She had to.

Something must have been on her face, for his eyes
turned hard.

"You love him," he said softly.

"Faolan, I don't have time for this."

She ripped her arm from his grasp and stepped into
the shiftroom. He did not try to stop her, but stood stiffly
at the edge of the threshold.

She turned to stare at his handsome face, memorizing
every bit of him, drinking it all in like a starving woman.

"I'll be back."

"Sharra, don't do it."

Closing her eyes, she blocked him out as she readied
for the shift. With all her mental strength, she drew a
picture of the scene: the backseat of the blue car, the
back of her brother's head in the driver's seat, the chase
with Tanner and Greyson in a dog fight down the

street…every little detail that she could picture as if she were already there in the thick of things.

The blocks began to build in the frontal lobe of her brain. More and more, detail after detail, until the small pile became a giant pyramid of information. When there was nothing left to add, she gave the command and sent it to the mainframe, praying that it would work.

The agrylium connected to the floor, sending the blocks of information down to the mainframe in one endless stream until her mind was clear. Peace filled her heart as she felt the Vault accept her request.

Opening her eyes, she peered into the Vault. Faolan was still there, waiting. His eyes were hooded as he watched her from the threshold. Her heart hurt at the sight of him. In that moment, she knew that she couldn't lose him. They had a special bond, and she wanted that more than anything. It would be so easy to stay. Yet, she had unfinished business with her brother. Until that ended, there would be no peace for any of them. And no matter how much she loved, Greyson would always find a way to destroy it. That thought was enough to harden her resolve.

"I love you," she whispered to him.

His face brightened as the soft words reached him. He raised a hand, palm up to her.

"Sharra. Come back with me."

She shook her head, and closed her eyes, for there was another man that she loved, too.

Taking a deep breath, she sent a silent plea to the white ball in her head.

Please shift true. Please.

The threads pulsed bright in reply. An unnatural calm set over her body. She welcomed it with open arms. With no need for assurance, she gave the final command to the mainframe.

"Shift."

Chapter Thirty-One

Chicago, Illinois USA
1986

The brightness of the shiftroom was gone. There was no time to wonder if the impossible shift had worked or not, for the answer was immediate. The sound of the moving road, the feel of the cloth seat under her legs, the jerking of her body, it all told her she had made it into a moving car. And when she recognized the back of her brother's head in front of her, she nearly jumped for joy.

Yet, her joy was short-lived.

As her brain registered that the shift had worked, Greyson jerked the wheel hard to the left, and slammed into the back fender of another car. The force of the hit flung her body against the passenger door with a *thud*. The sound was blocked by the grinding of metal against metal. Like nails on a chalkboard, it tore at her eardrums, making her cringe. The smell of burning metal filled the car.

"Come on!" Greyson yelled from the front as he ground the cars together.

Through the piercing sound of the screeching metal, Sharra gathered her body, ignoring the awakening pain in her side from the last knife wound. She knew that time was critical. She could see the other car. It was her mother's. The exit ramp was almost upon them.

She didn't wait to contemplate the consequences of her next actions. All she could think about was that Tanner was in grave danger.

Desperation took over, and with desperation came adrenalin. It pumped into her veins as she lifted her body from the floor and flew across the backseat to grab Greyson's seat belt.

With a jerk of the seatbelt, she caught his neck, and pulled with all her might. Greyson clung to the steering wheel with a hand as he grabbed at the belt. His eyes bulged as he pulled at the seatbelt around his neck. His face was turning redder with every second, but Sharra didn't care. She had one thought, and one thought only. She had to stop him from detonating the bomb early.

In those first few moments when Sharra had the upper hand, the cars broke free, but it was too late. Through the windshield, she could see her mother's car had moved into the exit lane, right where Greyson wanted it.

Letting go of the seatbelt, Greyson grabbed a hunk of her hair as he struggled to keep the car in control.

Pain ripped through her scalp. She screamed, and let go of the seatbelt.

With a jerk of his arm, he pulled her part way over his shoulder by her hair. Though she tried to pull his fingers away from her hair, they were relentless in their hold. When he saw whom he held, his eyes widened for a second and then turned red with rage.

"You!" he yelled into her ear, making her jerk. "How did you get in here?"

"By shifting, dumb ass," she said through her teeth. "How do you think?"

"You never give up, do you. And what do you hope you can accomplish?

"Stopping you!"

"Why? It has already been done. Ten years ago."

Growing suspicious Greyson peered at the car in the exit lane.

"Wait a minute. That's not Dad. Who is that? No, it can't be. It's Tanner, isn't it? You're going to ruin everything again! Well, I won't let you!"

"Haven't you learned that the Vault takes care of its own?"

He jerked hard on her hair as he growled, "Not this time, Sis."

With her head pressed to his shoulder, she bit him as hard as she could.

He screamed as he jerked her head back by her hair, letting go of the steering wheel to use both his hands.

Pain screamed through her scalp, forcing her to let go of his flesh. Her lips came back wet with blood. Yet the momentary victory was short-lived. In the heat of his rage, he flipped her body over the backrest and into the front passenger seat.

As they continued to wrestle, the car swerved to the left and veered over the line into the fast lane. Horns blared, and tires squealed as passing cars swerved to avoid them. The noise was enough to knock Greyson from his rage to look through the windshield. Dropping Sharra, he grabbed the wheel and jerked them back to the right.

Sharra righted herself in the seat in time to see the concrete barrier of the exit lane in front of them. She stiffened, squeezing her eyes shut, as she braced for the impact.

At the last possible second, with the squealing of tires, Greyson jerked the car to the right, yelling as he held on.

The force pulled Sharra's body to the door. She opened her eyes to see the concrete barrier inches from her face as the car slid by with only a hair's space to spare.

The car drifted sideways down the ramp, swaying back and forth as Greyson fought to gain control. While he wrestled with the wheel, Sharra grabbed for purchase, knocking something in the pocket of the center consul. When she looked down, she saw that it was the trigger box to the bomb.

It was right there for the taking. All common sense left her. The things that Lazarus had warned about not doing were gone. No time loop, or ripple, or paradox mattered. In that second, all she could think about was Tanner.

She dove for the box. Greyson saw what she was up to, and went for it a second later.

"Oh no, you don't," Greyson said as he grabbed the box at the same time, melding their hands together.

The car hurtled off the ramp, and onto the street into merging traffic. More tires squealed. Horns blared. Brakes were slammed as drivers veered out their the way in a mishmash of vehicles.

In the car, they struggled over the trigger as Greyson flew through the gap, and down the street. The noise from the street brought Sharra's head up for a glimpse out of the windshield.

Several blocks ahead and running perpendicular to the street that they were speeding down sat the elevated railway system upon its long running structure of metal and cement pillars.

Though Sharra couldn't see the crash site, she knew they were getting close.

Her mother's car was in front of them. Traffic slowed them down enough for Sharra to see Tanner's head. They went through one, then two intersections each one with a green light. When they came to the one in front of the overhead railway, the light was turning red as Tanner pulled up. Without slowing down he zoomed around the corner and disappeared from sight.

Greyson pressed the petal to the floor, and rocketed dangerously around the corner, through the red light. Adrenalin pumped into her veins as they grappled with the trigger box. Neither one cared about the traffic, or of the approaching crash site. It was all about the box.

Greyson's thumb stretched over the red button. She grabbed his thumb and pulled it away with all her might. He fought back, his face twisted in determination.

And when he threw a fist into her face, connecting to her right cheekbone, it was enough to whip her head to the side and loosen her grip on the box.

"Aha," he gloated, whipping the box into his other hand and out of her reach.

Her eyes widened as his thumb went onto the red button. With speed born from desperation, Sharra sent a Link to Tanner, praying that he would pick up the connection.

Greyson sent her a wicked smile as he held the box away from her.

"Say bye bye to your lover boy," he sneered.

She watched horrified as his thumb slowly came down to press the button. Outside the car windows passed a familiar row of brick housing.

"Tanner! Shift! Shift now!" she screamed into the Link.

Throwing herself onto her brother, she wrapped her arms around him, and thought of the Vault, sending the hurried blocks to the agrylium in her head, hoping to shift him before the trigger connected.

In that moment Sharra heard the distinct click of the trigger.

Like in a dream, time slowed.

A millisecond passed.

A rumble hit them as an explosion as bright as the sun flashed through the windscreen. Sharra froze in shock.

The second millisecond began.

Greyson slammed on the brakes as the shockwave hit their car. They skidded to a halt against the curb.

The bump woke Sharra into action. With little time to spare, she sent the command to shift.

Another millisecond elapsed.

Sharra felt the beginning of the shift.

"Tanner!" she screamed, but the Link was gone.

Overtaken by a fireball, her mother's car zoomed out of control, hitting a support pillar of the overhead railway. The force set off more explosions so intense that it consumed the road, the railway, and the apartment across the street.

The millisecond turned into four, or ten. It didn't matter anymore. It was too late to save Tanner. What was done was done.

In the space of a blink of an eye, the fireball barreled down on them where they sat frozen in the car.

The Vault took over, drawing her back. With her arms tight around Greyson, they blinked out as a wave of fire crashed into their car.

Chapter Thirty-Two

The Vault

Sharra screamed Tanner's name. The torturous sound echoed through time and space as she and her brother were flung back to the Vault. They landed on the floor in a sitting position. Sharra's body was draped over Greyson as she hung on tight. The last image of the fiery explosion still burned in her eyes. The thunderous explosions rang in her ears.

The second they appeared into the shiftroom, Greyson pushed her off his body, and sat up. When he saw where they were, he jumped to his feet, his face contorting with rage.

"What did you do?" he said.

"You killed him!" she cried, and pounced on him.

With all her force, she rammed him with her shoulder, knocking him out of the shiftroom. He fell to the floor and rolled to a stop inside the Vault chamber.

The whole scenario felt familiar to her: the struggle, the shift, and now the Vault. As she followed her brother out, it came to her why.

Dash.

Yet this time it was her brother, and much more serious.

The majestic row of spirals began to increase their spin, stirring up the cloudmass at their feet. The sparks ignited within the cloud, sending tiny flashes of light around the pylons. Within her head, the tiny ball of energy grew agitated as it tried to reach out to the mother cloud. Sharra pressed the ball back as she tried to reach Tanner through the Link.

There was nothing but dark silence.

She turned on her brother. As she faced him across the floor, all family ties drained away. She saw nothing but a stranger, a man willing to kill, a man wanting to destroy all that she loved with no recourse. Anger burned in her heart as hot as the fiery explosion of a moment ago. Her fists balled at her side.

"I hate you," she said through her teeth.

With a growl, she rushed at him, using the force of her anger to push him further away from the shiftroom. Using his weight, he stopped them fifteen feet out.

"Whoa, whoa, what's gotten into you?" he said.

"You! You bastard!"

"Tsk tsk. Swearing, are you? If Mom could hear you now, she would just freak out. Ah, but she can't. Too bad. I would have enjoyed seeing her expression."

She felt the shiftroom at her back. It was still too close to Greyson for her comfort. Like with Dash, she couldn't let him shift at any cost. If he got away, her future would be a living hell, that is, if he let her live. And her parents... once he found out he had failed to kill them, he'd be back to finish the job. None of them would be safe until Greyson was locked away.

Her eyes narrowed as she peered at the man who was her brother. Her blood boiled with anger as she thought of all the hurt that he had caused them.

"You are no brother of mine," she said.

Greyson raised his eyebrows. A tiny smile hovered on his lips.

"Well, we finally found something to agree upon," he said. "Mom should never have had you. We were fine before you came along. And now look how things have turned out. Mom, Dad, and now, Tanner. All that's left is you."

Forgetting about her training, Sharra hurled herself at him, giving into the rage that coursed through her veins.

Spinning around, he shook her off, and grabbed her from behind. With the hard bands of his arms, he pinned her to his chest.

"Argg!" she cried in frustration as she kicked the air in front of her.

"You never could stand to be beaten," he said in her ear.

His angry breath brushed the hair next to her ear. Yet, it was the rising wind of the pylons and the expanding particle cloud that concerned her more.

"This is not some sibling rivalry," she spat out. "You tried to kill Mom and Dad! But you know what? You failed! Do you hear me? You failed!"

"Delusional as usual. You saw the explosion. I know you did. I heard you scream. There's no way they could have survived that. And we both know that they didn't because our timeline has been set. That's something that can't be broken."

A swish of the Medical doors hit her ears. Someone walked in. She peeked over to see who it was, but the wind grew stronger, whipping her hair about her face. It caught in her mouth. She spat it out to speak.

"They did survive," she said, raising her voice against the wind. "And you want to know why? It's because we saved them."

"That's impossible. You can't change our past. It's not allowed."

"Is it really impossible? Look around you. You know nothing of the Vault. And I'm glad. For, my brother, you've been played."

"I don't believe you."

"Look over there by the Medical doors. With Katie."

Ignoring the rising turbulence, Greyson shuffled them around like one body attached at the waist until they faced the Medical doors. At the far end of the Vault near the doors to the Medical Facilities, and beside Katie stood Lilly and James. Their hair was blowing around their shocked faces as they stared at their two children. Katie had a hand on their arms, holding them back.

"Greyson, what are you doing?" their father called out.

"What should have been done long ago," Greyson answered.

On the other side of the Vault a shiftroom flashed bright, signaling an arrival. A moment later, Sharra felt Araylai reach out to her. As Sharra's father and mother tried to reason with Greyson, Sharra made other plans, for she knew there was no reasoning with a madman.

Have you heard from Tanner? Sharra asked.

Araylai scanned the Vault. *Isn't he here?*

No, and I can't get him on the Link either.

He will show up. Your brother... Do you need help? I have a knife, and a good view of him.

Does it have to always be knives?

It is an easy shot. The Vault is agitated. You should move.

Sharra felt the presence of the cloud closing in on them. Like a heavy hand it pressed against her back, reaching out to her, and to the ball of energy squirming in her head. It wanted something from her, but what? That was the question. She had been there before, in the cloud with Dash. It had wanted something then. She had been too afraid to listen. Now, she was too angry, and the cloud felt it. Yet, the feeling from the pylons would not go away.

Sharra? Araylai said. *Do you want me to take the shot?*

Sharra shook her head, pushing the presence of the pylons aside long enough to answer.

Thank you, she said, *but this is my fight. A blood challenge. You understand.*

I do, as my honor is bonded to your honor.

Honor to honor.

Sharra dropped the connection for it became too hard to hold. Her father's voice reached her through the growing haze in her mind. He was talking to Greyson.

"Listen, Son, we can sit down and talk this out," James said as he pulled free from Katie.

He raised his hands in appeal to his son as he took a step towards them, and then another. His face was drawn with worry. It hurt Sharra to see her father that way.

"Let me go!" Sharra said, renewing her struggle in his arms.

"Shut up!" Greyson yelled into her ear and squeezed as he dragged her back a step. "Father, I suggest you stop right there. I'm not afraid to hurt her."

The bands of his arms grew harder. The pressure on her ribs became unbearable. She couldn't breathe to cry out. She lashed out, kicking at his legs. The hard sole of her boot hit his shins.

He cried out and squeezed tighter. Each kick of her legs forced him backwards bringing them closer to the expanding cloud.

The pylons grew more agitated the closer they got. Each spin of the metal spiral columns sent a gust of wind around the vaulted chamber, creating a whirlwind effect. It was with the same voraciousness as when Sharra had clashed with J.D. Dash. It worried her, for Greyson had not been there, and did not know of the power festering at his back.

Lazarus and Faolan appeared from out of nowhere. Both struggled to stand against the growing wind. Both were tense with worry, impotent to help, for Greyson had her too close to the cloud.

Sharra locked gazes with Faolan. Those silvery eyes spoke volumes as he tried to come to her. There was no time left for last minute revelations. He loved her and she loved him, and that was enough for her.

Like all important moments of life, she learned a great lesson while held captive in the arms of her brother.

Love was the key.

Love was what made the world right when everything else went wrong. Love was the bond that made life worth living even in the direst of circumstances. Nonetheless, love, the kind that went to the very soul of a being, was the kind that was worth sacrificing a life for.

That was what Greyson was missing. He had no understanding of love, and thus the value of friendship, relationships, and even life itself.

He was the one who had been lost all these years. Not her.

As this thought came to her, her vision scanned those gathering in the Vault. From all around the vast chamber appeared agents: Maxum, Grimm, Viktor, Zoe, Tony, even Cael. Each took a position in front of a shiftroom, joining Araylai, and Katie as they stood guard over the portals into time.

This was her real family. They cared about her, put their lives in danger for her. She was not alone.

Lazarus held up his hands to Greyson in the universal sign for peace as he fought the wind.

"Your father is right," Lazarus called out against the windstorm. "We should talk about this. You don't have to harm anyone. You have our full attention. I'm sure we can work something out to your satisfaction. Speak. I am listening."

"Speak to you? You've ruined everything! If you hadn't recruited Sharra, none of this would have happened. It's your fault that people are dead. Not mine. Lives have been ruined because of you. And now, you have forced me to get rid of Sharra myself."

"It's no ones fault. What happened was meant to happen."

With his hands out front, Lazarus took a tentative step towards them. Ignoring the wind, Greyson matched it, stepping back with Sharra, keeping the same distance of floor between them.

"Sure, you can say that," Greyson spit out, "but my parents were supposed to have died in that accident, remember? So what are they doing standing over there?"

"Listen, Greyson. Your whole family has been stuck in a time loop. The car accident was the catalyst that started it. Now you are all free."

"Free?" Greyson laughed hysterically as if the thought was beyond funny.

"Yes, free. Though they didn't die in the accident as you had thought; in your timeline when you were young, it had to seem as though they were dead to bring you to this point, completing the circle of the loop."

"I don't care about a damn loop!"

"What do you care about then?"

"You are rich, Lazarus, to speak so casually of freedom." Greyson peered out at the other agents standing guard, and yelled to them over the rushing wind. "Lazarus tells you that you are free, but you're not. You've bound yourself to his bidding by following that damn handbook of rules. Those rules mean nothing. Nothing, I tell you. They only anchor you to the Vault, and thus, to Lazarus. Think about it. Why work when you can amass riches beyond your wildest dreams, taking what you want, with no one being the wiser? Hell, you can live on and on, wherever you want, whenever you want with all the sinful pleasures that this world has to offer at your fingertips. That is true freedom. Not this… this place!"

Lazarus nodded once. "That is true that this place, as you call it, gives you that ability. But with all things of power, it comes at a price. That price is what we pay back to all the societies of earth: past, present, and future. Long life is not enough. Neither does wealth bring real happiness. But family and meaningful work does. It is our duty and our privilege to pay the price for those things. All of us have accepted that."

"Well, I choose not to. Tell your agents to stay away from me. They're making me nervous. I just might do something… rash."

Greyson took another step into the storm brewing at his back. The cloud billowed behind them. A tendril reached out through the thickening air and found Sharra. She stilled under Greyson's grip as it traveled down the arm of her Vault uniform to the exposed flesh of her hand. Though her shield was strong, she did not resist its questing touch. She was tired of resisting, and so let it in.

It slid through the barrier of her weakened shield and into her skin until it found the nerve endings in her hand. A tingling began in her fingers. It traveled up her arm like warm liquid. Another tendril joined the first, and then another, each crawling over her Vault suit like questing fingers of a ghost. The alien threads in her head leaped for joy as it felt more of its kind enter her body. They slipped through gaps in the sleeves, neck, and boots to find her skin. The tingling grew as more particles entered her flesh and coursed up her limbs to gather at her spinal cord.

"Greyson, the cloud," she said weakly.

Greyson looked over his shoulder, at the cloud touching his back, and shrugged, "My shield is up. Is yours?"

"We are too close."

"Are we? I think they fuss for nothing. Look." He reached out and touched a tendril of energy, letting it crawl around his hand as if it were a living thing. His chest heaved against her back as he laughed at the antics of the thread. "See? Nothing."

He wiped it away with a flick of his hand. With only one arm around her, she struggled to get free, but he was not ready to let her go.

Wrapping his arm back around her, he said through the growing tempest, "I think that you and I should test the cloud. What do you say... a last adventure, together."

Another step and they were inside the cloud. The energy in her body leaped in excitement. She knew that the cloud wanted her, but not why, and it scared her.

Sharra violently shook her head. "No, Greyson. Please don't do it."

"We can end it here," he said. "You and I."

"No," she whispered.

His chest shook with humor as he dragged her deeper into the cloud. What he found so funny, she didn't know. There was something very wrong with his mind. His behavior went beyond thinking. He had tried to kill their parents, and would have succeeded if it weren't for Tanner.

Tears welled up at the thought of Tanner. She tried the Link again. There was still no reply. Her heart grew afraid. With the fear came anger for her brother. He had known that Tanner was in the car, and still he had pushed the button. It chilled her, for she knew that the killing wouldn't end. Greyson had to be stopped by any means possible.

Unknowingly to Greyson, he was handing her the means with each step deeper into the cloud that he took them.

In her body, the energy from the cloud was building. Soon it would consume her. It read her thoughts, for it had joined the threads in her head. When it understood what she was about to do, it leaped for joy. That joy gave her the strength to do what she knew she must.

A sense of calm washed over her. Through the haze of the white light in her brain, she reached out to Araylai. The connection was weak, for the light in her head was taking over.

Tell Lazarus that it wasn't his fault, Sharra said.

You need to get out of the cloud. Now!

It's okay, Sister of my heart. It's okay.

You cannot leave your parents. You cannot leave us.

Tell them that I love them. And Faolan...Tell him that I'm sorry... that I wished that I had more time with him.

The connection wavered. The energy in Sharra's head was taking over. She felt the connection disappearing.

Sharra! Araylai cried.

The white light burned in her eyes. The cloud was thick around them. Everywhere she looked, particles of energy flashed like tiny diamonds, beautiful, but deadly. As the wind whipped through the cloud, it churned it into a frenzy of sparks like those that came from high voltage wires, scorching whatever they came in contact with.

Sharra pushed against Greyson's torso, moving them closer to the spinning pylons. His breath was heavy in her ear as he labored to breathe in the cloud. The sparks zapped near their faces. She looked through the white haze of her eyes and down at his hands, and saw the cloud working on his flesh. Tendrils of energy writhed and squirmed as they covered his body, eating at his mental shield. Soon they would be inside him. Though the cloud had accepted her from the beginning, her heart told her that Greyson would be rejected just as the pylons had rejected J.D. Dash.

The whooshing noise of the metal blades was loud at their backs, drowning out the frantic calls of her friends outside the cloud.

Greyson squeezed her ribs. "Can you feel it?" he laughed into her ear. "I told you that Lazarus was lying. There is nothing here, but wind and dust."

"Then, let down your shield," she said.

She gritted her teeth against the power flowing in her veins, feeling the sparks gathering in her mouth. All she had to do was ask it, and she'd be free from him. The energy read her thoughts, and pulsed with gladness. It was there in her body, waiting to be released.

Her hand crept up to touch Greyson's hand.

Go! she commanded.

With a whoosh of light, the alien energy jumped from her flesh to his, demolishing his shield before he knew what was happening. As it attacked, the energy called out to the mother cloud. The cloud listened, and flooded in, cocooning them both in a white field of particles, blocking out everything else.

"Ouch! Stop it!" he said, as he swatted at his face.

"I told you not to go into the cloud," she said.

Greyson cried out, dropping Sharra, as the threads grew more aggressive. The harder he tried to brush them off; the more they came.

"Get off me! Get off me!" he cried.

Hundreds of tendrils jumped from the ball surrounding them to attack Greyson. They crawled over his body, into his nose, ears, and mouth, covering him in a writhing mass of threads. Sharra no longer cared.

Without Greyson's arms around her, she fell to the ground onto her hands and knees. When she raised her head, she found the blades of the center pylon inches from her face.

Whoosh. Whoosh. Whoosh.

It brushed past her face whipping her hair around her head. Power vibrated the air. With every breath, she breathed it in, adding more strength to the threads already swimming in her body.

She swiped her hair away from her face as she staggered to her feet. The wind shook her as she fought to stay vertical. The metal blades of the mother pylon cut the air in front of Sharra with a mighty hum. Beside it, the other eight pylons added to the noise, lending force to the wind as they spun.

Power snapped in the air and in her veins. The pylon was everywhere, in the air and in her mind. She struggled to think. It called to her. She couldn't resist it, and had to look.

In front of her, the metal blades of the mother pylon dripped liquid silver as it spun before her face. It drew her in like the spinning watch of a hypnotist. She peered through the brightness in her mind to the face reflected in the spinning blade, and saw herself staring back. Her hair was blowing everywhere. Her face was white with raw energy. Tiny sparks filled the space that was her pupils. She sucked in a breath at the sight of her face, and saw more sparks in the cavern of her mouth.

The mother pylon beckoned her closer. Her body listened, for the power within her was at one with the pylons. Even if she wanted to, she could not deny it anymore.

Dash was electrocuted in this exact spot. But not her. Hers was to be a different death. Closing her eyes, she let the pylon pull her in, holding her breath as she braced for the cut of the blades.

Chapter Thirty-Three

The pain before death did not come.

As Sharra stepped forward the metal gave way, sheeting over her skin in great rivets of liquid silver. Another step and she was inside the great pylon. Like a warm shower, it drenched her head, and slid down her body. Sheet after silvery sheet it came, and yet she felt dry.

In that instant the rushing wind stopped. All turned silent. No cries of her friends. No screams from Greyson. Not even the raging windstorm touched her ears.

A fresh calm settled over her as she opened her eyes. The silver was all around her, in the air, on her skin, inside her body, and in her mind. She opened her mouth to breathe, uncaring if she should die, and found air. Awe filled her as the reality of where she was hit her.

"How is this possible?" she whispered through the silvery liquid.

THE VAULT

Shiny particles like diamonds of light flashed in streams around her as the outer shell of the pylon spun gracefully before her face. She reached up to touch them, letting the liquid silver flow through her fingers. There was no pain. There was no sense of motion, only silence, and the insistent pressure that she associated with the alien energy pulsing inside her body.

A vision of time filled her head. The past became the present as the present merged with the past. The endless plain of the future spread out before her, century after century until it disappeared into a plain of eternity. Yet it, too, merged with the others until there was nothing.

Time was everywhere, and simultaneously nowhere. She finally understood the concept. What was time, but the passing of events? Inside the cocoon of liquid silver time had no meaning.

In the silence of the silvery prison, she felt the liquid metal join with the threads coursing through her veins. Together they streamed to the space between the agrylium in her head. A bond was formed, liquid metal to liquid metal. With the bond came a new mind, an alien mind. It filled the deep recesses of her brain where it swirled in a molten pattern, waiting for her.

"You're alive," she whispered in new understanding.

The revelation made everything clear. All those times when the power of the Vault had disturbed her, it had been trying to communicate. She had brushed it off like everyone else. Even after the threads had taken up residence in her brain, she should have realized it. Looking back, she was sure that they had tried to tell her, and still she had lived in denial.

Now that she understood exactly what the Vault was, there were no more excuses. This time she was ready to listen.

A sense of happiness flashed into her body from the warm presence. The emotion merged with her, saturating her whole body in a glow like she had never felt before. While she reveled in the powerful sensation, it slowly melted away. As it left her, another sensation, a darker one crept into her mind, one that she was all too familiar with.

Pain.

Her gut wrenched as the strength of it washed through every nerve ending in her body until she was consumed by it. She tried to cringe away, to protect herself from it, but the pylon held her captive with its mind.

"Please! I can't bear it!" she cried, writhing in its shared pain. "Why are you doing this?"

The entity heard her. The pain lessoned, leaving Sharra deflated and weak. She sagged in relief. And yet, the entity was still there... a tangible thing. She felt the weight of it in her mind, and knew that it was waiting for something.

"What do you want?" she asked it.

It swelled with excitement inside her mind.

Though a residue of pain remained, the alien excitement quickly covered it. The electrical impulses gathered in her mind's eye. They began to form a pattern, laying down lines of colors, some larger, some smaller, like a machine laying down threads to make a cloth. When pressed together the lines of color made a picture.

A black square of nothing floated in her mind.

"Is that suppose to be space?" she asked.

The picture changed, growing outward into a large cube of emptiness. As she watched, lines dropped down from the four corners of the cube to merge in the empty space of its center. Where they touched, the space broke open. New lines emerged from the hole. From the lines was born another smaller cube. The lines solidified, tilting the new cube at an apposing angle to the outside cube, connecting them together by the lines from their four corners.

Sharra stared at it with her minds eye. She had seen the form before and struggled to remember where.

The picture changed again. Like a camera, it zoomed in on the smaller cube to the very center where the four inner lines of the larger cube intersected inside the smaller cube.

It hovered there for a second before zooming in on the point where the four lines intersected. The picture opened up. There was the Vault chamber with the nine pylons of agrylium metal rotating in the center. The picture focused on the center pylon. Within it, Sharra could see a shadow of a figure, and knew that it was she.

The picture zoomed back out showing her the nine pylons. Out of the center that was the Vault chamber emerged billions upon billions of threads. More kept coming, so many that no number could name them. Each led to a moment in time, past, present, and future. They fanned out so thick that they formed a solid sphere of time that reached out beyond the space of the first cube.

The Vault was everywhere, and simultaneously, nowhere.

The revelation shocked her.

The entity wasn't done. The pictures changed. She was back inside the Vault complex. Successively, she was shown pictures of rooms filled with people. Each apartment was occupied. There were even children there, running in the hallways, splashing in the swimming pool, even playing near the Vault chamber. Sharra could hear their laughter in her head as if she were there among them, and felt the joy of the entity fill her.

The images were wiped away. The laughter and joy cut off. The pain came back, growing stronger as fresh pictures of empty rooms flashed up. Gone were the people. Gone were the children. All that remained was an emptiness that time could not fill... sad and lonely.

With the loneliness came a gnawing hunger. Sharra grabbed her stomach as it filled her own belly, understanding what it was trying to say.

"You are hungry."

The hunger was replaced by hope. It was the kind of hope that came from desperation.

Again, it showed her the people, humans and Arderians, this time placing them in the Vault chamber close to the cloud. It was hungry, but not for flesh and blood. It was hungry for something else, something that surprised her.

"I understand what you need," she said.

Everything finally made sense: the turmoil among the agents, her own troubles, even Lazarus' most guarded secrets. He had known all along that the pylons were alive, and that the agrylium was a living part of it. That was his secret. And now she knew it, too.

Those that lived within the Vault were intertwined with the entity by the agrylium in their head. They could not time travel without it, nor have long life and good health, or any of the other benefits that came with it. Simultaneously, the entity needed them, more specifically, the electromagnetic energy that they gave off. That energy was what it required to stay alive. It was what it used to create the Vault – their home.

Symbiosis: two different beings dependent on each other to live.

With the revelation came wisdom, and Sharra knew what she had to do.

She touched the agrylium tattoo with fresh understanding. "I will help you get what you need. I promise."

The energy particles jumped inside her body, nearly knocking her off her feet as an alien joy exuded from every pore of her body. The liquid metal of the pylon caught her before she fell, and held her steady within its cocoon of warmth.

In those few precious moments when time and space had stood still, and when two entities, one human, and one of liquid metal, came together as one to form a partnership, Sharra had forgotten all about the tempest going on outside the protective wall of her cocoon.

It came crashing back as her focus returned to see her brother on the other side of the wall of metal, swatting at the wispy threads that covered his body. Disgust for him filled her heart, for all the pain he had caused, not just to their family, but also to the people of the Vault.

The entity felt her disgust. It tugged at her mind, asking for more. Without thinking about the link, she answered it, letting it glimpse a memory or two, thinking that would be enough.

She was wrong.

It followed the path of the memories to her frontal lobe before she could stop it, and began to devour all that was stored there. Everything that had happened to her, from the time she had been born thus far, flashed inside her head as the entity relived her life in a matter of seconds, feeling all that she had felt: joy, shame, hurt, grief, even love, all of it. Nothing was kept secret from it, not even the most recent events, nor the reason why her brother stood at its feet.

Sharra felt its focus leave her frontal lobe, and turn to the human at its feet outside its metal perimeter. Fresh understanding flashed as bright spots of light from the alien energy pulsing through her body. It was soon followed by righteous indignation as it felt the pain in her heart over the years of loss and suffering, feeling it as if it were its own pain.

She sensed its anger growing in her mind, and did nothing to suppress it. Connected as they were, her own anger grew along with its, until they were as one mind, and one thought.

Though she spoke no words, the threads inside her body responded, breaking through her flesh to swarm through the liquid metal, and out into the Vault. They entered the rising cloud, feeding it with angry energy.

The cloud around Greyson grew thicker. Greedy tendrils wrapped around him like squirming white worms, attacking him with a vengeance. She felt them enter his body, and rush to his brain. Through the entity she saw her brother's naked mind, all the defects and instabilities that drove him to act out his madness upon their family, and in turn, upon the Vault.

It was there, all of it: his plans for steeling the original Training Contract, the deal with J.D. Dash, the manipulation of Viktor and subsequent kidnapping that led to Ardus, and worst of all, the premeditated plans for murdering her and her parents. Bile rose into her throat, and stuck in the back of her mouth. She swallowed it down.

"Why, Greyson?" she whispered.

The pylon felt her pain. There was no denying the instability of Greyson's mind. The pylon saw it too, recognizing the threat at its feet for what he was, and grew angry.

Fed by their combined anger, Sharra's and the alien's, the particle cloud responded, surging over Greyson. The cloud attacked his flesh, covering his body in sparks. Greyson fell to the floor screaming as he beat at the cloud, but to no avail. The torturous screaming peireced Sharra's ears as she watched her brother writhe uncontrollably under the attacking blanket.

Dark smoke began to thicken around Greyson's body. The sight of it broke through Sharra's anger. She squashed the anger down, remembering who she was, that she was not her brother.

The Vault had killed for her once before. If she let it happen again, she knew that it would destroy her.

"No," she said to the entity.

The cloud persisted, covering her brother in a heaving mass of sparks. The dark smoke around his body grew thicker, rising into the air to mingle with the cloud.

"No," she said again louder. "Not this way."

The cloud refused to listen, for the entity was consumed with a rage too thick to break through.

The screams of wracking pain pierced her ears, and tore at her heart as she watched the black smoke increase.

Raising her hands inside her liquid prison to the tempest outside, she gathered all the mental strength that she could muster, and commanded the cloud in a loud voice.

"Stop!"

The tempest of a windstorm, the cloudmass, the massive array of sparks, and the nine pylons: all of them stopped in mid-action as if someone had paused a movie. With that one command, even time itself stopped.

To Sharra's relief, her brothers' piercing screams ended. All turned silent except for the loud beating of her heart in her ears. Her breathing became laborious as her hold over the Vault sapped her strength.

As the cloud settled back, a space of flooring cleared in front of the pylon, revealing Greyson curled up in a fetal position. Burnt patches still smoldered on his jeans and jacket. His arms covered his face. The hand that she could see was red from where the skin had been burned.

A bit of exposed flesh on his calf above his sock was also raw.

Sharra slowly lowered her arms. Greyson wasn't moving. She stared at her brother through her silvery prison. His body was laid out like a gift offering at her feet: the sacrificial lamb.

"Greyson!" she cried.

Her chest heaved for air as she fought back the horror. It was Dash all over again.

"Let me out!" she cried to the pylon.

The pylon listened. The metal thinned around her. She pushed against it, and found her path unhindered. With a few steps, she passed through the wall of the pylon, and was outside. The smell of burnt flesh hung in the air. Tears blocked her vision as she dropped to the floor beside her brother. Reaching under his arm, she checked the pulse of his neck.

"Please be okay," she whispered as she pressed her fingers against his neck.

There it was... a pulse.

A tiny sob of relief escaped from her mouth.

"He's alive," she sobbed to herself, or to the pylon, she didn't know. "He's alive."

All the horrible things he had done washed away. No matter the past, he was still her brother.

She moved his arm off his face. The flesh underneath was raw. The hair that was left on his head still smoldered. His eyebrows were singed to nothing. Without a thought to her hands, she patted out the fire in his hair and on his clothes until the smoking stopped. As she patted, Greyson stirred under her hand, and moaned.

Grabbing Greyson by the arms, she dragged him to the edge of the circle of the cloud. With a wave of her hand, the thick white wall opened before them. As a pathway formed through the cloud, she dragged her brother's body one foot at a time to freedom, groaning as his dead weight pulled the muscles of her shoulders and back.

At last the cloud gave way to the open air of the Vault.

A few feet out from the cloud, Sharra let go of Greyson's arms. They dropped to the floor with a slap, and didn't move. Breathing heavily, she fell to her knees next to his body in exhaustion. Behind them the passageway closed, hiding the lower section of the giant pylon once again.

The threads that the pylon had fed her were still in her body, swirling around, lighting up her brain. It made it hard for her to see.

"Sharra!" she heard Faolan call out.

Through the haze of her eyes, she saw a lone tendril break free from the receding cloud and float to her. She raised a hand to it, no longer afraid.

"Don't touch it!" Faolan said, stopping a safe distance from her.

"It's okay," she said.

And it was. They were linked, her and the entity.

Faolan stood back as the tendril touched her skin in a gentle caress of power. The energy trapped inside her body leaped in response. In gladness, the stream rushed to meet the tendril. Light flowed through her nervous system as the alien energy left her where the tendril touched her skin to merge back with the cloud. Her body emptied of the fiery energy until all that was left were the threads from her initial encounter. With what mental strength she had left, she gathered them together and herded them back up to the spot between the agrylium in her head, and into their protective ball.

As the last of the energy settled down, the haze left her vision. She raised her eyes to Faolan who hesitated a few feet away. She read the uncertainty on his face. A tear escaped and fell down her cheek. She wiped it away, wondering where it had come from.

The sight of the tear broke Faolan. Rushing to her side, he gathered her in his arms and pressed her to his chest.

"Sharra."

His voice trembled as he said her name. Her arms went around him, soaking in the warmth of his body. He kissed her lips, sharing his fear and joy in that intimate act. Tearing his lips away, he pressed her to his chest and held her close. Her ear was on his heart. It beat wildly, sounding loud to her after the quiet of the pylon. She welcomed it, and moved in closer.

"I thought you were dead," he whispered, kissing her hair. "When he had dragged you into the cloud…"

"I'm okay. The cloud didn't hurt me. It didn't hurt me."

"I can't believe it. No one has survived in there. It's a miracle you're alive."

"Yes, it is," she whispered, thinking of the entity that was the Vault. "I think it likes me."

Faolan stiffened in her arms. She lifted her head to search his face. His silvery gaze was on her, studying her with an intensity that made her nervous.

"You know, then," he said.

"Yes."

His face turned hard. "How long have you known?"

Beside them, Greyson's hand twitched. Sharra was saved from answering. Leaving the comfort of Faolan's arms, she went to her brother. Gently she touched his arm.

"Greyson," she said.

A low moan of pain came from his mouth. His eyelids fluttered, but did not open. Slowly he dragged his arm to his body and rolled to his side to curl up into a ball. He began to cry, deep and guttural. The horrible sound echoed around the Vault chamber, for the pylons were still immobile and the cloud subdued.

Lazarus who rushed in after Faolan helped Sharra to her feet as he waved over Cam and Cael. Cam, prepared as always, was pushing a floating gurney over to them. He brought it parallel to Greyson's body, and lowered it to the ground.

"Can he be saved?" Sharra asked Cam.

Cam looked the patient over with a calculated eye.

"It is too early to tell. We need to get him into a medical chamber right away."

A med pen was pressed to Greyson's neck. As they watched, Greyson turned quiet as his body relaxed into a medicated stupor.

"Cael, help me with the patient," Cam said as he unrolled Greyson from the fetal position and stretched him out on the floor.

Together Cam and Cael lifted the sedated patient onto the gurney, and floated him away from the cloud, past his stunned parents, and through the frosted doors of the Medical Facility.

Sharra gazed across the floor to her parents where they stood looking totally confused and overwhelmed, and felt the ten long years of grief lift from her shoulders. All the pain, all the trouble caused by Greyson was over... finished. He could no longer harm anyone. Faolan, Viktor, Lazarus, Araylai, Katie: they were all safe. The list went on and on.

She was finally free. She wanted to cry with relief, but held it back, for the feeling was too new. The old way of living in constant dread still sat there. She knew it would take time to let everything that happened sink in. Fortunately for her, time was on her side.

"We should move, too, before the pylons wake up," Lazarus said as he gazed thoughtfully at the silent giants resting within the cloud.

It wasn't the pylons that were asleep. Sharra knew that it was the humans who slept in ignorance. Yet for some unknown reason, she had been awakened. And by the look of it, she wasn't the first.

She slid a glance at the two men beside her, remembering a sentence here, a knowing look there, putting two and two together. There were so many questions she wanted to ask, but bit her lip instead.

Later.

The awakening was a gift, the same as life was a gift. It was not to be taken for granted.

Sharra felt the mother pylon through the cloud that separated them. The connection was still there, gentle, but insistent. Though the pylon was silent, she knew it was waiting patiently for her to release them, trusting that she would.

"I'll take Sharra to the Ward. Cam should have a look at her... just in case," Faolan said to Lazarus, as he tucked an arm around Sharra's waist, and led her away from the cloud.

"I'm fine, really," she said. "You know that I am, because you know what's there."

Lazarus sent her a sharp look. She met his stare, unafraid.

Lowering his voice, he said, "You and I, we'll talk about what happened here later, after things settle down. Until then, keep it to yourself. Some secrets are too dangerous for the public. For now, we have two new guests who are totally confused as to what is going on and need some reassurance from their daughter."

Sharra turned to her parents and smiled shyly at them. When they saw her they waved. They weren't alone. Sometime during the last few minutes the other agents had left their posts and were standing around her parents. Maxum and Grimm were talking to her father. Viktor was standing behind Katie, guarding them with a watchful eye as the tiny girl answered Lilly's questions.

Zoe and Tony stood off to the side strangely subdued. Tony was holding Zoe quietly in his arms. Her head rested upon his chest as she leaned into him. His face was pensive as he stared out into the cloud while stroking her short blond hair. There was a sense of renewal about them. Sharra was glad. Though they both had strong personalities, Sharra had come to like them and wished the best for them. Life was lonely enough without someone, and especially within the Vault.

Seeing them together made her think of Tanner. She craned her head around Faolan's body to search the Vault, but the trainer was nowhere to be seen. Neither was Araylai. She tried the Link again. It was silent.

"Have either of you seen Tanner?" she asked both Faolan and Lazarus who had taken her free side. "He's not linking. Neither is Araylai."

"Faolan gave her a squeeze. "I'm sure they are both around somewhere. Tanner probably went back to double check that the crash went as planned. You know how he is."

When she looked at Lazarus, his eyes turned hooded. He looked away before she could ask, saying nothing. Sharra brushed it off, figuring that the Head Director had enough to deal with cleaning up this mess. She understood. For now that the Vault was secured, and their lives at peace once again, her future was looking good, and his would be back in order.

She had her parents back in her life. She had Faolan who loved her, and she him. And she had a new responsibility to the Vault. What more could she want?

When Tanner returned she would have a talk with him in private. It had gone on long enough. Though she loved both men, she had to make a choice. It wasn't fair to any of them. She was not her brother. She had to do the right thing. And no matter how much it would hurt him, she was letting Tanner go.

Her heart broke a little at the thought. And then she pushed the pain aside, and mustered up her resolve. She was not her brother.

Reaching up, she gave Faolan a kiss on the cheek, marking her decision.

"What?" he said.

She stared into his eyes, and whispered, "I love you."

"I love you, too." He kissed her lips.

She pulled away, and blushed. "Stop. We have an audience."

"I don't care." He grabbed her to his chest and kissed her again, bending her back with the force of his passion. She kissed him back, forgetting all about the people watching them as his passion spread to her until they were both out of breath and they broke apart.

Cheering broke out around them. Sharra looked at the happy faces surrounding her, and smiled back while she held onto her man. Whatever the future held, she was sure of one thing: love was the answer.

"That's enough," Faolan said, unaware of the emotions overflowing in her heart.

"It will never be enough."

He laughed, and let her go. "You greedy thing. Go to your mom. She's been waiting for you."

Chapter Thirty-Four

The method was easy. The task was hard.

Picking the spot was never a problem. It wasn't something that Sharra had to think about. When she had walked into the greenhouse, and saw it, she knew that it was the right place.

The wooden tub filled with bushy white daisies sat on the floor at the end of a row. The plant was so thick that the greenery draped over the edge of the tub.

She crouched down and stared at the plant. The white daisy heads smiled up at her. Formerly, she would have smiled back, for she loved their velvety white petals and sunny centers. It was such a simple plant compared to some of the more exotic ones that she had growing in the greenhouse. Yet that simple plant held great meaning to her, and that's why today her lips were pressed together, for the deed was a solemn deed.

There was no room for laughter. No room for happiness.

Pulling the bush aside, she searched for the dark soil near its roots with her hand shovel. It was still wet from the morning watering. The shovel sank into the dirt next to the edge of the tub. The roots broke under the sharp blade as a narrow dent was opened up in the dirt.

Leaving the shovel in the hole, she opened her other hand. On her palm sat a piece of twisted metal. It might have been a rectangle at one time. It was hard to tell. The edges had melted and flattened. Black shards were imbedded into its thin warped casing. Though it was extremely damaged, there was no denying of what it was.

When Araylai had placed it in her hand, Sharra knew that it was a Com-Link.

"Tanner's?" was all Sharra could manage to say.

Araylai nodded. Around her body, her aura was dark with grief.

Sharra saw the aura, and knew the truth behind it.

Tanner was dead.

Tears came unbidden to Sharra's eyes. Her vision blurred as she turned to stare at the mutilated piece of metal in her hand. Araylai shared her grief. As she spoke, her words were soft and sad.

"When he wouldn't answer the Link after the explosion," Araylai said, "I had to go back and check. It wasn't like him not to respond. I knew you were worried about him too. And since I could do nothing for you in the Vault, I shifted out to the crash site."

"Did you see him? Was he still in the car?"

"The flames were too intense. And when the fire department arrived, it took them all night to get the site under control before anyone could approach the car."

Hope stirred in her heart as she grasped for a lifeline.

Her voice trembled as she said, "That doesn't mean he was in the car. The Com-Link could have been knocked off before he shifted."

"I thought the same, but when Tanner did not show up, I went a little forward in time, and had a closer look at the evidence gathered from the scene. When I read the coroner's report…"

"Please don't tell me there was a third body."

"There was… evidence to suggest_"

"No," Sharra cut in with a violent shake of her head. "I won't believe it. I can't. Not Tanner. Not Tanner."

Tears shined in Araylai's amber eyes as she fought not to cry.

"I'm sorry, Sharra," Araylai whispered.

Tanner was gone.

The man who had been her friend from the beginning, who had teased her in his good-natured way and made her laugh, who had taught her to stand up for herself, and trained her to be strong, both of body and mind. He was the one who loved her first, the one who always had her back. He was her rock, her salvation. And now he was gone.

Great sobs welled up from the depths of her soul as grief hit her hard in the chest. Her knees grew weak as her body was wracked with uncontrollable sobs. Araylai's arms came around her and held her, crying with her as they both mourned the loss of a friend.

Sharra rested her head on her friend's shoulder, and cried until the tears were spent and there was nothing left in her, but the dull ache of loss.

When she had seen her parents settled into an apartment, and left in Maxum's and Grimm's capable hands, she had fled the Vault, seeking refuge at Faolan's townhouse back in the nineteen century. Faolan had gone with her. It had been awkward at first, for he knew that she had loved Tanner. Yet Faolan's love for her had never wavered. It had been his quiet acceptance and comforting embraces that had finally softened the anguish in her heart.

With the passing of time, her grief lessened to a dull ache. The time had come for her to face the people back at the Vault.

And so, the two of them returned to the Vault, hand in hand, each with a better understanding of the other. For Sharra, the pain of loss was still there, and would be for a long time. Though she had gained her parents, it had come at a great price. She knew the guilt associated with Tanner's death would never go away.

Today was a new day. It was time to try to move forward, for her sake and for Faolan's. And this was the place to start.

After one last look at the ruined Com-Link, she dropped it into the hole, and pulled the shovel out. As soon as the shovel was gone, the roots and dirt fell over the Link and buried it. A tear escaped, and ran down her cheek. She sniffed, trying not to cry. She had done enough crying already.

"Good bye, Tanner. I will never forget you."

She wiped the tear away with the back of her hand, and stood up. The barrel of daisies looked undisturbed, a fitting memorial to Tanner. The sunny flowers will always remind her of him, of his sunny disposition and cheeky smile, and she was glad of that.

While her thoughts were on the daisies, the PVC came on.

"Lazarus Maitland requesting entrance," it said.

"Let him in."

She set the hand shovel on the workbench, and left the greenhouse. Lazarus stood inside the threshold of her apartment. A shadow still haunted his eyes. Though he smiled in greeting, it barely reached the corner of his eyes. She understood, for she felt the same.

He had exchanged his suit for a Vault uniform. It fit him like a glove, making him look the part of an agent of the Vault. Not that he wasn't an agent. He had been from the beginning, longer than any of them. She was just used to the executive suits. She liked him in the uniform, and she told him so.

"Trying out a new look?" she asked. "It suits you."

Smiling at her pun, he looked down at the uniform, and touched the agrylium logo on his chest. A strap to a satchel resting on his back ran down the front of his chest.

"It's been a while since I've put this on. Feels good."

"What's the occasion?"

"Nothing special. Well, don't tell Katie that. She told me to put it on, and then went on about an overdue vacation, spending time with family, and the like. She said that she has it all arranged, and that I wasn't to argue with her. Even convinced Faolan to fill in for me while we're gone, not that time will move much on this end, probably a day, or two."

"Faolan shouldn't be able to get into too much trouble in two days."

"I can't remember the last time the two of us had gone away together. I'm actually looking forward to it. Especially after…"

He turned away and cleared his throat. Pain filled the lines of his face, aging him. There was a vulnerability about him that hadn't been there before, a shadow of loneliness that weighed on his shoulders. It almost broke her to see it, for the man had been so strong, a pillar to them all.

Sharra felt the lump return in her throat. She swallowed it down along with the tears that threaten to spill over.

"A vacation will be good for both of you," she said through her tight throat. "I know that it helped me."

The living room turned quiet as they gathered control of their emotions. Finally, Lazarus lifted his head and smiled sadly at her.

"With all that's happened, we never got a chance to talk," he said. "I know things haven't been easy for you, especially with Greyson. He will never fully recover. His mind is gone: Brain Shifted. It was never strong enough to withstand the rigors of shifting. It takes a certain kind of mind, and his was not it."

"What will happen to him?"

"The agrylium has already been removed and returned to the Vault. Cam has done a great job with the skin grafts. No one will ever know that Greyson had been burned. Once he's well enough to be moved, we will put him in a suitable mental institute in his timeline where he'll get the best of care for the rest of his life. Don't worry. Cam will install a Memory Block in Greyson's mind, just in case. He won't remember anything."

"Not even me?"

"If you want it that way."

Sharra thought about all the pain and suffering that Greyson has caused in her life. It made her decision easy.

"Yes. Delete me from his mind. All of it."

"Consider it done."

"It's sad really. I won't miss him. The people here are more family to me than he had ever been."

"And we feel the same about you."

"Even with all the chaos that came with me?"

"Even with that. I must admit that for a long time I wondered why the Vault wanted you. I think I know now."

"The Vault wanted me?"

"Yes."

He took out a folded piece of heavy vellum paper from the black satchel strapped to his back, and passed it over to her. She unfolded it and began to read the spidery writing. It was all there on the page: her name, birth date, Charlotte address and timeline down to the exact date when he first had contacted her at the job fair. It stated that she would be different from the others, someone that would help him when he needed it the most. It said that she'd discover the true identity of the

Vault, and that it was okay, that the Vault wanted her. The note finished with a warning: she would bring great pain and loss to him and to those around him. And yet, knowing this, Lazarus had gone ahead and recruited her anyway. It made Tanner's loss even more devastating to her.

She folded the letter, and handed it back to him. It went back into the satchel.

"It's a funny thing: time," he said with a snort. "There are many time loops in this place. This letter is another one. I've just written it not ten minutes ago. I'm on my way right now, shifting back in time to leave it on my desk for my past self to find. You see I am going to tell my past self to find you and recruit you, that you would be someone special to the Vault. And you are. The Vault has chosen you. You cannot deny it. We all saw it. Sure, the others don't understand what really happened. And I'd like to keep it that way for now. But I know that it took you in. Why, Sharra? What did it want?"

This time, Sharra held nothing back. She had made a promise to the Vault, and she meant to keep it. Lazarus needed to know the truth.

"The entity wants to live," she said, starting with the obvious, "just as we want to live. For the Vault to survive it needs us, but our numbers are too few. In the past how many people used to live here? I've seen the empty apartments and know that the Vault can hold hundreds. Yet there are only what? Forty? Maybe fifty of us? That is what it needs, people. We bring life to it by the electromagnetic energy that our emotions give off. Each time we arrive back from a shift, it feeds off the exultations, the fears, the joys, the satisfaction, the whole range of emotions that we feel as humans. And now we can add the Arderians. That's what makes the blades spin and the particle cloud react. In turn it gives us a home, a meaningful job, and a longer life, just to name a few of the big things. We cannot go on as we are. And the Vault cannot survive without us. The few that have been added, Cael and Immari, are not enough. I promised that I would help get what it needs. Will you help us?"

"It spoke?"

"I can't explain how, but yes, it spoke with me. We are connected, the entity and I. It told me many things. It showed me the Vault's true nature, and where this complex resides in the stream of time. I also know that the agrylium in our heads is not just metal, but a living part of the entity. These are some of the secrets you've been keeping from us. What I don't understand is why?"

Lazarus rubbed his face, and sighed. "It has always been that way. I recruit for it when it tells me to, and that's it."

"Yet Faolan somehow found out, didn't he."

Lazarus nodded, confirming what she had already guessed.

"It's the reason he left," he said. "He couldn't understand why it would be dangerous to give agents full disclosure on the subject. And I wouldn't bend. I had to protect the entity. That was my first duty."

"Maybe you should have listened to Faolan. Keeping it a secret hasn't helped anyone. The Vault needs our full cooperation, and to have that we need to tell recruits the truth. It's the only way we will have peace."

"Full disclosure?"

Sharra nodded. "Full disclosure."

He tilted his head, pursing his lips in contemplation. After a moment he said, "Maybe it would be wise to listen to you, Sharra Lane. After all, the Vault has chosen you to be its mouthpiece. Who am I to hold back change if change will make things better."

"'For the betterment of mankind.' Isn't that what we do?" A cheeky smile lifted the corner of her lips. It was something she had learned from Tanner.

A small chuckle escaped from Lazarus.

"How can I argue with that?" he said.

"You can't."

"You're right, I can't."

They smiled at each other.

Lazarus paused as he studied her. "I remember the first time that I saw you, and wondered what my future self had seen in you. After the meeting, I remember thinking of you as a lump of coal."

"Well, that's real flattering."

"Look at you. You have turned into a diamond, a jewel worth a king's ransom. Don't ever downplay your own worth as I had done. You are special."

Sharra recalled that initial interview as well. She had felt unworthy under his gaze... a nobody, and had dropped her eyes to her lap. It felt like a lifetime ago. Maybe it was. Whatever the case, she was no longer that timid girl. Her recruitment by Lazarus, and subsequent training under Tanner's hand, had made her into the woman she was today. For that she would be forever in his debt.

She stared back at him, eye to eye. "We are all special."

"Yes, we are. Which reminds me: since your parents are staying, they need to be properly introduced to our ways. I thought, since you are their daughter, that you might like to take them under your wing, and help them through the training process."

"Me? There must be someone more qualified. Tanner, he…"

"Tanner was a great trainer. One of the best the Vault has ever seen. He will not be forgotten. But, if as you say we need to fill the Vault, that means that all those new candidates will need to be trained. Just think on it. You don't have to decide right now. I've already loaded the Training Program into your file, just in case. You can have a look at it while I'm gone. Use your parents as test subjects, and see how you feel about it. We can talk later. I'm sure Tanner would approve of you filling his shoes."

He reached into his satchel, pulling out a small wooden box, and held it out to her. It was Tanner's card box, the one that used to belong to his mother.

"This is for you," he said as he set it into her hands.

Tears came to her eyes. She blinked them away as she looked down at the faded polish of the top of the much-loved box, and thought of all the times they had played cards together. They were memories that she would treasure forever.

"Tanner would have wanted you to have it," Lazarus said softly.

"Thank you." She pressed the box to her chest.

"I need to go. Time is marching on, and I've got a few more errands to do before I can leave with Katie."

She followed him to the door. The box was still at her chest. In the hallway, he turned around, and raised an eyebrow at her. It was a look she knew all too well.

"Oh, and Sharra."

"Yes?"

"Try not to break any more rules while I'm gone."

She laughed, and raised a hand in goodbye. As soon as the door swished shut, and she was alone, she sent a link to Faolan.

With Lazarus' final warning in her head, she said, "About dinner with my parents. I think we should postpone going to your home in London until they're assimilated. The past will be theirs soon enough."

Chapter Thirty-Five

In the hallway propped against the wall next to Sharra's apartment door was a large military duffle bag. Lazarus had set it out of sight before entering her apartment. He hadn't wanted her to see it. It would have caused too many questions…questions he was unprepared to answer.

Lazarus picked it up, and slung it over his shoulder. As he headed to the lifts he heaved a deep sigh.

Another secret, he thought, pressing his lips together.

On the main floor, not a soul was around. The hallways were quiet, except for the clipping of his boots upon the polished floor. He listened to the silence with new understanding, and wondered why he hadn't noticed this before.

Sharra was right. There was once a time when these halls were filled with life. When troubles had been few, and friends aplenty. How could he have forgotten? He was the caretaker of the Vault. He should have noticed.

Well, thanks to Sharra, they had been warned. He knew what to do to make things right. With a little time and effort, this place will be whole again, and at peace.

But first, he had one last errand to do.

The shiftroom flashed bright as he made the jump from the Vault to the Training Facility. The last time he had been there was when he came to shift Sharra to the Vault for the first time.

Time had not touched the place. Besides the Vault chamber, it was the one constant thing in his life.

The agrylium spirals that graced the sides of the entranceway to the facility began to rotate in greeting.

Hello to you, too, he said, knowing that the entity was there, listening.

The spirals said nothing, yet he felt the entities presence. It had always been there. Now though, he was more aware of it as a real creature with real needs. And so dared not take it for granted.

He headed to the living room. There was a man sitting on the couch. Hearing the footsteps, the man stood, and turned around. It was Tanner. The Vault uniform was gone, replaced with jeans and a white t-shirt.

"I've brought your things as you asked," Lazarus said as he dropped the duffle bag onto the couch.

"Thank you," Tanner said.

Tanner jammed his hands into the pockets of his jeans as he faced Lazarus. Fresh worry lines creased his unshaven face. His hair was a mess, as if he had just gotten out of bed. Dark circles were under his eyes.

"You don't have to do this." Lazarus said.

Tanner's face turned grim with determination.

"Yes, I do. You didn't see her, Lazarus. She looked so tortured. I shouldn't have pushed her to choose like that when I did. What was I thinking? I wasn't. I was being selfish when I should have been thinking about what she was going through." He swiped a hand through his hair, tousling it even more. "God, I'm such an idiot."

Lazarus set a firm hand on Tanner's shoulder, and tried to comfort him the best way he knew how... with words.

"Love is the one factor that we have no control of. Man can do great things, travel through time, and fix the world, but try to control who we love, the way we love, is an impossible feat. Love makes us do crazy things, and at the most inappropriate times. Yet it's love that reminds us that we are alive, and that life is worth living. Don't throw it all away because you think that you have made an irreparable mistake."

"I can't fix this."

"You underestimate Sharra. And yourself. None of us are perfect. There's no need to punish yourself."

Tanner closed his eyes, and shook his head, and said, "It's too late for me now." He opened his eyes to stare blankly at the wall. "Someone had to make a choice, so I made it for her."

"You didn't have to go this far."

"Dying seemed the easiest way. A clean cut. No more wondering. The future is clear."

Tanner's blue eyes turned glassy with unshed tears. Lazarus swallowed the lump that came to his throat. Goodbyes were so hard.

"You will be missed," Lazarus said.

"I'll return someday. Don't we always? But for now, I need time…"

"How much time?"

"I don't know. Maybe a lifetime, maybe two, when the pain is gone and I can face her again, and not… break."

Together they walked back to the shiftroom in silence. Lazarus hated to see Tanner go. He had come to depend on him. Yet, he understood Tanner's need to disappear.

They stopped outside the shiftroom between the rotating spirals. Katie was waiting for him back at the Vault, and he still had the note to deliver.

Lazarus had one more thing to say, not only for Tanner, but also for himself.

"Faolan is a good man," he said, and meant it.

"I have come to see that," Tanner admitted. "If I didn't think that he wasn't good enough or what she needed, I'd be fighting tooth and nail for her. He'll take care of her. She will soon forget about me."

"Where will you go?"

"Does it really matter?"

"No, I guess not."

Lazarus could not prolong it any longer. He hugged his friend, and stepped into the shiftroom, knowing that Tanner was waiting his turn to leave. He sighed, and pasted a sad smile on his face.

"See you in the future, my friend," Lazarus said.

Tanner eyes met his one last time.

"The future," he said.

Lazarus gave the command, and shifted.

TIMELINE GUIDE

Antonio Rossi:
guild member, age 29 from Florence, Italy
Year 1658

Araylai:
heir apparent, age 24 from Ardere, Ardus
Year 2252

Faolan:
swordsman, age 28 from Rhinns, Scotland
Year 764

Cael:
Umbra scout, age 28 from Ardere, Ardus
Year 2553

Greyson Lane:
IT, age 23 from Chicago, IL USA
Year 1989

Grimm Hannay:
quarry worker, age 65 from Glasgow, Scotland
Year 1975

J.D. Dash:
sailor, age 31 from Boston MA, USA
Year 1853

Katie Hyde:
orphan, age 17 from London, England
Year 1789

TIMELINE GUIDE

Lazarus Maitland:
Earl, age 48 from Compton, England
Year 1741

Maxum:
centurion. age 47 from Rome, Italy
Year 1000

Sharra Lane:
accountant, age 24 from Charlotte NC, USA
Year 1996

Tanner Holmes:
Delta Force, age 33 from Bangor PA, USA
Year 1982

Tatiana Ivonovic:
ballerina, age 25 from St. Petersburg, Russia
Year 1895

Viktor:
shuttle tech, age 26 from Federal Ukraine
Year 2253

Zoe Fox:
model, age 22 from New York City NY, USA
Year 1987